A Rhapsody in Blue

JONATHAN LOVEJOY

Armageddon Publishing

Cover: *The Storm*, 1874
by William Adolph Bouguereau (1825-1905)

ISBN-10: 0692333649
ISBN-13: 978-0692333648

For every Carol Ann

And the first angel sounded, and there followed hail and fire mingled with blood, and they were cast upon the earth: and the third part of the trees was burnt up, and all green grass was burnt up.

Revelation 6:7

Clocks and Monsters

1

The burning of nighttime real estate presages their arrival. When the forests and fields of suburbia are aglow with the dark revelation in blue that no, this was no ordinary fire set, and the flames of Hell on Earth must burn with an endtime fever, a warning that the end of the age is near. And sadly, I have awakened in the bed next to my own teenage daughter at night—myself an Armageddon flower in gold leaf petal, planted, picked and plucked in endtime lust, having seen the comet in the sky already which burns this self same fire tinted white. But this time, as my breasts still ache from the night's perversion come and gone, as my brunette shapely lies in my big suburban bed with me in shapely repose, this time I see the nighttime horizon through the bedroom window aglow in unearthly and otherworldly blue, from the trees that burn somewhere beyond my sight—burning blue and black fire.

The fields of my complacency, the forests of my endtime audacity have at last been set aflame, as Meadow Oppenheimer lies in my bed, caressed in her end of the world sleep, fully 21 and beyond what moral code society has imposed on us—that what we do behind closed doors is our own business, and nobody else's, including her absentee and wealthy father, who was stupid enough to put his hands to my throat when I laughed at his naiveté that night, when he proposed to know what Meadow and I chose to do behind his back. *My God,* he said, *you're fucking your own daughter,* Mr. Million Dollar corporate climber said to me—gathering himself up for the proverbial song to the heart—the sword in the gut and the song of the harp, as when he looked at me, I could not help but cover my mouth to hide a self imposed snicker and grin, as I listened to him say in bewilderment, *but all I wanted from you was a little love and respect...*

Well, you're not getting that, I had said, in the busty white sweatered repose of last winter. In the cold of one year and a half ago. In the cold that hides in my heart from the heat of summer, and the burning of the earth in blue and black fire.

As I stand at the nighttime window of revelation, my breasts still ache with a sweet memory, or lactations that have not come and gone—

the front of my white silk gown dampened with the echo of what was done—which was not a dry nursing this time, but as much wet nursing as a mother ever gave her daughter anywhere from one to twenty one. And while I touch and squeeze this memory in hands dampened, I take little comfort in this endtime perversion, Miss Carol Ann Oppenheimer, in disbelief at the end-of-the-world sounds that I hear barreling at us throughout the night. These are the big, low booming sounds they make, like a bassoon as big as a mountain, as though there were a creature named a trumpeter swan sent from Olympus—sounding like the announcement of a great ship about to depart for waters unknown.

The creatures do not screech, as one might think they would—but they have the sound of the rapture in their voice, as if it were to echo the Trump of God, in a great and long honking sound never before gleaned by men. *Snow dragons,* some call them, or *angel eyes,* and rightly so, as they are known to have emerged after the Great Southern Faultline appeared across Antarctica, after the strongest earthquake ever recorded on Earth had come and gone. *We were so lucky,* the scientists had said, *not a single casualty came from this massive quake, except that the landscape of the great continent has been changed forever.* And studies in video and pictures had revealed the emergence of these strange and beautiful creatures in flight—bearing the classic resemblance of reptilian flight—though not quite serpentine, with skin (or scales) as white as the landscape they emerged from, with eyes the color of the deep blue sky above them, which glowed with a determined energy of purpose—to equal the power of their deep, moaning voices.

And to the scientists' unbelief, to the world's eschatological shock, the most watched and studied event in human history occurred as the video somehow was recovered and posted, making its way around the world as lightning shines from the east to the west—as seven gigantic, monstrous things emerged in beauty, with one of them landing nearby the scientists' camp, rearing back as if to blast a warning to be heard, but instead blasting an alabaster fire pitched in royal blue, swirling in blue and black flame, until the scientists camped near the faultline were consumed to ashes upon the ice, and these too were burned until it was as though they no longer existed.This, happening from the mouth of the gigantic creatures, said to be the largest flying creatures known to man, towering well over 300 feet when raised up, so that there is no structure under a 30 story building they cannot look down upon.

Preferring to fold these massive wings away when they have their calling—which is to lumber around the cities, the forests and fields of the countryside like death pitched snow white, with eyes that glow in blue flame, breathing an end of the world fire tinted this self same ocean and icy blue. The schools and the amusement parks have not been spared, as these demons have landed in the midst of paradise to breathe their breath of warning upon the population, until so far, in just these six months since their arrival, a billion souls have been wiped out in the fires and the explosions, as the creatures do not engage the military without inner knowledge, being chased away by them in flashes of manmade fire and vapour of smoke; impervious to what so-called injuries are sought and wrought for them, at times, meeting our defenses where they lie—coating the tanks with this blue fire hot enough to make the metal glow orange, melting them with fervent heat, making them to none affect. Coating the skyscrapers at the bottom with flames undeniable and un-fightable, until there can be no beauty of a Nine Eleven implosion, as the concrete and steel melt and go away at the foundation, so that the world may see fifty and one hundred stories sway and fall like a tree under a logger's calling from God.

And not one of these seven white Armageddon stars has been hurt or killed, as they do not possess the human arrogance of ego telling them to fight needlessly onward in place of flight, having a genius for attack and retreat (as if retreat were necessary)—seeming to have abandoned the noisy and doomed city scapes for the green and pristine countrysides—appearing at farms and farmer's fields as if directed—burning the houses great and small to nothing, setting vast areas of crops and trees aflame, leaving evidence of the scorched and charred earth for all to see. And lately, the snow dragons have drifted their sights and sensibilities to the suburban sprawl, to the gated communities of aspiration and cheap luxury, until whole neighborhoods are helplessly burned to the ground as the people run—often hearing the warning in the earthquake rumble of their great stomping feet, these gigantic monsters of fight and flight—hearing their low, moaning voice at night like a trumpeter swan from Hell, to frighten the children of suburbia, and the children of violence and adultery, who see the mountainous blue flames appear in the streets before them, before the realization of their own mortality. It is oftentimes the last thing they will ever see, as they wait in fear with th e rest of the world, for a visit from one of the 300 foot snow dragons, and the burning death in blue and black fire.

Seeing the blue glow beyond our mansion lawn. Feeling the protection of the divine will for now I turn from the window of revelation, away from one of the seven vials of blue fire poured down upon the nighttime landscape afar off. Staring at the beauty which is my exotic princess in her queen's bed, desiring to repeat that which cannot be discussed among the population which lives and dies, as death has come to claim it, on the eve of the Second Coming. Such words in their opposite context, I must play as a melody from Beethoven, as I wake this Meadow from her slumber, that she may watch me remove the white and silken gown from my bare skin. Bottom underwear on, knee firmly implanted upon the mattress, I must lean over to offer her this gigantic and heavy hung breast in search for comfort, to exercise my gift born and bred.

And she lifts the bosom to her mouth as I lean forward, to hungrily give suck as I glance back toward the nighttime window in the bedroom darkness, feeling each suckling raise me like the pulling of a rope at a flagpole, which raises the cloth higher and higher towards its peak and purpose. And I must respectfully call upon the name of God himself, in a deep and gruff voice of surrender, shaking my head in disbelief that such feeling is possible, that I can be brought to this devastation from a nursing alone, as she settles into the knowledgeable sucking rhythm, as I hear the air begin to flow out of my lungs on its own, to give voice to the spirit that flows out from me, as my entire body begins to tremble and shake like the petals of a doomed flower in an earthquake, somewhere over the fields of Armageddon.

3

The hellfire that this world is set upon is blue. And this, wrought by the seven angels sent from God. As to whether these angels are divine or demonic, whether they be fallen or no, is not for the world to know as it burns with judgment, as nearly 1 billion souls have already been cooked alive in royal blue heat from on high. As to what form of fire was prophesied in scripture, who is to say? *The elements shall melt with fervent heat* is all that is important for us to remember, I suppose, whether we ever even cared that there is a Bible to remember or be concerned with, or whether we are as obsessed as Jack and Rexella Van Impe. All we really know is that these are seven snow white, monstrous beauties of fantasy specimen phased into our reality—whose eyes betray the same bright, almost royal blue of their liquid blue and black flame laced with traces of white, or even vice versa, blue and white flame laced with echoes of pitch. The end of the world burns in blue and black fire, with red and orange explosions of man's work going up in vapor of smoke, with even the fool's button having been pushed more than once already, sending the thermonuclear hopelessness into the sky somewhere in the desert middle east, in someone's feeble attempt at battle towards one of the flying white monsters. When this hydrogen fireball had cooked the middle eastern desert landscape to a charred and glassy remain, there were still seven, count them, *seven* dragons afoot and aflight, whose scales are as white as snow, and whose breath is set on the blue fire of Hell's earthly creation.

From our wealthy suburban post in pastoral Virginia, the distant mountains and hills have been on fire in the twilight, so that in the nighttime distance, a single, high forested mountain peak burns like a blue torch in the blowing summer wind. And video of these forest fires do a latter day justice to the impossible, showing whirlwinds made of pure, blue flame, whirling from the ground high up into the low and smoke filled clouds, to confound scientists everywhere as to how flames of this color, let alone flames at all, can be produced by living, breathing animals, and burn with a heat previously unknown outside of thermonuclear fire. And these seven creatures live and breathe to blow this flame with greater frequency, until it seems at times that every inch of the ground is in need of water, which has a lesser affect on this particular fire than any other on earth. It would seem that if they chose, they could take up residence under the ocean in their calling, and melt the very ground at the shores beneath the sea. And these seven monsters bear no resemblance to smallishness, being gigantic enough to carry away elephants in their claws if they so choose, with mighty wingspans that glow as white as the snow dove, seeming to be tinted as the glory of the Almighty Wrath of God.

And nearly all of the tallest buildings in the world have already gone not spared, as these animals were sent forth in this task early, all of them making violent and fiery work of the bottom of these heavenly structures, melting the bottom of these buildings in broad daylight, some of them filled with screaming, hopeless workers somewhere far beyond Nine Eleven, where the feebleness of airplanes carry only a spark of these white monster's power. And when their flames pour in burning liquid from their gigantic, 30-story frames, this fire makes its presence known as an agent of death and determination, sticking to the buildings in roiling, boiling, flaming chaos until the steel structures are melted inside, and the tops of the skyscrapers begin to sway, and the bottom collapses to where there can be no beautiful, divine implosion like Nine Eleven, where the buildings came down in the most perfect clouds of demolition dust ever conceived by the heart of God and man—no— these buildings collapse at the *bottom*, as the sawed through trunk of a dying sequoia, and the 100 story structures begin a daylight topple in the violent wind and rain of their departure in gray, and they fall slowly just one way down, to where 1000 feet of man made desperation topples like a redwood toward the burning forest floor. What every camera, what every little phone and I-this and I-that device, what every 100,000 dollar bar version for the mass media captures— eyes all aglow from helicopters and news vans scattered abroad and about— these skyscrapers turn themselves into an end of the world leaning, in the raining of hailstones and concrete stone and glass and broken steel showered, until they create the impossible fall down, down and downward, to where the wind of their demise is sensed even through the television screens, until their toppling in the wind and rainstorm is complete, and the cloud of endtime dust and debris they raise is followed by the earthquake of their unbridled and lightning bolt devastation.

A Rhapsody in Blue

And the seven dragons of eschatology, as they burden the heart and mind. From somewhere burned so deep in my memory, beyond my own sensibilities alike in kind.

Ephesus! Thou dragon of judgment—pour thine blue fire of revelation down upon the earth. Thou wicked and corrupt place along the timeline, having forsaken thine first love, which was Christ the Lord—burn and grieve from the fire of thine punishment! Weep and howl from what judgment and pain hath come upon thee in the night.

Smyrna! Burn this vial of fire down upon the earth! The peoples from somewhere along the timeline that are persecuted—search thy tormentors in this end of the world flame.

Pergamon! Pour this vial of blue suffering upon the earth! For the myriads of them who choose not to repent! Who choose not to humble themselves before thee, their time is beyond redemption, where they are tormented in this flame!

Thyatira! Thou dragon of wicked intent! Pour thy fiery judgment down in blue flame upon the earth! To burn every witch and warlock who doth smear the name of the Almighty—who masquerade in goodness, who claim the white light of the Holy Spirit and Christ consciousness, but whose loyalty is to their father the Devil, the god of the underworld! Who seek to smear the name of righteousness for unrighteousness sake in evil darkness, these shall go up in this rhapsody in blue! Their souls are reserved for the Great White Throne— their damnation is reserved for the day of judgment!

Sardis! Pour this fire of judgment down upon the earth! Awaken the sleeping saints of God, who no longer follow after the faith, who believe that the righteousness of God is as the comfort of slumber, who hath no cross of righteousness to bear! Burn their unbelieving hearts in the curse of this life, until their backslidden bodies lie charred in the ruins of ashes, and the burned dust of the earth hath no further memory of them to grieve!

Philadelphia! Alasehir! Burn the persecutors of God in blue fire! Pour thy vial of judgment down upon them. Let them who laugh at the peculiar people be damned in this azure and ivory flame— in the cerulean that whirls in the heat of blue touched by ebony-white. Pour this vial of judgment upon them who mock the endtime children of God! The scoffers, the unbelievers, the idolators of latter day poison—them who lust after what ungodly pleasures that still grow and prosper among the burning towns and trees.

Laodicea! Thou greatest heart of blue flame! Pour this vial of judgment down upon the earth before thee! Cook the lukewarm church of unrighteous intent! Blaze their non-committed flesh in a fire too hot to endure. As the spirit of the Almighty hath spewed them forth from his righteous mouth, as he hath cast those hypocrites aside, lay their lives asunder in a coffin! Let their bodies be consumed with every work of man! As they give themselves over to every enddtime perversion unnamed! Every behind closed doors act unspeakable. Let us hear the mothers and their daughters scream for mercy that hath come and gone! Let them watch the brick and balsom wood of their churches go up in smoke, and fire the color of the sky in creation! Laodicean dragon! Burn those Pharisetical and Saducean monsters as they engage in secret, when they are not in their modern cathedrals, sending false praises to God! Awaken their fat and needless slumber in heat beyond measure—watch them run and scream to the burning heavens for relief—watch them weep and howl for redemption that is no more! Watch them blaspheme the name of the Lord, from the shadows of a reprobate mind—a spirit that hath turned to latter day lust—to endtime pride, to eyes lusting after the end of the age, to partake of every forbidden and secret pain and pleasure that burns them from within!

reams of clocks and watches don't need much interpretation. There's not much going on there beyond the passage of time, the physical passing of our condemned souls along the timeline. And finally, when the spirits make their way into our dreams by way of this warning, I suppose it means that yes, we're running out of time. Time to do what, I don't really have to imagine. And what do my daughter's dreams, recurring, of her and me on fire mean? And these are cursed (or blessed), with lack of ambiguity, being that the fires in which we burn are blue tinted black with the requisite angry screams coming and going, the so-called weeping and gnashing of teeth. And while I move from the morning window of dreams to the crescendo of screams, to wake her up from the nightmare innuendo of fear and tragedy, it seems, I am again confronted by the marriage of reality and fantasy, the reality of the burning world around us, and the fantasy of clocks and monsters, the fantasy of ticking watches and screams emanating from burning blue and black fire. For it is what color the world was on fire with even before the dragons came, which had blazed to the surface of mankind's dealings with one another in public and in private.

But for my daughter and me, the concern is a private and wanton lascivious need born and raised, and nurtured up in the most unbelievable intensity, for if another living soul were to even suspect that my birth daughter and me were lovers, what end of the world consequences and ramifications would there be?

And I have felt the pressing of these outside forces anyway, these forces of the forbidden, that seek to burden my conscious with why I am leaned over with the belt strapped around my thighs, with my wrists bound up behind my back, with my mouth gagged so tightly with a black stocking. Feeling the pounding of her into me from behind, with nary a false breath at all come from either one of us as we focus in on what experimentation we have given ourselves over to , the counting of pounding strokes within ourselves, so married to wearing that which pertaineth to a man strapped on and hanging down in the sexiness of its surreality.

Why is a strap on phallus, hanging down in realism from a woman, so much sexier and so much more appealing than the fantasy of a real penis grown from her? Because a real penis suggests masculinity, which is the enemy of feminine power and beauty. Only when masculinity is channeled through femininity, can it be transformed into the universal, the sensuality that captures the hearts of all women and men. For a woman to merely wear and utilize masculinity, then to internalize it for her bleak purposes, that is the sensual fire that burns the modern woman alive at her groin, at places which cannot be accepted by many, nor can be mentioned or discussed by many millions more. *Amazonia* is the latter day truth, which is why the divorce courts are filled to the brim, as one of God's supreme curses and prophecies from the Garden itself is being fulfilled before Armageddon—before Antichrist—that Eve's desire shall be to her husband, and he shall rule over thee. When this dynamic is breached, when the wife does not surrender and submit to the husband, one of two truths is born from the soil of their union—either the marriage is stressed and unhappy, or the marriage is stretched and undone. The curse of Eve removed the paradise of emotional equality in marriage. A man has to lower his natural emotional masculinity like a flag over a battlefield cemetery in a long term union, lest there be stress and stretching until there is no field of tranquility for the rabbits to run and play in.

These are the modern forces that burn. With the lust of wayward woman, who has decided that she would rather be single than surrendered to a man, or even subject to living without the ring and the certificate of marriage, to enjoy the benefits of the union without the shackles of it. And yes, I am guilty of this to the highest degree, as I literally for no good reason, ended my husband's attempt to have me as a possession—to have none of me as his, not even my love and respect, which is all that he really wanted from me as the twentieth year approached, but which I refused to give him because it was blocked by a new lust, an end of the world lust that has risen up and overtaken my physical body. It has overtaken me again this fine morning, as I stand in the middle of the floor of my bedroom, the belt having bound my legs immobile at the thighs, bent over so that the macromastian breasts hang so far down toward the floor, as my daughter pounds away like a lady lumber jack at the felling of a tree, one not yet having been set on fire from what now plagues the world to the edges of every continent, from sea to every other shining sea.

And as the revelation of clocks and monsters begins to take over my body in the pounding, as the wedding of the waters and the fire take place in my body, I understand now, all of a sudden, that my time and allegiance to this high tone house and neighborhood are coming to an end, as the fire approaches daily, as the foghorn voices of these monsters are heard in the Virginia countryside. As my eyes roll back while my mouth is gagged, as my voice takes on the pitiful, tortured bellowing howl of one who endures the unendurable, I know as surely as Oppenheimer is my name, that my daughter and me are headed for the Virginian prairie, where the cropfields hold the flaming forests and future burning woods at bay.

19

Jonathan Lovejoy

*P*art of the power of what I do is its secrecy. The other parts are composed of various degrees of unbelievability. Nobody would believe or care that my daughter should be wearing a sign across her big breasted body, "I fucked my mother." Or "She fucked her mother."And those are the signs down through the motherline—part of that unseen iceberg of endtime perversion. The idea of fathers and their daughters is old hat. Who batted an eye of the Mackenzie Philips revelation? Who cared even? But the world awaits the fiery revelation from the first famous woman, that somewhere beyond the babysitter and the aunt and the family friend and the foster mother and the stepmother, lies the reality of the pornographic asthetic. The reality of a certain blood that burns blue hot in some mothers—so many of them not really understanding the source of their perverted punishments—the source of their mother daughter obsession—the source of their refusal to embrace their own motherhood, but instead to cinch and starve themselves into a middle aged pervertedness, where youthful femininity is no competition for the mature, curvy beauty. It is a revelation so privately common, so covertly pervasive and so deep, it would deliver the world an apocalyptic shock, to know that some mothers and their grown daughters are given in to disrobing, to taking the paddle board down from its hiding place in willingness, after nudidty has been achieved, and paddling deep, simple turmoil into one another's backsides, to where the years of it produces a special kind of pain that dispatches heat to the groin, whereupon the right rhythm, the right intensity, the right echo about the room, the right thought, the right self stroking of the nipple, can send the body into an otherworldly tremble, which is a variation on the Witch's Crown, which is an orgasm achieved without apparent stimulation. This, a woman's orgasm, which is not given to many among us without the mundaneness of vaginal touching. Whether giving or receiving one of these to my Meadow— it happens to my body, in the unearthly glow of the impending dragon fire, in the electronic lure of Lifetime Television, in the end of the world mother daughter obsession that looms.

There are times when I have delivered the first blow to her naked backside with the big paddle, and the strain of her voice's struggle against a yell flows into my body with the force of a wayward spark, which will ignite a visible tremble that surprises me, that I sometimes am thankful that she didn't see, though I cannot imagine why. From whenceforth cometh the flash of puritanical shame, when I beat perversion deep into my daughter's body and soul? Frankly, I wonder whether, sometimes, if I am the only one whose lust runs so deep and complete, until I feel my spirit confirm to me that no, I am but one of many, and this is something that is deeply common to both man and womankind, women with a whore's libido, with the sex drive of a serial killer, whose perversion is activated by the strangest things—some pushing up against the sink during the dishes, some stripping to toplessness when they vacuum, some putting their daughters over their knee well up into the college years—some requesting massages from their daughters upon the husband's back while they watch, some keeping a daughter who might have a functional illness like epilepsy home well up into the late 30's and into the daughter's 40's, where the mother in her perverted 60's is not shy in the behind close doors breast comparisons or breast punishments with canes and rulers, to where only the briefest tapping of an old fashioned 12 inch ruler across the mother's nipples is enough to start the moaning banshee and the earthquake in her body.

Mother Daughter Perversion
Has become a thing of beauty to see
An end of the world diversion
On the eve of eschatology

Somehow, I know it is the revelation, the last great secret left to reveal to a wicked and adulterous generation, that hypocrisy runs wider and deeper than what was previously thought possible, and this form of human depravity is, and has been a reality from as far back as East of Eden, and has remained a secret through the ages of eternity, to the posting of modernity and beyond. It is the cup of bitter wormwood, where is the cup of the forbidden, tasted so sweet upon the lips, so savory upon ever nerve of the hips, in slips and trips and short clips so hidden and unrevealed.

To the air around me, from my spirit out into whatever room or space I'm in, I must flow this revelation into my reality like a Captain's Log, that the ghosts and spirits who listen may live their ethereal death and dying in shock, that humans have such audacity to grieve, to act as though there are no consequences for their actions, who act as though there is a God given right toward hypocrisy, and that going to the endtime worship auditorium of the damned, the Armageddon coliseum is enough to cleanse us from our sins. For even though I have not done it, even though I cannot force myself to accept this gift, I know somehow that the whole thing is based on something the Bible calls "justified by faith" where what my daughter and I do is more than covered by what was written in John 3:16. I feel the calling to this, and I known that soon, under the light of a summer Mountain Moon, I will give my heart and soul to the God of this faith, to keep me from plunging into the lake that roils and rages in liquid flame, where their worm dieth not, and where the fire is not quenched.

Upon the heavy hipped bottom of my exotic Meadow's 21 year old backside, I deliver these blows, so happy to see the Asian (or is it Egyptian) tint of her eyes in deep suffering, her looks passed from her father's grandparents both Greek and Asian-Indian, an Asian- Indian great grandmother who never married—this exotic, raven haired beauty having reached across time to settle so heavily upon my daughter, so much that many thought she was a child I adopted from the Middle East (not China), with the Kardashian-esque looks so heavy with eastern sensuality and Egyptian belly dancer curvaciousness, which hath made her ripe for the picking.

My husband's grandparents never married—the Greek and his Asian-Indian concubine—and their only daughter was taken by a blue eyed German named Oppenheimer. Pictures of Elizabeth Anne Oppenheimer are not without power, so many seeing the origin of my daughter's looks, the same Greek, Asian-Indian harmony in her face, as is in the pasture of my daughter's beauty, which sought the name Meadow Elizabeth Oppenheimer. Even before she was born, I knew that what my mother had done to me had already corrupted he roots of my daughter's tragic family tree.

She is the possession that I own. So mature, seven years in appearance beyond herself, so that she could pass for her mid twenties even when she was eighteen, and the depth of her sensual understanding like that of a soul that has lived and known another life, somewhere along the flow of time and history.

A Rhapsody in Blue

These are the sins of Li Pompeii, as they burden the heart and mind. Those passed down through Elizabeth Oppenheimer, then down to the girl Meadow, whom I nurture and possess. And this poor little thing which she was, meets at the crossroads of our human history, both memories leading down through her ancestry, to coalesce into she—having been given such an exotic draw to the sadistic minds around her, having a quiet strength tempered by vulnerability—a core of womanness underneath the powerful beauty that radiates, until she knows and understands like few beauties in history, that human beings cannot be trusted, and their tendancy is as the buzzard over a ripe woods, to circle over the scent of weakness and death until they find it, and pick its dying and dead carcass clean. Meadow is a used and abused soul of sweetness and vulnerability, which makes her prone and primed to lonerism, and perfect for the company of a grieving mother.

Here, at the end of a dying age, I see the coalescence of a secret and modern day tragedy, this, in one mind and body of a girl named Meadow Elizabeth Oppenheimer, whose secret life is as the Armageddon Flower, which slowly dies under the gray clouds of a nuclear winter. The curse of both bloodlines passed down to her, where one is the pleasure of the forbidden Mother Daughter Dynamic, and the other is the forbidden pain of it. It is the painful side, flowed down from Oppenheimer Mountain as a river that I see, when I close my eyes to the seven terrors that seek to burn our world to ashes in blue.

I can see Li Pompeii, the unmarried woman of average size in the old country, known in her Chinese farming village as a half Indian freak of nature and ridiculed, even before she met her Greek American soldier husband, who was smart enough to recognize the beauty she possessed when he saw it, though she was no beauty about the face as was he. He was struck in the heartstrings by a spirit that played him invisible, at what macromastic treasures that hung from her chest to her belly in greatness that her own family, her own mother had seen as an ugly curse. So when soldier Orin Tulsanari went to Li's mother and father, to offer to bring her with him back to America, they agreed with smiles and thanksgiving, with only the smallest dowries in payment necessary.

Orin brings Li Pompeii to America, with promises of a wedding that never takes place, but with enough fire of attraction to hold them together for ten year until Orin dies, leaving Li alone with their young and impossibly beautiful daughter, whom Orin knew the name of even before she was born. The rather thin backed and gigantic breasted mother Li, is left to raise a beautiful girl she despised over her common law husband's grave, leaving her to have to work their little dirt farm to keep them fed and in the small, isolated Virginia house they live in.

This seed of mother daughter hatred played from the old country, done in isolation without pretense, as the Chinese Indian mother who barely spoke English, who speaks what of it she knows in a thick and hateful Chinese accent toward the beautiful half Greek bitch she is cursed to raise—this Mother Daughter hated occurs in secret, from the time the little girl Elizabeth Ann Tulsanari is ten, until she escapes her mother though grades and a scholarship to the University of Virginia—where Elizabeth Ann eventually meets the blue eyed German descendant, whose parents had come from Germany to conquer the American game with ease.

John James Oppenheimer Sr, lucky enough to have seen the shy and reserved beauty in the library, whose hair was pinned up all the time, without a brush of makeup on her pale, Greek, Indian Asian beauty. Oh, but what Oppenheimer luck and ignorance this was—what good, behind closed doors fortune this will be! How many nights of unbridled and secret pleasures would the Oppenheimer mind be privy to, as he enjoyed every mysterious line and faded scar upon her long and heavy breasts, or upon the unusually thick hipped balance in fertility below! Oh, what glorious figure this woman hath hidden from all but the woman who gave her life, and took it from her so abundantly!

Now, she is free from the abuse of the farm, cursed only with a son to give suck to the long and swinging breasts, the son who never remembers the scars on his mother's skin as he gives suck, as he draws life from deep inside the daughter of Li Pompeii, who was left alone on the farm to age in bitterness—with only the occasional visit from her well to do Elizabeth Ann—whose visits are of a secret magnitude and intensity unheard of, unbridled, and unseen by the public eye in the latter day, but only imagined in the heart alike in kind. Elizabeth Anne Oppenheimer, who visits her Asian Indian mother on the farm, every so often for so many years, to satisfy the end of the world craving her mother hath implanted like a drug, until it becomes part of the private fuel that powers a secret life—the need to be physically abused in private by her mother, whereupon breast torture is the norm, and where the new scars hath become a curiosity unspoken of by her husband over the years, as she is careful to keep herself chaste and hidden as the two of them age, as John Oppenheimer Senior indulges his younger mistress, his lithe and waifish little Jewish brunette concubine, to take the sensual place of his Asian Indian beauty of a weird wife with the big hanging bosoms, who visits her mean band bitter Asian Indian mother with the big, hanging breasts somewhere deep in the farmlands of Virginia.

Through the Oppenheimer bloodline, this vision passes to me, in growing, end of the world clarity, until I see the Asian Indian woman Li Pompeii in her old, long skirt of gray peasant cloth that covers her down to her bare feet, topless in macromastian glory, with her daughter bent over in epic and quiet obedience, wearing only the white underwear bottoms, her hands clasped willingly behind her back, her breasts grown to such long and swinging maturity as her mother's. Elizabeth Anne, Meadow's paternal grandmother, is bent over with the length of her breasts exposed, her thighs already welted from the caning strokes, now enduring the sensual agony she feels from her mother's cane being struck repeatedly across her hanging breasts like two great bells hanging down, until a deep and loud woman's scream is heard from her mouth, and her entire body wavers in its balance from the explosion of energy passing through.

*U*pon the energy of this breast caning, I feed, delighted endlessly by my daughter's natural masochism passed down, her ability to bring her body to shaking from whatever abuse I need to give in sadism, whether it be the heaviness of the paddling board, or the lightness of the cane that stings. There is a special peculiarity to our perversion, where our deep kissing is so often followed by her standing and bent over in the Pompeii Position, bent over with her hands clasped behind her back untied, that I may sting her breasts from the cane until she has to cry out, eventually having to cry out in a lightning bolt of feeling that traverses pain, into a pleasure known by so few that have lived and died. As I cane my daughter's exposed and hanging breasts to my satisfaction, my vision is of the Elizabeth Ann aesthetic, passed down to her as a gift, to join the Carol Ann River from Turner Mountain, to where the deep and abiding sadism is born.

These two meet in my daughter's mind and spirit, until I wonder if either of us can remember what is normal in sensual expression, until I am bathed in thanksgiving for the gift she possesses, for the prodigy that she is. Being so thankful that she was never like other girls, obsessed with their cutesiness and their boys and phones and beep-beep cars overpriced and weekend excursions to nowhere in endless chatter and public misbehavior and money spent—debit cards on the same end of the world fire that so many of their houses soon will be. I am so selfishly thankful, that the endtime suggestion that haunts us actually came from her in a fear revelation; *"Mom, we have to get out of this neighborhood"* is confirmation for what I had been feeling myself, that its long past time to be running from the dragon fire, before this wealthy neighborhood begins to burn its own rhapsody in blue.

It is time for us to ascend, to the heights of what isolation there be that awaits, that we may descend in kind, to what depravities there may be that must come. That we may begin our journey through this part of the timeline, to hide from the wrath of the Almighty, to hide from the breath of the seven terrors that go to and fro, whose purpose it seems is to tear creation apart with fury, then burn it to smoldering cinder and ashes. And somewhere nearby, so far away, as my daughter remains bent over, in the phantom memory of the Pompeii Dynamic, somewhere afar off is the voice of one of the animals, as a great foghorn of rage echoing as the trump of God, which makes me light into my daughter's bosom with fiery speed and skill, making her have to breathe and cry out from pain alone, which prompts me to have to step away, to pull the thin red member up about my hips, and commence to strike her breasts again. This, I do. Determined to make them bleed if I have to, to garner my own satisfaction. This renewed fire of intension, this new flame of intensity infuses her, and I see her glance at the red member and close her eyes, or rather they close on their own in the tell tale roll back sign, and her young voice soon gives way to the spirit within, and I watch her react with remarkable gusto, as the intensity shakes her body visibly in the Witch's Crown, causing her to swallow after the yelp, and bellow deeply in her own disbelief in the power of what she just felt.

"I feel like I came in my tits," she says, shaking her head, as I drop the cane to the floor nearby, escorting her to the mirror. I admonish her to stand up

straight and true, wasting no time sliding the red member into her rectum, relishing the sound of her own deep and loud woman's voice cascading all around me. The sound of her tortured voice blends with the sight of her tormented breasts in the mirror, to harmonize with the Elizabethan melody played, causing me to slowly bend her over, that I may see her great breasts hang down to touch the dresser in her reflection, which draws a feeling from every part of my body at once, all of them coming together somewhere along the core of my being, to cause me to have to stand still in moaning, and accept the quaking that shakes me in grieving from head to toe.

Turner Mountain

Jonathan Lovejoy

She's fifty seven and all ass, this woman. The woman who haunts my dreams and visions like one of those end of the world dragons out there— the woman who sat on the edge of her bed in panties rolled down to her hips where she nursed at my oversized breasts like a starving calf. And I never saw this as anything other than normal, even being thankful that Daddy was always gone—always away on some business trip or another—not in the arms of any other mistress than the one made out of the lust for money—being so glad and proud to feed the hips of that assy wife of his and her breasty daughter, which was my mother and me respectfully.

As I hear the chiming of the endtime whistle train, in the rain that is born from pain itself—I am tormented in my waking hours by the phonecall I just received, by the arrival impending, by the coming over of Mrs. Irene Turner Stewart, a woman not short on beauty, even greater than I, though not extraordinary as her granddaughter Meadow—the woman with a gift for sensitivity of the breasts *and* hips—this anomaly passed down through me to her prodigious and precious Meadow. As I prepare in my heart to leave these suburbs behind forever, I don't know whether the memories of her torment or titillate me, as I am heavy burdened by the weight of what I was often charged to do. Having to strip Irene down the bare flesh of who she was, a devoted wife and mother of one—and stand with her in the daytime dark of middle class suburbia, in the halls of cultured civility, and deliver to her what was her grandest devastation, which was to feel my bare hands in bare skinned whacking against her big, naked backside, a set of hips hardly ever seen on a normal sized woman, wide enough (as he sister says) to show a movie on, which is made apparent in the tight, gray business skirts she loves to wear, underneath the making blazer tops cut to show them off, so that there is not a woman in the room of any race or weight or shape whatsoever who is not intimidated or impressed by what they see. A classic low rider, a bucket butted behemoth of bound up secrets, too impressive in a pair of jeans to go unnoticed, so that there is no possibility of her walking down the ailse of a grocery store or department store without getting a glance or a stare, being such a sophisticated and mature beauty besides. But she is not a horse assed woman—with giant, high bred, hard horse haunches—this is nothing of the kind. The width and curve of her hips is Opraesque in magnificence, the glory of Gail Kingness in what is truly extraordinary on a middle aged white woman, adding to the already powerful nature of what beauty she possesses. Irene Turner is a memorable sort of Amazonian female, having a presence enhanced by the bright, twinkling eyes of knowing, where there is no getting around her knowing stare, no escaping her glare, no pulling free from what part of you she wishes to me made aware. And for me, more often than not, Irene wishes to know how Meadow's long and swinging breasts have tasted in my mouth. So that she may carry this fantasy into the abode of her private dreams, so that as she does her old fashioned duties upon her husband, upon my father in riding and writhing, she may imagine the feel of them in her own mouth, as she shakes to her husband's utmost and utter amazement.

Irene Turner most likely considers herself a pioneer. A leading lady in the private army that marches toward Armageddon's fiery flame, having been so unafraid to introduce me at the age of nine to her desires—which she first called "the butt game"—where she got me to give her a stand up spanking in her blue jeans. I can remember the bellowing, the coming grunting and gruff groaning like it was yesterday, which neither delighted nor disturbed me as much as it merely confused me, as to why *"Momma wanted [me] to spank [her] butt so hard."* And curiously enough, it was something she had never had the courage to ask for from her husband—but it was born and raised up from memories of her own childhood, and the spankings she received from her mother ad nauseam.

Irene had noticed that even as a little girl, the spankings did not hurt as much as they heightened a feeling between her legs, that sometimes went far enough to shoot a lightning bolt of pleasure through her entire young body. And this exchange of energy, Irene's mother must have known about, gathering them both to nude over the knee spankings when Irene was 16 years old, but done under the pretense of discipline, so that what deep perversion it was remained hidden from the mother's punishment minded psychology. But these were the pleasures of what abuses Irene had to endure, for the rest of the physical abuse was borderline brutal, often leaving her in tears and despair. Oh, what sins and iniquities flow the motherline, along the branches of our accursed family tree!

Irene Turner. So unabashedly unashamed she was, to introduce her nine year old into the motherline perversion. To eventually have her nine year old daughter (which was me), to strip her bare and wail the tar out of her upon her happy flesh, which she relaxed and took seriously the second time, until I can recall that when she shook and screamed, it frightened me something fierce.

These are the greely eyes. The witch eyes. These are the eyes of Mrs. Irene Turner Stewart that stare. The look across my fine kitchen table at me in knowing, just this side of a determined wink, with the black mug of sweet crème coffee in her beautiful white ivory hands.

Jonathan Lovejoy

*S*omewhere just south of my mother's Richmond home, we languish in complacency, us three. My mother insisting upon being unshy in her vulgarity, "when are you going to let me put the wood to my granddaughter's ass," she says over her sweet coffee, which makes my mouth drop open in unpretend shock, as if I don't really understand the source of such a brash and unbridled statement. Truthfully, I am amazed at its audacity, as the open reflection of our closed in secret. To actually hear it expressed aloud by another human being is another thing entirely. And it only serves to highlight the astounding nature of what dynamic there is between us—the modern mother daughter dynamic unrestrained, and whatever hidden perversions it entails. To hear these words spoken by a church goer, a do-gooder, a woman of sophisticated ways and means—educated with a master's degree in sociology, though it was something she never really needed—this solid, well to do Lady of the Hips, who is unshy to her daughter about her lust for her granddaughter, languishes in complacency here in our fine kitchen of wealth, where the Oppenheimer divorce money flows us down the Wealthen Stream.

We languish in *White Anglo Saxon Privilege*, oh, so *White And So Pretty*, until Meadow comes down the stairs in the blue jeans and extremely curved in waist, sports bra filled with the promise of antiquity, her beautiful face anguished with worry and distress. Meadow pulls her mother and grandmother from their morning leisure to the living room TV, where the morning news shows are burning with a different kind of blue and black fire, one of lyrical intent and purpose, in reality for the world to see. It is the burning of what has escaped until now, the fulfillment of prophecies at long last—not the melting of some ancient and beautiful statue somewhere in the world, or the toppling of another skyscraper, or the scorching of a fleet of planes or an airport—not the plunging of a train to its fiery death from a raised bridge trestle, or the collapse of some aptly named roller coaster at an amusement park. This, the setting of another group of fine homes on fire, and this, the tell tale fires of this endtime diversion, so that the world would know that this judgment was sent by what angel of death this is.

Somewhere in the heart of Richmond, in a neighborhood so familiar to us all, we hear the report of the latest dragon attack, the latest exercise in latter day Hell on Earth, where the worm of their worry dieth not, and the fire is not quenched. Somewhere in the heart of Richmond, in a neighborhood of old money, big, old brick houses and trees and golf course landscaping all aflame—this, to my mother's devastation and chagrin, having to sit her shapeliness down before it falls down in swirling, whirling revelation that life as she knows it is over, and that the part of Richmond that is on fire contains the burning remains of the life she once knew.

Mother had awakened with a burning unction in her body this morning. A desire that she had not felt in a long while—something that goes beyond just missing someone, well beyond the desire for their company. It is the same heat of attraction that calls one forth from the distance toward someone they otherwise have thought little about, when the promise of certain appetites may be satisfied. Oh, there is plenty of love between us, I suppose, what there is of it that has never really been lost. We have always gotten along as well as a mother and daughter can be expected. Hardly a week passes where the phone is not buzzing or beeping, with the voice of my Queen on the other end who, even as I transcend my 40th year, is still so clearly in charge of who I am, no matter how independent of her I have aspired to be.

This promised land of mother daughter dominance and control, this mother lode of emotional gripping, she hath found and achieved, discovered in the secret luck of a miner in the gold hills guided by God, guided by the spirits of what is by birth meant to be, until I am captured, and has remained so these many years of my adult life. The craving for us to come together hits every so often, like the proverbial friends with benefits, to where we have had to park somewhere in secret along a country road, and commence to tongue sucking like there is no tomorrow.

I suppose for me, for her, for so many souls spread out across a condemned landscape, the fires of revelation display a future screen, telling us that no, there is no tomorrow, and whatever it is that you do, you must do it quickly.

And for Mother, this very morning, the sensual feel of her daughter's body, the deep kissing of her daughter's lips, the anguished, agonized tremble of her daughter's flesh has called to her as she wakes up, so that she knows she will have to rise up from the early morning slumber. A heightened heat of burning. A flame unfelt for such a long time. It is a spark of lightning I felt myself when I opened the door this morning and accepted the surprise hug, breathed in the sweet perfume, felt the strength of soft lips against mine. And with me in my robe and gown, having wondered who on Earth it could have been. Is it irony, that we talk all the time on the phone about every mundane thing, yet when the importance of a visit arises, I receive no word from her whatsoever?

What in the world are you doing here is the requisite sound from grateful lips of mine, that my Queen hath descended in the latter day, in the shadows of the seven angels with the seven vials, to bring me whatever twisted comfort there may be between us. It begs to wonder, that here in Shangri-La, at the front gate of Paradise, what prying and peering eye may have seen the hippy, sophisticated woman kiss the younger version of herself, the mysterious and busty mom of the mysterious and busty Indian looking girl named Meadow. Across one of the hilly, golf-coursey lawns is one of the houses containing a busybody bitch of the highest order whom I cannot stand, but I make do with what upper class company she provides, at least appreciating her constant flatter and fawning over Meadow's beauty, my beauty, my house's beauty, and when she meets her, my mother's beauty. The woman is so very 'looks conscious,' it becomes annoying after a while, that she can see no man or woman through the veil of their outer appearance, where the judgment of their character lies for her.

And this condition is not hers alone to be blamed for—it is a human condition hidden in hypocrisy, so surreptitiously hidden in our secret motivations. But this secret is betrayed by us, especially when we go out, or when we watch the television, or when we gaze upon the stage of even the local cathedral church, that mankind is secretly, openly, subtly, blatantly obsessed with beauty. And the loveliness that has captured me, that has tormented the soul of who I am sits now in the driver's seat of our silver Mercedes SUV, rolling the miles north into a smoldering Richmond. The three of us hardly perceiving what luck, chance or chaos hath touched my mother's life, prompting her to wake up this morning with the burning desire to drive the miles south of town to see her daughter. For while she was en route, even before she had darkened my door with the shadow of her arrival, even before the corruption of her finger hath touched the doorbell unredeemed, two of the seven mighty dragons had descended upon Richmond, in the wake of her departure, and had made no peace with restraint, and began to cook every inch of the historic town in the fires of alabaster blue.

A Rhapsody in Blue

These dragons are the most frustrating of tragedies, being impervious to all forms of injury attempted by man, breathing every poisoned vapor as easily as we breathe oxygen, not batting an eye when the missiles explode in their faces, nor flinching or twitching when the tank machine guns send the night tracers at them like fireworks, as the world slowly begins to realize how much trouble it is really in, as this is a new and unknown species of animal, the origins of which are a total mystery, as we learn that yes, they are invulnerable to every manmade weapon we have devised to kill with. They have been known to bite down upon an oil rig with the gusto of a bear on a salmon, hardly breathing a different cadence upon the explosion that ensues. The beasts are at home in the blossom of fire, they flourish in the bosom of flame; its seems that they feed upon the energy of whatever is thrown at them, and it appears that there is a natural shield around them to enhance their invulnerability, which is why the missiles never really make contact with their skin.

Whatever magic or unknown natural science this is, the world is baffled— knowing only that these things cannot be killed, as full on battles that the beasts are forced to engage in when they are cornered reveal the incredible, that whatever fear and vulnerability they once showed has flown away upon unmuted wing, with the noise of fiery and foghorn voices pitched in fury, as if they have increased in power since they have arrived, as their purpose and intent grows apparent, which is to only kill, steal, and destroy.

It is a spectacular thing to watch the tanks and planes and helicopters take their best shots, always in futility as the weapons have no affect on these monsters, the poor soldiers inside the tanks saying their prayers to whatever God they pray to—as the angry monster rears its white dinosaur head back in a breath angrily taken, lunging forward with mouth wide open, fire the color of the earth ocean as seen from space, pouring over the unfortunate vehicle whether by land or by the air above, the planes and helicopters exploding instantly in their own fiery orange deaths buried in the blue, the tank machines literally melting, glowing orange in the superheating of their so-called barrier, until that orange turns yellowish white underneath the dragon's unearthly blue flame.

The breath of these fires from the dragon's mouths has a curious reaction with the air, causing a heart unseen and unheard of in a normal fire, where it seems that nothing manmade can withstand it but for an instant. The sight of these white creatures with their ocean blue eyes aflame, with the whirlwind of their river fire all aglow is something not quite monstrous, even though it remains terrifying to the sight and the imagination—as the drifting of the towering funnel cloud through the man made structures lends itself to tranquility upon viewing, watching those snow white demons their bidding in war is truly a thing of beauty to behold, especially in the fading light of the evening day, when the stars from the impending fall of night become visible.

And my mother was either blessed or unblessed, lucky or unlucky, subject to predestiny or chaos, when she woke up this morning in the spirit of Mother Daughter Lust, which rose her up from her bed in end of the world grieving and emptiness, devoid of the feeling of purpose beyond this life, beyond the immediacy of lusts and instincts satisfied, the years of church services and listening to the Gospel to none affect, as she feels nothing of eschatology in these vials of liquid judgment poured out upon the earth. Seeing herself as a good person, who is worthy of whatever heavenly reality that might exist beyond this life. She has given to charity, given food to the hungry, given mercy and goods to the poor, had more than a few wayward children pass briefly through her home on their way up in society—why should she worry, what is there for her and Raymond Stewart to fear?

Fear and despair coalesce, and form the clouds of grieving over our journey north into Richmond, as the first drops of this morning rain have begun to splash downward, as the first drops of rain have begun to fall. The rain has little effect on the blue burning remains of the town around us, as the three of us peer through the SUV windows, through the shimmering waters of a grieving earth that fall. For reasons unknown to logic, by a logic unknown to reason, they chose this fine and historic spot to bring the blue and white pain to, leaving no stone unturned, and no stone unburned to their liking. Survival interviews say they *"sound like the loudest foghorns you've ever heard, and you know its them because suddenly there's this blue glow coming from outside your window; there's this rumble like you're in an earthquake, and all you want to do is run to the basement..."*

Those who were witnesses and lived to tell the tale, say that they were privy to the monster's appetites for destruction, as some houses were bitten down upon in the shattering of glass and brick and wood, as people were lifted from the rubble and devoured like fish in a barrel at Sea World. The Richmond attack confirmed what many had already reported but none had seen, that yes, people were being *eaten alive* in these attacks, being devoured in screams underneath the screams of lightning, and the roaring blasts of earth shattering thunder.

The burning landscape that is my mother's property is hardly diminished by the swirling wind and rain. The fire decorates the winds of war. Adding color to the name of God's will and purpose in the earth around us. The neighborhood looks as though a bomb were dropped, or as if it were attacked by a fleet of war planes without mercy, until there is nothing left but trees on fire and the smoldering remains of brick houses devastated. Yes, brick houses, broken and scattered about as if they had been made of straw kindling and wood, suggesting that they met with a force more immediate than the force of flaming heat initially.

On the street where my mother lived, the houses had been knocked down, clearly, the way they would have been if a tornadic wind or a bulldozer had gone through. In my soul's memory, by privilege of the vision the Fates allow me to see, as the temperature drops so rapidly around us, as the wind threatens to drive us back into our fine SUV from this smoldering rubble, I see the giant white menace Smyrna, descending in fury on this part of Richmond, his descent announced by a long and direct stream of liquid fire blasted from its open mouth, bursting into a ball of flaming blue energy upon the first grove of trees that stands nearby as a monolith of charred black sticks.

This great, flying monster swoops its gigantic body down past the burning trees to the first house, without a blast of second fire at first, and begins to crash into it like an angry child stomping through a sand castle when a parent says no, this sand being bricks and old money dying. And I hear the pain of rage in the blue eyed dragon's voice as it claims the children of the first house devoured, as it literally eats two of their three daughters alive in rage and fury coalesced by instinct into hunger.

And I see this great monster, the dinosaur formed to latter day power, move from house to house in quick and like manner, satisfied now with merely turning the houses to rubble without new flame as of just yet. And then I see the beast turn toward the grand old brick mansion which is my mother's home, where Raymond, Ray Stewart hides in the arrogance of defiance, refusing to go below in his home, refusing to believe that this is King Kong or Godzilla; that no, this monster will not eat my house and home, this monster will not dare touch my house—a thought seeming to enrage the beast anew, by default, causing him to rare backwards in the tell tale sign, and blast my mother's house in a spew of dark blue, liquid fire—a spew of liquid flame poured. Then through the burning curtain of a house, the beast crashes its great mouth through the upper portion of the house to where my father's arrogance awaits in form, locating him by scent and sight in the burning chaos, then snapping its great jaws shut upon what it sees in human screaming, leaning a partial remain behind to tell the tale of this—part of a right arm and right leg.

And this painful, fearful revelation is confirmed to me in reality, as we stay out here in the cold summer rain, sifting through the smoking ruins of complacency, the smoking ruins of prosperity—at the charred remains of Raymond Stewart in the ashes, and my mother nearly fainting where we stand, being escorted away from the ashen gray regret to our fine SUV, where she sits now wet and devastated in the storm.

An umbrella is God's mercy in the mist of sorrow. We have no rain gear, the three of us, not understanding when we left Brandmere Estates this morning to drive here that the world would begin to weep in mourning, but being lucky enough to have had a forgotten stash of tiny umbrellas in the back. It is a byproduct of the social dynamic, a consequence of benevolence bestowed by Fate, because we are always ready to lend such helping hands in hypocrisy. These umbrellas come in handy when Irene has to take her hand from her sexy, middle aged mouth and open the car door and stumble again into the rain, running down the street in indeterminate determination, not knowing where she is going or why, but being compelled to wander the Ruins of Athens, which was the road her delusion lived and died upon.

Walk the ruins of Athens Road, in the suburbs of Miller Creek Crossing. Mother, daughter, and granddaughter, to embody the three generations of Eve, here at the end of the second age of man. I hold Irene's arm tightly as we take our brief walk through the fiery devastation, where there are no fire trucks and ambulances and Red Cross cars to uplift hope and sanity. Gone are the days when billions of dollars were spent in emergency rescue missions and disaster aid—these endtime disasters are not simply a part of human life on earth—there are no more federal disaster areas declared, as the whole country is one great big federal disaster area now.

We walk lonely through the remains of burning life, our nostrils and lungs heavy with the scent of cinders and ashe, our breath thick with the air of eschatology, trying to make sense of the fiery blue puzzle put forth around us, and the black charred remains where glowing red embers still have life among the flames of blue. The fascinating walk through Miller Creek is the darling of this media age, this media obsessed culture—for what was an elegant old landscape, where brick mansion homes were nestled among woodsy stretches of hidden tranquility are now open country, where the burned remains of a small forest stand painfully in the rain, and where only the suggestion of houses are scattered in debris to the near horizon. Miller Creek in Richmond looks like it was hit by an F-5 twister, and exposed to a leering, peering endtime population.

When the music of hypocrisy is stripped away, the ugliness of original sin is terrible to behold. When the paint and prettiness of cultured civility is burned and charred away, when the elements of mankind's earthen façade are mixed with fervent heat, what lies underneath is the unimaginable truth, the revelation of the human condition, the foreshadowing of mankind's ultimate fate—which is outer darkness, where there worm dieth not, and where there shall be weeping and gnashing of teeth. Underneath the smiling prettiness and good natured civility and false charity and phony politeness is a burning soul of wicked intent, with whole forests of dark motivations created by the fires of sin, where all pretense toward goodness are ignited by the cause of a curse inherited from the Garden of Antiquity, where man is no longer capable of avoiding unrighteousness—where Gene Roddenberry's Star Trek Universe will remain science fiction, where the cold spirits of death and hopelessness will always haunt the streets of desperation, where because iniquity shall abound, the love of many shall wax cold, and the poor will always be among us. Where modern society is geared toward laziness where compassion is concerned, and apathy on climbing the hills of understanding. We go fast and hard toward the great precipice, spreeding like Thelma and Louise over the cliff, where the Great Canyon dive is the death of clarity, a corpse laid out but decorated in the fine linen of political correctness, and false politeness given for survival and advantage, but not in salvation and absolution for sin.

It is a world on the edge of annihilation. And what final form shall this devastation take? These are signs of the times we live in—these are the great wonders under Heaven spoken of and prophesied about, where the heavens are passing away with a great noise, and yes indeed, the elements are melting with a fervent heat. His ways are so far above our ways that it cannot be fathomed, his thoughts, beyond our imagination, his motivation, beyond our comprehension. The end of our understanding is the beginning of his, this great and powerful god I must soon get to know—the wonders of his greatness go to and fro about the earth—the majesty of his glory is unfathomable to man!

This is only the beginning of what he has planned. Only the echo of the start of mankind's total devastation, which will commence in end of the world drama first, dare I say in the revelation of the Redeemer, dare I say, as the eve of the Second Coming of Christ unfurls. This, I hear. This, I see in the heart of my soul's memory, where I feel the annihilation of the entire earth, and the devastation of the civilization of all mankind. The beginning of this, with the appearance of the seven angels of blue fire, with the destruction of mankind in grief, and flame, and vapour of smoke, to burn away the mask of hypocrisy in screaming, that the truth may be revealed underneath—that the reason for our impending demise may be shown to the Almighty's sovereign contact, that his own need to justify this judgment before our eyes is satisfied, even before we are taken by our escort angel in death to the Great White Throne, to learn whether our name is written in the book of life.

And in the magic and burning morning, as we wait for the fires of God's judgment to fall as great drops of rain, mankind goes on sinning; we go on marrying, buying and selling, eating and drinking, dying and being born, blessing and cursing one another, in tragedy and triumph, joy and sorrow, in light and darkness, in eternal life and salvation, and death and eternal damnation. Oh, thou wicked and adulterous generation, how can you escape damnation! How can you escape these signs up from beneath the earth, that it grieves the Lord that he made mankind, and the time for his righteous undoing of us is at hand!

The power of the human soul is paramount in Creation. Mankind is the fifth dimension of life. God the Father is the first—God the Son is the Second, God the Holy Ghost is the third—the heavenly hosts, the holy angels are the fourth dimension of life. And the ultimate power in Earth, underneath the heavens where the four dimensions rule, is the fifth dimension, which is the collective souls of humanity, which are at war with the spirit of the first four dimensions, which have been corrupted by the fallen angels, who the spiritual begotten of their father the Devil, who have corrupted God's creation beyond what his righteousness can endure. And his decision to create the fifth dimension of life must be rectified and reversed, and set right once and for all, to where mankind is made pure and clean by the sacrifice that God himself hath made, and the purity of our souls are reunited with him in glory.

Bt as I walk through the charred and open remains of burning life in the rain, I am confronted by the other side of God's nature, where love is encompassed by judgment, uncompromising and pure, knowing that Hell was created for the Devil and his angels, and that whosoever is not found written in the book of life will be cast into the lake of fire.

*G*od *is mad as Hell.*

It is the quiet and collective spirit of the moment as we drive. The unspoken truth that flows into the barely breathable air around us.

In the shadows of the night—the dragon silhouettes glow cold and snowy white. They walk tall through the smoking guns of war all aglow, seeming to be the height of fifty stories, though what exaggeration this be, I cannot tell. The beauty and tragedy of war glows simultaneously around these creatures, often content to slip behind a skyscraper as cover, ironically drawing fire from a doomed war machine below, until it seems that half the building has been blown up by tank fire and airplanes, even the occasional blast from a long range missile shot with pinpoint accuracy from a ship just off shore. There are those who believe that the tides of World War 3 have come rolling in; though oddly enough, not with malice toward our fellow man, so much as our visitors from the cold north deep.

And it seems that they have grown in stature and strength since their arrivals, as they were not yet fully grown when they first made themselves known to us, as they flitted and flew about almost timidly, with emphasis on attack and retreat, go back and repeat, flow back and reheat the concrete landscape to a fervent melting down the street.

And it seems that they are content now, as any seven cities around the world seem to be set ablaze anew at any turn along the timeline—they are content with old time stomping and raging by the doomed buildings, to give those stupid enough to be inside them a real show for their money, as they lumber past in a storm of earth rumbling noise—leaving the fools grateful that the monsters decided not to turn their heads and blow those trumpeting voices in blue and black fire. People around the world have refused to give up, in the cities not yet destroyed by one of the Seven Sisters, by one of the fire stars from Heaven, as many stubbornly commute to work into the buildings that still stand, as if the world still had a chance at normalcy—as if the planet still had a reason to turn and live for man.

In the smoke and silhouette, the giant monsters rise ten, twenty, thirty stories into the evening air, their eyes lit up all aglow, the memory of their dragon heads burned so bright into the consciousness of every human being on earth—for their seems no jungle savage that has not stopped pretending not to know, to not cower in fear at what liquid and fiery death these monster soldiers, these angels of death are capable of. There is hardly room left in the sentiment of man for any other concern, for any other interest downloaded from the radio or television into consciousness, as if seven white tornadoes gigantic and swirling white with lightning blue have come ashore, and have taken over the comings and goings of man.

And these summer months have not been spared the ravages of what weather cycle it is that is overdue, as the earthquakes rumble at many more times the frequency of any time in human history, oftentimes finishing what job the dragon hath begun, having brushed himself so lovingly, so unlovingly, and so hatefully against a doomed building under cloak of night, as the smoke of their battle with mankind rises around them in the darkness, to reveal the glow of their skin and scales in fire and snowy white.

These are the hardheaded mothers that scream. The young and jaded women in their corporate dresses and skirts, lost in stubbornness though the Freedom Towers are long gone, having been turned back into the shattered pieces of clay they were born from, having been sent back to the graveyards from where they were risen, with no more tears of sorrow and mourning left to cry for what transpired when the pitiful arrows were flown from the east, to turn the two concrete originals into powder and dust.

These are the poverty mothers. Pledged to die in the cities not yet descended upon, rather than let chaos and loss of control come in and take their lives—for these are lives so hard fought and won on their climb up the ladder of income, in their pursuit of the new American Gothic, which is to sit at a desk on a computer all day and tap away—while busy, hopeless callers who need customer service get lost in a hellish runaround of automatic phone menus, customers with no hope of speaking to a human being behind the veil of phone and electronic forestry grown. These are the corporate mothers, content to wait for the eyes of the dragon fire, who hath descended from the first heaven, with power breathed from beyond the second heaven, to where the wrath from the third heaven is at last given and shown.

These are the modern mothers who wait—with every excuse of stubbornness, who no longer understand female empowerment, nor the beauty of feminine strength and virtue, but only the lust for sex and money, the lure of what pride and avarice their corporate time will buy for them. These are the wayward wives and mothers, who have bound themselves up in the corporate chase, who do not fear the approaching eyes of the dragon, but rather wait for it in hatred, to gaze at long last at the fiery blue eyes that stare. These are the secretaries and corporate assistants who walk the carpeted corridors of corporate concern, in and out of the elevators up and down, heeding no warning, no recommendation for the possibilities that must be, for the tragedies that must befall them, for when the trumpeting voices of eschatology must rise and fall, and the myriad of flaming glass, concrete and steel must soon begin to glow in blue flame, and fall to earth so completely down around them.

This is no longer the eve of eschatology. This is the sunrise of its arrival. The morning. The Dawn of Realization. Where the light of Revelation is shown. The impending arrival of the trump of God. When the dead will rise to their destiny in eternity.

It is the so-called Second Coming. But of who and what—does this name bear mentioning here? What judgment of God hath been wrought upon the world, burning in blue and black fire? These are the homes of the privileged.

The houses of ill repute. Witchcraft has taken its modern day form—where domestic violence, child abuse and adultery are grown like moss in the forgotten woods, which bears viewing to be appreciated, when the female babysitter, the blonde white doll, decides that the little Carmen doll of thirteen is too beautiful, too sensual for her to miss the opportunity, the chance to file the experience away into her blonde doll memory. The deep tongue kissing she engages, the west coast sunny side up in smiles and laughter concealing, hiding the teenage heart of pedophilic darkness, where her little craving, her seventeen year old craving is to give this little thirteen year old a body shaking pleasure that she may see it happen, and file it away for the psychological safekeeping, the fuel for the fires in which we burn, the flames of what drives her from here, down the timeline to her future before the Lord—a lifetime of intense, self-martyred dedication to youth girls, where her craving is raised and lowered deep into her 40's and 50's in vampiric instinct, to where her own trembling against little girls, young teenagers and young women number into the scores of happenings—a serial killer of little souls—the souls of little girls without a rudder to guide them in the moral sea, the ocean of secrets that cannot be spoken aloud, of what Ms. Milton does to them in private, of what shakings and breathing, what yells and bellowing Ms. Milton, youth pastor and Jr. High School 7th and 8th grade teacher hath done.

This is not the eve of eschatology. This is the morning day of its arrival. When the waning crescent light of the sliver, the sliver of the silvery moon doth shine in brilliance, above the hidden bright and morning star.

There's no need to strike another nuclear fire. This, the prevailing question asked and answered over Tokyo Bay, where the Japanese gave in to the stubbornness, and decided that the next time one of the Angel Dragons made its next appearance, they would be the first to put a stop to it. But the only thing they succeeded in doing was creating a bigger mess than had already been started, as the white dragon's steps had already caused an earthquake off shore, and its rising sent a small tidal wave spreading inward, which swept hundreds to their watery deaths, turning so much of the city nearby the bay into a pile of watery debris as the monster came ashore, his arrival in the wake of the brightest manmade flash in human history, made by a device as what hath never been wrought before, that mankind hath never had the courage or the stupidity to strike—the hot, fiery winds doing damage to the city at the shores of Tokyo Bay. The monster had emerged from the nuclear fire unscathed and angry, the fire of his blue eyes burning as he stood high in the waters off shore, towering 30 stories into the air in exclamation point that no, there is no vulnerability here to speak of, no cracks in this end of the world armour.

Oh, but what does it say about the heart of man, when the nuclear fire was struck in grieving? So many have already died in the tidal wave and the earthquake—how many more must perish on an untested theory? We must sacrifice a few lives, they say, to that we can save many millions more. And so, the already devastated coastlines of Tokyo are on fire of revelation, but this, not the blue fires of judgment just yet, this, the orange and yellow fires of foolhardiness and solutions tried outside the sovereign will of God, where the blast wave is so much bigger than proposed, sending a wall of flame ashore past the tidal wave debris, past the few hundred bodies afloat in dreams beyond this life—deep inside the outskirts of the city, to light sensibilities up in flames of realization, that there will be no manmade solutions to this problem, that this is truly the end of the age, and the fires of judgment are going to burn in the manner of our choosing, either the red fires of human stubbornness and stupidity, or the blue and black flames of revelation sent from Heaven above.

And this 350 foot beast from beneath the earth rises out of the water and comes ashore into the city, bent on total destruction, his eyes big, bright blue against the smoke and soot—not from the nuclear blast but from his own nostrils, spreading wings too massive for description, to give the elegance to his stride—rising briefly upward to move his progress speedily forward, floating down into the heart of the screaming population—as they hide in their cars and trains, trying to leave the city for parts unknown, for a place so far away from the death they were promised, and from what dark reward awaits them in the world beyond this life.

The fires of Tokyo do not burn in the theater of my mother's mind, as the heart of her grieving forms the future of our inner suffering. The sensual woman is in charge of us, even before she speaks the fateful words—*I want you two to go to your mother's bedroom and take off your clothes and wait for me. I'm going to have a drink and I'll be there in just a few minutes. Don't talk*, she snaps at me, as I try the verbal bewilderment, as I try the logical, psychological deflection but to no avail. I take Meadow by the arm and escort her obediently, reticently up the stairs of our magnificent million dollar suburban home, a collection of luxurious collections, a clutter of treasures replete with pressures and the sorrow of the privileged.

Meadow and I glance at one another in disturbed wonder, knowing that we are no longer in charge of the secret life we have wrought—that what behind closed doors energy there was is transformed, is drafted from us like the atmosphere from a world lifted by the gravity of a passing planet—this planet being Irenia, Goddess of Mother Daughter Perversion, of which is so pervasive in the world around us, but remains a hidden taboo, even at the end of the age, as the poverty mother hath stripped her teenage daughter bare behind closed doors and begun the belt whipping to exhaustion, and then commences to lay upon her daughter who is nude; this heavy breasted poverty mother in her bra and underwear, to hump and grind upon the daughter between her open legs spread apart, until the daughter's punishment and humiliation are complete, and the mother's dark instinct is satisfied.

Irenia, the Goddess of Mother Daughter Perversion is at rest in our kitchen at the counter, taking a drink of resignation, that her husband is dead and gone, her house and former life is dead and gone—and so too are her inhibitions, the natural barriers that have kept her from this over the years, those barriers that had relegated these thoughts to her private bath and sleep fantasies, unbeknownst to her husband, who was cooked and eaten by one of the dragons, the one the world refers to as "Spike," because of the great platelets that run up and down its back in beauty of design, the dragon *Laodicea*, the largest and most formidable of the seven dragons from beneath the earth.

In the same Laodicean hypocrisy that blankets the rest of the world in shadow, Irene removes herself from the wine of the whited grape, the white wine of her desperation, and she comes up the stairs and goes quickly to where we wait for her in obedience. The woman of mature and sophisticated beauty inquires of the whereabouts of our paddle, retrieving it in the authority of desire, the authority of Prosperity, having Meadow and I face each other and hold onto each other naked, which tingles the nipples of my breasts to no end, as I watch my mother—the mature, sophisticated blonde woman of substance, as I watch her rare back and bring the paddle with crashing assurance to my daughter's ample backside, which makes her strain against a loud yell in my ear, the experience of which I have never felt or imagined, which trembles the inside of me like a mind warning of an approaching earthquake.

And this, Mother does again with skill, until my Meadow is broken and weeping in my ear, which lights a flame in me that runs its course from my tingling nipples onward, until my hips are on this self same fire of trembling, and I have to breathe to resist the exclamation point in my own voice, as the energy explodes deep into my body from what I see and feel, to shake me once mightily from head to toe. This, my mother senses. This, I know she hath seen, which satisfies her enough to end Meadow's paddling, and inquire as to the whereabouts of the strap on phalluses.

She locates them, she finds them in the warning breeze, the warning winds of our eschatology, strapping one upon myself and upon my daughter. This woman who is my birth mother, yes, the woman who gave birth to me, she kneels down before us and begins to suck and fellatio the both of us as if they were capable of a fountain, as if they fountain of her sexual youth were contained within—these being the expressions of her inner self unleashed, the animal grunting she displays and unleashes, the spit she allows to fall in choking from each of us strapped on—a feeling that goes beyond any I have had, that even touches my daughter deep enough to make her close her wondering eyes and hold her head back in surrender, that the beautiful and sensual mother of her mother is burdened by this end of the world lust unseen, and unimagined by so much of the condemned world outside these privileged walls.

When she is done, she escorts us to the bed, where Meadow is told to lie down, with the extension of herself one inch times eight into the air, powerful and prepared. My mother, Irene, climbs on top of my daughter, sliding herself down upon her, to impale the last of pretense to death, to end all speculation of what behind closed doors reasons there be for living, to give in to the impending loss of tomorrow.

Mother yells a powerful grunting as she slides down on my daughter's phallus, reaching back and removing her bra, the last barrier to fall, to fully reveal the origins of my own perverted past, of whose milk I have tasted as a teenager, as I lay in her lap and nursed her fully clothed like a suckling child in the Heart of Memory. But in this present day, in this latter day, I hear her speak expressly, for me to get behind her, and to put it in her, which I attempt to do, until she herself lubricates the tip of it with the spit of her deviant play, allowing me to slide it into her backside as she yells so loudly in the surrender of a tortured soul, where loss of dignity is the benchmark to the future.

I am inspired to the sadism of the moment. Pushing it past her resolve, sliding it so deeply up inside her until every inch is pushed in, resting behind her, holding onto my beautiful mother while she leans back against me in uncertainty, betwixt whether or not the feeling is a comfort or discomfort, pleasure or pain, agony or ecstasy. But her body decides for her in instinct, as she begins to hump herself against both phalluses, feeling Meadow against her womb at the front gate, and me at the barrier to it at the rear, the knocking of both spirits at the forward and rear of her center being too much for her to bear easily, causing her to lower and shake her head wildly and accordingly.

And this, she continues to do, as the feeling rises to a slight degree of madness within, when I take both her nipples in my fingers and pinch them without ceasing, giving such a renewed and instinctual flow to the center of her groin, as Meadow holds on to Irene's curved and mature waist, watching her own mother's mother grind herself to oblivion, to activate what dormant sensibilities lie within, as Meadow's own body begins to course with this hidden depravity we share. My own head begins to swoon and swirl with the advent of new desire, as my hand slides down to my Mother's center, which makes her push her head further back against me in new and desperate concentration, to infuse the three of us with the knowledge that yes, our Mother needs to cum, and she needs to cum quickly, to avoid her body's death and devastation, to give it new life, and life more abundantly.

And so I oblige this, rubbing the front of her with skill as I have been wrought as a woman, with one hand at the front of her and the other at her breasts, until she begins to grunt repeatedly in a crescendo of madness, until the nuclear fires are struck inside, and her grunting is shaken by the explosion of flame inside her body, that convulses every inch of her like the arrival of our impending devastation, passing through her like an earthquake over the battlefields of Armageddon.

*T*ongues deeply probing, our mouths wide open, my beautiful Mother

and me, to continue our legacy behind closed doors, as the eve of

the Second Coming of Christ unfurls. And I am by no means a religious

woman, even knowing in my heart where I'm going if I die today, if one of

these dragons finally does to our house what it did to my father's house and

what it did to his body, taking him out of this world with one sharp bite and

epic swallowing, where he slid alive into the fiery pit of the monster's

insides, until he succumbed to the heat of acid pain in the darkness of Hell

on earth. What is it to be eaten alive by the Devil? Surely, none have been

so unlucky, and then lived to tell the horror story of their painful death, as

the ghost of Timothy Treadwell hath done.

In the heat of unfathomable lust, I am devoured, overtaken by the whim

and desire of this beautiful woman, this woman of seasoned and bottle

blonded beauty in her upper 50's, having achieved that modern Nowhere's

Land of female aging, where youth is far spent, and no longer a factor in her extraordinary sensuality. But maturity hath only served to make more sensual every feature, every curve, every feminine nuance of her form from head toe as Hippolyta, Goddess of Themiscyra.

Tongues deeply probing. Mouths wide open in what the French call a kiss sometimes. Fully clothed in our suburban best in our foreplay, heels on. Dress tightly draped upon the woman in her high 30's to the edge of 40, which is me. Skirt and blouse fit for the office is she, the blonde mother and daughter are we. Neither of us with knowledge of what must be a continent away, upon the fabled Golden Gate bridge this very day, when the gray descends over the bay like a prophecy, and the thunder and lightning begins.

Mother removes her belt, leather and black, and tells me to take off every stitch of my clothing. And this, I do, as she gathers the stockings of legend from somewhere in the grand bedroom, and my naked legs are tied at the ankles. Then I am bent over to where I feel the elongated breasts swing toward the floor, at truth that runs through the women of our families, breasts that flop and hang downward to varying degrees, the champion of this being my daughter when she is unclothed, the girth of which are macromastic, so that even at eighteen, they hang down to her waist in perfect fertility Goddess beauty.

Obediently, I am bent over for Mother, as she does not yet make work of her skirt and blouse away, leaving them in place, leaving them tightly done up in authority. And soon, I hear the high pitched "yip" fly out of my own mouth, after I feel the snapping sound upon my ample backside, to lash a welt across the ass of my white skin. And there is the inglorious pause, as she gathers another stocking of legend, and commences the ties that bind the wrists, tightly up and behind my back in grieving.

Here I am bent over, ankles tied, wrists tied, breasts hanging down untied, as though an invisible weight were hung from the two of them. And Mother gathers her strength in full this time, raising her arm high, bringing the leather down in a crashing blow with skill, to where the tip of the belt bites a chip of skin from my backside, a yipping that I actually suppress, held in by shock and disbelief, of the level of pain this is, and the level of perversion this is, unfurled from the core of our spirits, and the heart of our visions and dreams.

This is but the second of seven blows, I count, until she lays the belt aside, touching the places on my skin raised and red, to marvel at how Fate decided to marry the words welt and belt by pure sound alone.

"You've got seven of the best welts on your ass I've ever seen, she says. "Where's your camera?"

"You serious?"

"What do you think?"

"There's a closet full of 'em," I say. "You know John and his tech fetish. Sometimes I think he wishes I were a robot."

Mother goes into the closet, retrieving the smallest and simplest looking thing that masquerades our space as a life essential, though it may be one of the most trivial of all end of the world truths in technology for the home. We do not shoot movies, we do not shoot the news, we do not shoot commercials, we so not shoot entertainment for television. This, a high powered, high priced toy.

Mother pulls this silver thing, takes a brief moment to orient the inherent skill that all suburban women seem to have as amateur cinematographers, and she laughingly puts the camera right in my face, to capture what is left of my humiliation on film, and the tears that stain a rosy cheek or two.

"It hurt, didn't it?"

I only laugh a little, and lower my eyes.

"You're lucky you're such a good welter," she says. "Otherwise I'd probably still be hitting you."

Holding the camera steady to my face, she says, "What if I told you that you were going to get another whipping tomorrow?"

The types of fear are many, and uniquely distinguished. Among these is the Fear of Pain, which washes through my brain and down through the rest of my body. The apprehension, the nervousness in my eyes is to her fervent delight. She moves with her little camera down to the rest of my body, filming the welted and reddened skin on my fair skinned hips. Taking long and slow inventory of her work, scanning the back of me up and down, from the welted buttocks to the two that decorate my left thigh.

"Magnificent. These are the biggest *welts,*" she says, toughing them with her free hand, fingernails done so pretty in pewter, to match the melancholy of the skirt she wears so tightly. She is soon done, the documentary of her deviance delivered, sent into the brief span of her near future, to gauge its worthiness to satisfy her inner craving. She unties the stocking from my wrists, and then from my ankles, and escorts me to the fine space of a bathroom, in the house that Jack built. The camera is turned off and placed on the dresser, as a guest turned away, uninvited to the privacy of future events. These events are upon us. As she begins to slowly undress in front of me, not taking her eyes from mine, to watch her daughter's awkwardness, to absorb the effect of this otherworldly deviance on my psychology, as a mature daughter at the dawn of 40, with a life and a daughter of her own watches her mother undress after having belt whipped her.

From within the bags she brought with her when she arrived this very morning, Irene produces like a magician the instruments of her needs, the manifestation of desires born. She slides the straps up around her big hips and tightens them in front of me, as the crème colored member hangs down in realistic form from the breasty lady in front of me, that I may receive the visual which is the best of both worlds. With the member hanging down, she pulls the white enema bottle from the black bag, and fills it to bursting with water.

It is as though the memory of our past is resurrected, born from an imprint that began on my sixteenth birthday, when I was in the tenth grade, and Mother was a secretary in a prestigious law firm. I stand in obedience to this inner voice we both hear, facing the mirror as she holds the bag up with one hand, and slides the enema nozzle so smoothly into my bottom from behind. I lower my head and bellow like an animal, as my entire body rings with a shot of orgasmic energy, that stops just short of causing a visible tremble, as one who teeters on the edge of a great height, but is kept from falling by unseen Fate.

This is Mother Daughter Perversion. As the eve of the Second Coming unfurls upon the earth, burning blue and black fire.

Mother holds the enema bag up with one strong hand, holding the nozzle in me with the other, as I lower my head repeatedly and moan loud enough to wake the dead. And when I am filled to bursting, when the water in me blows backwards from around the nozzle inside me as I tense and scream, she exclaims her mighty approval, her satisfaction in the requisite "oh yeahs" and "oh yes's" hanging the bag upon the towel hook nearby the mirror, keeping the nozzle deep inside me to prolong my suffering, as my bowels are filled with water. In the mirror, I witness the suffering woman bent over, the pain in her expression colored by ecstasy, as the mature woman gets behind her, until the younger woman feels the fullness of the mother's mind slide into her from behind, pushing the member into her proper place, while the enema nozzle remains in its improper place, to increase my suffering two fold, and four fold the impossible pleasures ignited from within. How, pray tell, doth water ignite the burning of blue and black fire within! To where my womb begins, in the trifecta of pleasure, from my groin, to my backside, to the breasts I must heartily pull upon, I am at the mercy of what is passed down through the motherline generations, as she carefully, skillfully slides the member all the way in, pushing the nozzle inward as well, until every inch of my groin and bowels are plugged.

In the mirror, I see the lovely Irene close her eyes and hold her head back, as if enduring an unendurable wave of brief pleasure through her body. She reaches forward with both hands to my nipples, anchoring the member and nozzle in place with her body. And as she begins to tweak and pull both nipples, it is as though a chord of energy hath been plugged in, and I feel her begin to bang against me in slow rhythm, even while the enema nozzle remains in place, keeping my bowels full with water, as she begins to bump and grind her member deep into my groin with a sustained rhythm—a slow, steady bumping against me from behind, that continues to build pleasure inside my body wave upon wave, until I hear her voice tell me "hold that water in baby, so you can cum on that cock." And whether or not she is aware, the words reach into me, to tickle my sensibility, to raise up a wave that climbs to unbelievable heights, then it begins to fall mightily toward the earth upon my wailing, weeping voice until it crashes, to send the wail into a scream in the air around us, and a trembling that shakes my body from head to toe.

And it is this mighty weeping, this earthquake trembling of mine that guides her into a harder rhythm, involuntary, to where I glimpse the shock upon her face as it happens, when she must call the name of Jesus as the wave starts at the center of her body, then shakes her rapidly from the core of her spirit, until I hear it flow in the end of the world trembling through her voice, as the energy explodes inside of her, and passes in waves of trembling thought every curve and inch of her body.

A Rhapsody in Blue

Jonathan Lovejoy

A Tale of Two Sisters

others and Daughters at the end of the world, as they burden the heart and mind. As the eve of the Second Coming of Jesus Christ unfurls, here at the end of time. My mind is lifted upon these ungentle breezes, three thousand miles west of tragedy, to where sublime devastation is born.

It is the tale of two women. The mother of Chinese descent. So beautiful in the middle of her fiftieth decade, being driven in the rain by the smarter and younger version of herself, her daughter of this self same descent, equally as beautiful in the land of thirty. These two drive on toward the Golden Gate Bridge, to partake of what business lies on the other side through the rain, after they cross the bridge of legend, in modern silver luxury. This, they do in unique motivation, being singular in the purpose of Fate, that they are the only ones who traverse the bridge at this part of the timeline, the only ones who have given in to the feeling that is pervasive, among all the sensual mothers and daughters in their rainy cars—in this spot along the human journey, they are the only ones that the spirits may judge fully, who have acted upon this end of the world feeling that tugs, as the mother being driven in the smart and silver ride, reaches her left hand over to the driving daughters right knee, to touch it unsurreptitiously, but keeping her gaze forward in the rain.

Of this Asian mother's sensibility, there is no resistance from the daughter, this Doctor of Psychology, who knows from where all of her patients speak, having lived under the burden of the unspeakable herself since she was a little girl, after the father was so conveniently dead and gone. When her mother so conveniently inconvenienced her daughter's future with this truth, that among the evil population, it is a shame to speak of those things which are done of them in secret, that none would surely believe.

In the driving rain, the mother slides the driving daughter's skirt so casually, so uncasually upward from her black booted leg, until the skin of her daughter's thigh is exposed. The sliding of the fabric across this Asian daughter's skin slides a wave of quivering across the core of her soul, emanating from the nerves of the physical body, pushed along in an energy intangible and therefore unstoppable by the beautiful mother's determined and intimate Cantonese, the likely symbol of this impending, when the daughter of thirty three understands what surely must be.

For a quarter of a century, she knows what must be. Drawn into the full blown power of this deviance when it is engaged, when those that must partake of it come under its spell, as one who is bound by the alcoholic drink, or by whatever legal or illegal drug of choice there must be. In the daughter's heart of hearts, her eyes are already closed, and her head is already leaned far back, to feel the completion of the wave, as the exquisite mother must slide her hand far to the region of her daughter's inner thigh while she drives, speaking still in the secret tongue of the two of them, a recitation of poetic musing, intermingled with the clarity of truth, "*my hand is warmed by the fires of thee, at the center of thy beauty, I call to thee…*"

And upon this recitation, she slides her hand to completion, to the daughter's delighted dismay, to increase the power of sensuality, the power of secrets that drive, that motivate end of the world humanity.

And the daughter drives on in the rain, so comfortably hidden in the storm of every passing car, and those who would leer, and peer to break in. The mother works her hand in squeezing upon her daughter's inner thigh, to where part of her hand rubs the center of where the daughter sits to drive, until the daughter must slow her driving to minimum proper speed in the rain, and hold her mother's hand in its proper place at her underwear cloth hidden, by the fabric of her skirt gathered and pushed upward in grieving.

And from this inner grief is the reprieve of addiction, as any who have their chosen method of relief from the pain of this life, they express themselves in the open as an end of the world secret revealed, as the storm of eschatology grows, and the feeling they share with mankind grows exponentially; that these are the last days, and there is no further reason for behind closed doors façade, there is no further reason for hypocrisy in secret, there is no further reason for pretense in the dark, where deviance is born and bred, and where depravity is nurtured and grown.

And this rubbing against her underwear cloth lifts her up and transports her backward into the Heart of Memory, to where her and her mother were guests in a professor's home when she was but a girl of 12, when they found their way so surreptitiously to the bathroom upstairs, when the mother sat on the toilet with her lovely red dress folded up and away from her bottom, while her daughter straddled her thigh in such a fervent and hopping grind upon it, the mother's twelve year old flower in bloom, after she hath watered the petals of this rose with her lips and tongue upon her daughters young nipples, until her twelve year old beauty shook her head and spoke her girlish Cantonese—as her young body had threatened to begin trembling on its own.

In the locked bathroom of this lady professor's house, unbeknownst to the unwitting guests below, the daughter moves from the mother's thigh to a full straddle, as the mother sits on the toilet seat with her underwear still so tightly up in its proper place, as is the twelve year old beauty's underwear as well, to grind the front of herself against her mother in a fever, while the mother holds the back of her young daughter's hair in pulling, staring at the daughter's face in a pitiful defeat, that the sight and feel of her twelve year old's desperation is about to achieve the impossible in the core of the mother's spirit, and light her body in a burning of blue and black fire. But the mother strains to wait while the daughter bounces, the sounds they make so ingeniously covered by Mozart's piano from down below, as the conversation at their after dinner table has deepened to the throes of mankind himself, and the elements of end of the world immorality.

And when the mother looks again at the beauty of her twelve year old's innocence corrupted, the unearthly beauty of the child's expression contorted, twisted with desperation to achieve, her teeth gritted and grimaced in the effort, the mother's body flares upon its own, and she pulls her daughter's hair with a strength unbeknownst, as she shakes upon the toilet sitting, her daughter's twelve year old, raven strands wrapped tightly about her hand, as she covers her daughter's mouth with her other hand, to hide the emergence of a twelve year old yelp of suffering.

From the Heart of Memory, the 33 year old daughter emerges to the rising of the waters, splashing over the bridge in front of them as they drive, to produce a scream of fear from the both of them, as their shimmering gray view is suddenly lit up in a flame of royal blue, in fire that is alive with purpose, clinging to the steel cables of the bridge in front of them, then to many of the cars far out front, as the source of the flame and the rising water reveals itself in furious aggression upon the tall bridge support, as burning cables begin to snap and fall down around them, pulled and bitten apart by the mouth of the angry dragon.

In the Fear of Death, in the terror of the unknown, the mother and daughter join the rest of the people at this place along the timeline, as the white beast Pergamon rocks the bridge in dangerous instability, towering high above the bridge road, the deadly claws visible as they tear away a supporting cable or two, as the fires of judgment begin to coat the tall, rusted metal support, and the road in front of them begins to crumble and collapse into the raging waters below.

And they are privy to the unearthly desperation, as the animal sounds is foghorn voice loud enough to wake the dead, as the gigantic, snow white jaws beneath eyes of royal blue life reach down to the road unbroken nearby, and clamp down upon a black luxury SUV, raising it up in a ball of exploding orange flame, then tossing it free from its mouth in rage.

And the mother and daughter face this end of the world reality again, as the mouth of the dragon makes its crashing, clamping presence known to them, flipping their silver luxury ride with wild abandon many car lengths backward, away from the broken road, smashing them tossed upside down like glass and metallic debris onto the bridge road in the rain, leaving the two of them bloody and broken upside down in their seats, with the mother unconscious as though she were dead, and the daughter seeing the broken world around her in a fog of confusion, thunder and lightning, and the sting of icy cold wind and rain upon her skin.

Jonathan Lovejoy

$\mathcal{T}$he dragons are protected by a barrier of pure energy, so that nothing can penetrate their natural invulnerability. The fullness of their design seems to be destruction by fire, as if nature made sure that they could fulfill this purpose without interruption. Shoot at them all day and all night—nothing will come of it but balls of fire and great plumes and puffs of smoke, until more harm than good is done, bringing more damage to the surrounding landscape than what the dragon itself seeks to accomplish. And it seems that every country's military believes that whatever magic it can conjure is the solution, as the collective humanity will not bow down to the monsters' inevitability, as no one seems to learn their lesson, flying fleets and squadrons of planes in the dragon's faces every chance they get, as if they are obligated by Destiny to make fools of themselves—unable to do more than waste ammunition over the three hundred foot monster's heads. And every so often, the nighttime skies are alive with many lights and shades of fire, especially when the monsters become distracted by the constant barrage of fire from the planes. There is hardly a sight more spectacularly beautiful, than when the spiked plates along the dragon's back phase into a shade of alabaster blue (as prophesied by the legend), as the dragon prepares itself for another breath of fury—turning its attention from the city, town or countryside below, to address the problems approaching from above. The eyes take on a particularly bright glow in the nighttime air, as the mouth opens, and the blue fire pours out like a natural flame thrower toward the sky, touching many dozens of stubborn planes on fire of blue, which consumes each plane that it touches with a certain and fiery demise, as the planes streak downward in blue fireballs all over the sky, until at last there are no more left to waste ammunition, until there are no more left to burn—and the monster returns to its original purpose in fire and white.

In the evening day storm, along the darkening skyline of this West Coast City, the fires of human futility burn through the air at the monster created in scales of spectacular snowy white, as it spreads flames of royal blue along the buildings and city streets, until the view from below is as though it is raining blue fire from heaven—carried along by the wind and unaffected by the pouring rain. The appearing of these gigantic creatures is certain death, no monster of fiction is their equal. Towering the height of 25 to 30 stories in the lightning, roaring thunder and pouring rain, the monster raises up and takes spectacular and brief flight to the heart of the West Coast City, to the tallest hotel building it sees, where it senses the floors teeming with life, this life of the two legged variety, that proclaims knowledge, reason and higher intelligence, among its many audacities, one being to reject the incarnation of God in the flesh when he walked among us, then to reject him again through the generations after he hath ascended to the right hand of power and glory.

These masses of hidden pride and arrogance stare out the windows of the luxury hotel, over 50 floors of astonishment and fear, as the thunder calls them to fore, and the lightning shows them what for, of the white dragon beast that glides so gracefully outside their window. In the earthquake landing achieved by this monster, as the ground rumbles like thunder when it lands on its feet, the children scream to their helpless mothers and fathers in the storm, at what horror there is that towers outside in the lightning storm, trembling and cowering from the warning trumpet of a voice that comes forth, as the precursor to what must be, as the dragon's spikes glow as blue as the ocean in the evening storm, to warn of its impending judgment in blue and black fire.

Souls brave enough to not run and hide in bathrooms and closets stand in rapt amazement nearby the windows of false security, to see up close the eyes of their devastation, the otherworldly beauty of color and design, teeth gleaming in razor sharp fury under eyes of merciless intent and ruthless force and power. And these are the ones who stare death in the eyes of the dragon, who see death in the eyes of blue, in the smoke that emanates from the nostrils in the briefest echo of the earthly logic, dominated by the unearthly impossibility of its very presence, fearful enough to subjugate all of creation, and cause nothing but fear and dread.

And these are the unlucky few, who are privy to the dragon's expressions of purity, forced to acknowledge the looks upon the monster's faces of controlled rage, an anger of righteous purity, where there is no evil, but only instinct with determination, devastation and mercy. And in obedience to its otherworldly calling, the white dragon's head rears back in a grimace of anger turned dark, in a piercing gaze of instinct turned evil, the dragon lunges its head and neck forward, opening its mouth with purpose and determination, spraying fire directly into the glass sides of the fancy hotel, the fire blasting through the windows into the living spaces like an explosion in blue, burning the stubborn residences alive in flame, some of them drawing upon their audacity to seek refuge elsewhere after they have been lit up with fire, a few souls scattering into the hallways away from the burning in their apartment homes, running through the halls on fire in tell tale blue, as a sign unto them that look on in devastated awe and grief at the people burning through the hallways, the many women and children they known on fire, seeming to chase them, catching them and setting them on fire as well.

Some of them take common sense over compassion, hurrying away from the burning people and going back into their apartments, to listen to the screams and the pounding on their doors from the outside, a gathering of end of the world sounds merged with the voice of the storm, the crackling thunder, and the sound of unearthly rage and intent pouring forth from the mouth of death, in the deep, foghorn call to the end of the age, in the voice of doom and eschatology.

21

The seven major notes of the white keys beckon, in the voice of the seven monsters from the end of the age. These seven voices, which sound so much alike to the untrained ear, to those not given to wild thoughts and speculations of fancy. Most are not inclined to believe or care about the 13 year old girl from Pamlico Sound, North Carolina, who claimed to have heard such distractions in the dragon's voices. The child was so quickly dismissed as mad, and told by so many to wake up out of the foolish dream she was in to reality. And none have bothered to corroborate or fully deny her claim, which she admitted was given to her in a dream, which saw her at the piano matching the notes to the voices of the seven dragons—the seven deepest basses on the keyboard from C major on upward to B flat major. The world is not ready to receive this revelation, that the seven dragons carry the seven voices of music in white, these voices that combine to carry an endtime message from on high.

All that is known from person to person, from town to town, from home to terrified home, is that the foghorn voices of any one of these creatures is as the voice of certain death, more fearful than the charge of a hungry lion or an angry grizzly bear. At least from these there is the futility of running, the madness of standing up in useless defiance, the sadness of dropping to the opossum's stance on the ground, to wait for a reprieve from Fate, Destiny and God. But the sound of the foghorn trumpet, no matter what key they rise and fall inside, are a warning and reminder of certain death, that there is no reprieve, and no escape from the pain of this truth, that an appearance from any one of them can only be waited out in terror, that the sound they make is as the trump of God on the eve of the Second Coming, that a message of judgment may be imminent in the night wind, or even the gentle morning breeze that blows.

To hear the voice of the dragon is to hear one of the seven angels of judgment, sent to exact punishment on the souls, minds and bodies of the people of earth, upon those who have spent their lives in doubt and unbelief, who have rejected the Holy Scriptures as false or contradictory, as inaccurate or untrue—who have rejected the Spirit of the word as invalid, insignificant, or incapable. This is the voice of the dragon pitched in G, the great dragon Sardis, that returns to the cityscape in the cool of the evening, after the storm of lightning and thunder has passed, and the clouds unveil the light of redemption in the coming night.

The evening call roars throughout creation, pitched in Eine Kleine Nachtmusik, the voice of the monster that killed the great west coast bridge rust red, to reveal in the passing deluge of rain the beginning of the dreadful wrath of God. It is the voice of the dragon in G at twilight, nearby the edge of night that she hears, as she lies in the uneasy calm of the hospital, eyes half closed in reluctant rest and quiet apprehension of half sleep, lest her mind return her to the fearful dreams of the bridge dragon, and the mouth of razor sharp teeth under the eyes of blue—these teeth that clamped into the hood of her silver luxury ride like it were made of cardboard fiber, flipping her and her mother through the air as condemned souls of resignation, souls resigned to whatever Hell on earth they are in.

The eyes of the dragon burn blue in her soul, even as she finally allows her own Asian eyes of beauty to close, seeing the bridge immediately from two hundred feet in the air as if carried by the dragon's vision, lowering in lightning pace to the silver luxury ride below. Crashing into it with such force as to declare her awake again, to remember what was told to her not more than an hour ago, that the lovely mother Lena, the mother born Ling Chao, never regained consciousness when they brought her in from the slim remains of the bridge, and was pronounced dead in the aftermath of the storm.

Rachel Lynn Chao rests in the evening. Lulled to sleep by the sound of the trumpet. The horn of endtime revelation in the distance. Held prisoner in half sleep by the death of a forest of pines, in the burning of blue and black fire.

*L*eah Chao rides the wind. The winds of eschatology. Sister of Rachel Lynn Chao. Daughter of Ling Ling. Lena. Learning of her mother's death in the passing storm. This storm that passed away in the night, returning to deny the world the sun's renewal in the summer morning.

Leah rides the wind. The miles of grief and mourning. Through the burning miles of countryside, lit up so beautifully in the gray morning light. Flames undrowned in the darkn'd rain.

The younger sister of Rachel Lynn drives onward. Cruising from mediocrity, from a life resigned to no aspirations. A mother's dream dead on the vine. A violin gone silent. A mother's judgment that calls from beyond the grave. Ghostly eyes that burn like the California forest pine. On fire that reaches to the sky. Like the burning sequoia in the morning rain. That burns in the fire that is not quenched.

The violin. Why does every Asian mother suffer the heat of this self same melody. Music or academics. It will be one or the other. *So, its music? You don't choose the instrument. The instrument will choose you. That is why your fingers fumble on the black and white keys. Because the piano does not like you. The clarinet does not like you. The French Horn does not like you. This is why the bow and the string flow like water through your spirit. This is why your violin never screams like a dying cat.*

Leah Chao. Someday the world will know. The world will know that name.

This, whispered in the daughter's ear. Whispered upon the daughter's mouth. Kissed upon the eleven year old daughter's lips. *The violin,* she whispers. Words that tickle her skin. That tingle her young breasts to aching. Words that twitch her groin to an itch. Words whispered by a witch, whose fire in pitched in Azure.

Leah Chao rides the wind. Youngest daughter of Ling Ling. Sister of Rachel Lynn. Drawn to the other daughter of Ling. Drawn by the death of what churns beneath cultured civility. Drawn by the death of a secret.

A secret resurrected into her heart, and the heart of a sister in need. A sister that escaped death in the summer rain. A sister who lies in wait.

Burning.

23

The Japanese Monorail glides in fiery revelation through the night. Blazing through the countryside alive in blue flame, not slowing down at all as it nears the city, which has been spared thus far, as if awaiting this announcement under the clear and starry night, that what impending destruction there will be is soon forthcoming, and not a single soul within will be safe from these fires of truth that burn. The truth speeds into the early nighttime city all aglow, burning blue and black fire, ablaze both inside and out, appearing as a single line of fire sliding gracefully through the night, as a creature made of pure blue fire that knows its destination, rather than a train unfortunate enough to have been at the wrong place at the wrong time. It seemed that the dragon had known exactly how to spread the flame across the rapidly moving train, when it crossed over the high trestle, choosing not to devastate the bridge or the track in any way, but rather to light the train up with words unspoken, with a message of doom from the Throne of God. This message rolls rapidly along from the dark countryside into the brightened Japanese city, the metropolis of souls, in runaway fashion past the screaming onlookers who gaze in disbelief as it approaches the station with impossible speed, barreling though the station on fire from the dragon's mouth, as the would-be passengers look on in screaming awe, feeling the wind and heat blow past them in once-in-a-lifetime phenomenon, until the train blows past them in unrequited fury, in a rage never before seen by man, as if to say that they should all forget their ride in security and complacency, and gather themselves to a new and fearful reality—to flee, flee the wrath that is coming upon the city, when every skyscraper will be melted at the bottom with fervent heat, so that they will topple in a shower of glass and concrete to the ground, to lay a quarter mile's worth of devastation to the terrified strollers and streets below. These foolish onlookers, who still line up to be cooked in their own disbelief, who chose to stay and be killed in their own skepticism and scoffing, mocking defiance at the hand of fate, let alone the hand of God, of whose Son they have a growing hatred for, as the feel the approach of his impending day of glory.

This great city in Japan, which will soon begin to die in broad daylight, must endure the passing of a rhapsody in blue, the loud and horrific passing of a message of doom in the night, as it speeds away from the station and through the lighted city, to activate the screaming awe as it passes toward the city limits again, to send its glowing message to the other countryside, until in perpetual motion, along tracks designed to accommodate its uncompromising speed, which carry its song of doom, burning this endtime melody underneath the clear and starry night.

*I*n the gray mists of the morning dawn, Leah enters the San
Francisco Memorial Hospital in rainy footsteps of grieving. In the wake
of a stormy disbelief, she gathers her endtime information, the knowledge
of her own eschatology spoken in numbers to correspond to what room
her mother is in. As to the lovely older sister Rachel Lynn, there'll be

time to see her soon enough—but only after the business at hand is come and gone. It seems that all of her activities nowadays, though as mundane as ever, are laced with this same endtime finality, although this is the height and the depth of it for sure.

As she follows the doctor and the nurse to the elevator that awaits for them—mouth already open wide to receive them, to invite them into the floating metal coffin that it is—each step taken echoes her mind louder and louder toward the conduit space, which is the theater of her mind, that threatens to take her away from the sterilized walls of this reality, down the timeline to the walls of another. Though she is already twenty eight years along, the eleven year old China Doll that she was lights up her mind daily it seems. As the elevator closes its jaws of hopeful and impending doom upon their brief ride, the mirrored doors of it beckon to her Asian eyes to gaze at the truth, to see the sophisticated beauty which is her mother those many years ago, when Leah was eleven.

This is the ride of another rainy day, in the days before the fire dragons lived and breathed. Oh, but what dragons of fire are they that live, though accursed, burning blue and black fire! It is the ride home from the airport, where the 18 year old Rachel Lynn flies the gray skies in the storm, off to her ivy league refuge somewhere in the east, somewhere above and beyond the northeast mountain country. *"Obey the cliché,"* her mother would say, at the end of a stick every other day. *"Since you too dumb for music,"* comes the Chinese American accent, *"do your books..."* and this, to a fault, until all A's and the occasional B became the norm. 3.8 GPA, you say? Harvard, here I come, for the price I had to pay!

In the heart of Memory, Leah rides the elevator of eschatology, remembering the ride here from sister Rachel Lynn's airport ride to Harvard—three thousand and 25 miles east and away. In the Heart of

Memory, Leah sits in the passenger side of the cozy refuge of Camry silver gray, unable to grab hold of the ghostly feeling that haunts the pit of her stomach and somewhere beyond it, far down deep into her soul. *There is no buffer of protection between them now*, would be the words this ghost would speak to her if she understood, as she sits in silence, even careful not to breathe too hard, not to breathe too fast, lest the mist formed in her eyes should coalesce like raindrops on her passenger side window.

But the natural itching calls eyes to blink, and they betray the presence of secret pain. Leah blinks from the effort not to; and her pain appears from both eyes at once in two slow, steady streams. And the compassionate voice appears from the women drawing the car, uttered in her native tongue, as she reaches over and rubs the tears from her eleven year old daughter's eyes. This, in the compassion of complete understanding, as she feels their own tearing up inside, like the ripping of cloth pulled beyond what its weave can bear.

The Asian mother and daughter drive home in the silence of grief, the mothers' hands running her own special brand of comfort down her daughter's face as she drives, down her daughter's neck as she drives. Down her daughters's shoulders as she drives. Across her daughter's chest as she drives. Down her daughter's stomach as she drives. Down her daughter's thigh as she drives.

In the Heart of Memory, Leah disembarks the silver gray Camry ride, into the echo of a pouring rain. She and her mother take each rainy step in rapid succession to the front door, not caring at all for the closed garage door that hides a mess of storage. Shut up thy face, suburban garage— what does a car have to do with thee! The house door opens, upon the same wind that opens the mirror elevator in front of the adult young woman, who clip clops her heels behind the padded nurse's steps, and the cushioned steps of the doctor's padded feet.

Down the hospital hall of the fourth floor, they glide. On the death train, everybody rides. Down the hallway of the fourth floor Leah glides, in step with the little eleven year old girl in the Heart of Memory, who walks down the hallway of suburbia, toward the staircase in carpeted ambiguities hidden. Leah and her mother take these steps in the agony of preknowledge, which burns the mother from her waist down in what she has not known since her other daughter was eleven. And this same fire courses through young Leah, but to play a tune of fearfulness and dread, a lack of understanding for the sixth sense, the torment of this same ghost that had haunted her in the car, and had touched her body in trembling cold from the crown of her head to the soles of her feet.

Let's take off these wet clothes, her mother says, holding Leah's hand, a firm and measured grip, pulling her along into her master bedroom. A space subdued in exquisite beige softness highlighted and touched in whispers of brown. Nearby the beige and brown patterned comforter, she helps her daughter undo the little buttons at the top of her dress, and they both work to pull it up and over the little girl's head, laying waist to it upon the flour crumpled and forgotten.

Now, stand there, Mother Dear! Admire thy daughter's smooth, girlish young figure! Admire the eleven year prodigy of the breasts she has become! Pitched already in the key of C major, upon the body of youth incarnate. In her little t shirt, admiring the straightness of the torso yet undeveloped to curviness, see the shape of the future woman's little buttocks begin!

Mother! Lift thy daughter's white undergarment from her body! Cast it aside from thee! Now, mother, stare young Leah in the face, in her eyes as you kneel down! Lock eyes with her as you remove the pink underwear cloth—now, cast it aside from thee! Now, stand up, Mother. Thine Asian beauty is a warmth to your daughter. To contrast the winter cold that flows from thee!

Leah watches the beautiful woman undo the buttons on her white and frilly blouse. Each button one by one, down to the gray skirt—pulling each shirt tail out, then tossing it away. This, she does with the tight gray skirt—hardly taking her eyes from her daughter's. And then, at long last, the black bra is done away with, to where the globes are bulbous, left hanging for Leah to see. They hang in wobbling form and fashion, as the mother leans over to remove the sheer black stockings, and then they rest against her chest again as she stands up straight, so skillfully sliding the underwear down and away without hardly bending at all, kicking them away with her bare feet. There, the Asian mother stands nude, staring naked at her eleven year old daughter without judgment, without fear, and without remorse.

In the calm of uneasy acceptance, she sits on the edge of the lovely beige and brown flower pattern bed—smooth, beautiful legs closed tight, lovely hips spread wide underneath the slim waist as she sits. In her native tongue, she beckons, *come to Mama*, which Lea is inclined to do. Leah walks boldly, unboldly over to her mother, ushered calmly into her mother's lap. In her native tongue, she speaks, prompting the girl to stick her tongue out in silence. Then, the mother sticks her tongue to her eleven year old daughter's, and they kiss in what some call in the manner of the French, their heads swaying every so slightly in the unfelt breeze, the unseen lightning, the unheard thunder, and the unfelt sheets of pouring rain.

Then Leah must stiffen, she must stop the tongue kiss as the electric spark shoots from her groin to the rest of her body, as the mother's head finds its way up her inner thigh to Leah's proper place, to her improper place, resting her hand in the cleft of it, firmly against the front of it with no motion whatever, but pressed with skill and knowledge upon what place the signal call is born.

As to what feeling this bathes every inch of her body and soul upon, she does not know. She only knows to breathe—to endure the height of feelings only toyed with in the past—to suffer the blast of the forbidden unleashed, to feel it traverse the inches of her skin, down into her bowels, and up her spine and into the far reaches of her mind and body. From this position, with one hand between her daughter's legs, she rests her tongue upon the girl's nipple in pure wet, to feel the spittle die in tiny crystalline spark of her tongue to the nipple, painting the nipple with her tongue to full wetness, watching it harden instantly to a greater degree than the other. The mother blows a breath of gentle cold upon the daughter's nipple, to complete the beginning of Leah's devastation, to light completely the fires that burn within. With her other hand, she caresses the other nipple, leaning forward again, clamping, pressing her lips to Leah's nipple in full blown sucking and wetness, moving her hand violently at times—now going back and forth with her lips and tongue to bathe her daughter's dark nipples, her hand pressed still and steady at the girl's proper center—listening to her daughter's breath begin to grow unsteady, until there is no hope for a reprieve.

Upon this call to arms, in the distant light of devastation, the mother nurses in full her daughter's nipple in suckling and swallowing, as though drinking her daughter's future and phantom milk, as the blast wave gathers strength and momentum across the landscape of Leah's undoing, arriving in the form of a single, loud yelp from deep within her daughter's spirit, and a violent shaking of her entire body, somewhere deep inside her body and soul.

From the Heart of Memory, Leah steps out of one rain world into another, crossing the threshold into where there is the sanitized stench of death, and a hospital bed where there is the body of a patient, entirely covered with a white sheet from head to toe.

Rossini's Warehouse

25

The nighttime earth burns in fires of blue. Millions of acres scream in the agony of this blue flame, as seen from high above the

earth on the night side, working in tandem with the white lights of civilization to create a beauty of endtime devastation. This apocalyptic vision burdens North America and South America from top to bottom, as the shadow of night has fallen. As the earth turns into the darknes, where the truth of the cosmos is revealed in the glory of God, the smoke and sunlight are banished by the shadow of the earth, and the millions of acres of forestland are seen for what they have become—a hellish reminder in fire, and hidden vapour of smoke that this is the end of the age, and the reflection of mankind's inner burning is on display for every angel and demon to see. The trees of the Pacific Northwest are in grieving to be free of their prison of flame, as it seems that a full third of the forests are ablaze from what the white dragons have wrought, from what these avenging angels have brought upon the earth. It seems that whole states are burning in the fires of Hell, in picturesque Azure, azurean flame, to cause wonder as to what manner of survival could there be for the unlucky souls down below.

These travel to and fro in the fiery blue nightmare, in the wake of Presidential declarations of what is or is not a disaster area, as if such a meaningless swipe of the word or pen could raise a barrier of protection for them. Those brave enough to be on the forest roads at night do so in the terror of revelation, drowned in the fear of their calling, as the lowly photographer on the fields of battle, who braves the trembling terror to get just one more picture, to take just one more video of what death and destruction has been given. These are the soldiers in the battle to record the inevitable, to document the impossibilities of what prophecies have been fulfilled, driving the Pacific roads, bravely winding though the highland forests set ablaze by eschatology. Sometimes showing the fury of winds caused by the searing heat in the air, as lines of flame explode across highways to bridge the gulf between the lit and the unlit, until now both sides of the highways are an inferno of this otherworldly flame of nighttime beauty.

Sometimes, the trees give way to the open fields of farmland, where the devil is on display in a whirlwind of blue and black flame, winds that create a funnel of pure fire that rises to heights of unfathomability, whirling through the fields from one group of forest trees to the other, until it seems that every tree in creation is destined to burn. Many points

105

east of the Pacific forest trees, and the farmlands of northern California—these fire twisters have chosen a single night to reveal themselves in tandem, as exactly a dozen of them appear from the West to the East, the greatest of them residing the appropriate path through Tornado Alley, forming over a burning wheat field on the Oklahoma prairie, turning in end of the world nighttime splendor, as a tornado risen to the height of a fifty story building, made entirely of wind and fire.

26

Sometimes, I think I'm going to just drop dead from the way that I feel. There is hardly a description apt to be given, to bring into focus the Hell that has descended, that which presses down on me from the outside world and from within. These seven hideous monsters that came out of nowhere, burning everything in sight except for the very air we breathe—it seems that even I can feel the heat of an impending doom promised but not yet delivered—flinching at every sound, twitching at every shadow, jumping out of my skin once when my daughter shrieked, because the shadow of an innocuous little gray bird loomed over the blinds at the kitchen window, which in her mind was surely the beating, the flapping of dragon wings coming to call her home. I can remember my mother's reaction when Meadow screamed that bright, sunny day.

"God, you scared the shit out of me you little bitch. God DAMN it..."

My mother was so mean to Meadow that day. My exotic little flower I saw injured, as if a petal had been crushed and torn. I watched her move away from the sink where she had been washing the lettuce for our salad, and sort of sneak out of the kitchen as if it were a casual strolling away. But I know it was because her grandmother had humiliated her down to nothing in front of us, and frightened the poor girl more than she had already been.

They say that both triumph and tragedy reveals the heart of a person. And it seems that the sadistic heart of the woman who gave me life is revealed, since big dragon bit into her big old money house of brick, and took my father away. This late fifties fox, all hips and horny sensibility, all lips and lascivious eyes that stare—I see now the truest source of my melancholy, much moreso than the seven monsters that have set the world on fire of Hell. The burning of blue and black fire in my soul was set so far away, so far and long ago by the mean bitch in the kitchen, the stitch in the heart of my bitchiest memory, who even sucks the spaghetti sauce from her thumb as if it were the source of some hidden, secret pleasure.

I have tried as hard as I can to ignore the effect she's had on Meadow since she arrived. Meadow was always something of a depressive child. Even from when she was the sweetest and quietest little Carmen in the neighborhood, with those little Egyptian eyes, those big, doleful eyes— that long, jet black hair, that face of such eastern beauty as to make more than one woman get brave enough to ask me if she was adoped. No, I did not give in to self-righteous bullshit, some high horse nerve to act as though the women were racist bitches for asking. I just smiled.

She gets it from her grandparents, I'd say. That little Indian/Egyptian girl beauty, touched and colored so subtly, shaded with an echo of the orient. *Is she white? Is she Indian? Is she Greek? Is she Asian? Why is her mother white and she clearly is not?* All of her life, I have felt the condescension, the passive aggressive prejudice, the white supremacist hypocrisy, where the W.A.S.P surperiority rings an endtime bell in the air around me, in the land where white skin was once king, and the manufactured superiority of it hath been willed away by the Almighty. *My daughter is as white as you are, you racist cunt,* I wanted to spit and yell sometimes, when I would allow the blood of Irene Oppenheimer to boil inside. How often How often have I held my temper underneath? So afraid to offend the smiling Jenny's, one of the lust fulled Laodicean ladies, one of the hippy hipped heathers, so haughty in their high minded happiness and *fungalooga.* It's a sin and a crime where we come from to be real, to have a genuine thought, to express a real emotion—so much bottled up repression we are, that a reservoir of emotional problems curns lie that molten river that flows beneath what one believes is a mountain, but is really an unexploded volcano.

Holding it in, smiling the fake smile—pushing forward in phoniness and emotional half truth to infinity, until the human limit is reached at last, and the emotional output is transformed into that of a rabid dog, or a hungry lion, or a rattlesnake touched in the wrong place at the wrong time. I was raised in this phony repression, where evil emotions lie hidden just beneath the surface, where the faultline will appear after time as a warning, that soon the Big One is about to strike, to rumble that ground like not since the dawn of time, and carry end of the world devastation in its wake.

Yes, I was raised in this emotional repression, like the untouched breast that stays bound up and pent up, to where even the lightest brush past the unclothed nipple is enough to cause a sudden shudder. I was raised in this repression. By this closet supremacist, who believes without actually saying it that money is the honey, and white makes everything alright. Oh, its not anything she said over the years that made this a reality. It's the way my mother carried herself, the way she was so typically gathered to her *White And So Pretty* colleagues in upper class whoredom, women who had given themselves over whole heartedly to the groin aching pleasure that comes with the love of money.

And I noticed that even when young Meadow was 13, that my mother was unnaturally harsh with her behind closed doors, having coaxed me into allowing her to take her perverted fill of my little Carmen bird, whipping her brutally or spanking her to bruises with the hairbrush, or even strapping on the phantom member, even when Meadow was only 13, and causing her insides to ache standing up and from behind, slamming into her until a ghostly moan began to escape her own lips, as she ignited in her 13 year old granddaughter the fires of eschatology.

27

I was 13, when the spirit came to me. I was 13, when the spirit hath come.

Oh, Irene, daughter of privilege. Mother of perversion. What is it that the neighbors do not know, as you escort your daughter down the hall to the upper room? Oh, Irene, Goddess of Privilege! What is it that the neighbors do not know? Are you angry with me, Mother? I cannot tell. You sit down roughly at the edge of the bed, holding me tight by both shoulders, as if you want to shake me. You are so unashamed, Mother, to evoke the classic, tried and true—*how many times am I going to have to remind you about that attitude?*

But I'm sorry, Momma.

No. You're not. But I promise you, you're going to be. Because you're about to get the worst spanking you've ever gotten in your life.

Why, little Carol Ann, do you waste the tears in waiting? They cannot divert the tiding of this river of hers—this river of her perversion that must flow. This is the motherline, the River of Eve, this is the Eden River that flows down the time line, that flows through the Valley of Shadows, through Mother Daughter Pass, through Nightshade Canyon, where shadows of depravity are born and are nurtured, that flow in and around those accursed who ride down this river, to partake of what dark and sinister Fate there must be. This, the tragedy of fruit so perpetually forbidden, fallen from the tree from where thou shalt not eat.

Of this knowledge, you have waited 13 years, Mother. You have kept it bound and repressed inside, this desire to partake of this bitter fruit, beyond of which is the curse of bitter wormwood, and expulsion from the Garden of Innocence, from the Garden of Antiquity. From the tortured dreams of Eve, you rise up before me stern faced, determined, in fullest dour expression imaginable, where all pretense of intensions are absorbed and channeled away. In the sternness of motherhood gone intentionally awry, you begin to strip every stitch of your own clothing—so tall and broad hipped you are—breasts so magnificently supported by nature, so that they do not hang or sag, so that they are not the foreshadowing of my own, nor of the exotic daughter I will have someday. Thine are the breasts of a goddess, Mother Irene, that are gigantic and broad, that stick out far in front of thee, Mother, as a warning to those who might approach, that this is the endtime beauty of feminine strength, in the guise of virtue nonexistent.

After you are unclothed, my eyes are affixed upon them as they wobble big and strong, so strong yet so soft, as you bend over and strip me as bare naked as you. And then you sit roughly upon the bed again, but farther back so that I can lay flat and full across your lap. I can feel the smoothness of your thighs, Mother. The heat of thine self burns a fire upon my skin. And this heat is soon transferred to the back of me in bare handed bliss for thee, as you work such a profound redness into the skin on my backside in rhythm, until the spanking sounds are mixed with the sound of my own whimpering and crying voice, until the redness has deepened along the color wheel.

And when the line is crossed, when I am beyond endurance, you gather your strength in a rage reborn, concentrating each swat with finality, on one bruised side of my bottom, to send the pain deep into the muscle of my 13 year old resolve. And then the source of this pain reaches up to my blonde head, roughly guiding me to my feet. You stand your naked self up, Mother. Taking hold of my hair and my arm, pulling me to the very middle of the room facing the mirror.

Bend me over, Mother. Stand me up and bend me over. I feel the fevered pounding begin. As you slam the front of yourself into the back of me. Cursing me as a little disobedient bitch while your grab my sides with all your strength.

I see you in the mirror, Mother. So big, so strong, so Amazonian, compared to the spindly little blonde thing who is bent over in front of you. Pound the pathetic little thing into submission Mother. Slam into her that spirit which she does not understand. In the mirror, I see thy face, Mother. The fear and pain in thine expression is clear. I am a disobedient little bitch, Mother. A disrespectful little cunt, I am.

I see the pain in your face, Mother. The pain you grit your teeth in such an end of the world effort to bear. But you cannot grit your teeth any longer, Mother Dear. The awe and submission to terror is back in your expression. When you touch my nipple, Mother, of the spark which passes through me, I cannot tell. As to whether the trembling my body does is of its own volition, I cannot tell.

Hold on to my nipples, Mother. Let it anchor you as the agony bends you over towards my back. I can see the pain of devastation on your face, Mother. I can feel it in your body and soul. The siren in my ears rings loud from thee, O blessed Mother. The shaking in your body trembles me to the core. I have been a disrespectful little bitch, Mother.

But no longer.

The ocean liners have not been spared the occasional sighting, called a "dragon alert," where the goal is to speed to the nearest port, in hopes of getting closer to some degree of safety. But none of these sightings has come to anything like fruition, as the monsters have elegantly flown onward to whatever condemned coast they were headed for.

The people on the nighttime cruise ship do so in measured complacency, each one of them comfortable in their preordained dominion over the ocean waters. *I feel so safe out here*, one of them says, *the worst place you can be is anywhere on land. We're like a needle in a haystack out here. One little ocean liner surrounded by all this water? We're practically invisible to them.* And it seems that the wealthy crowd has settled into a rare place of end of the world comfort—a place where fear and panic do no preside. These are the privileged ones, who can use their money to escape into fantasy. To cruise the world in freedom from the terror of the masses, where they are free to breathe, and contemplate the glory of their earthly gain, to cruise the Wealthen Stream, grieving for the land of plenty.

These are they which are secure in their adulteries Wall Street wolfisms, corporate cruelties, political power mongering, legal loopholing, and every suburban secret known to man. These are they who cruise the waters of nighttime contentment. Two by two, the couples have taken to the waters. To escape the endtime fears that plague the land, the family responsibilities and worries on the back burner for now, all of them lucky enough to have escaped any such tragedies that have befallen.

None of them were in the Empire State Building that day, when the dragon melted away the concrete and steel from the bottom. None of them were in the Empire State Building that day, to feel the epic rumbling and creaking begin, then to hear the thunderous rumbling sound like that of an earthquake. None of them were in the Empire State Building that day. To feel the woozy sway of the world begin around them, the sway that suddenly leans more to one side, until there is no longer a sway to the other side again. None of them that cruise this nighttime ship of dreams, this modern day Titanic, none of them were in the building that day, when the skyscraper did its end of the world sway, careening so majestically off to one side nearly in tact as it fell, all 100 stories of concrete and steel falling in glorious union, as per the method of their execution for every skyscraper they have condemned.

These are they who cruise the Wealthen Stream. Those lucky enough to have been nowhere near the Empire State Building when it fell on that storm Saturday morning, when the building was so much emptier than it would normally be. When it seem the whole corporate world was at home in front of their fine flat screens, watching the Armageddon tragedy unfold. These are they which saw the end of the world happening from a safe distance. Those who live in paradise. Where they can see the masses at the River Styx, alongside the waters of poverty and mediocrity. Those who wish for them to have mercy, and dip their finger in the water, to touch it to their parched tongues, for they are tormented in this flame. But betwixt them is a great gulf fixed, so that none could cross over from either side. So that those in paradise cannot be touched by the accursed. By those born under this cloud of dark destiny, this cloud of perpetual want and need.

This is a ship of the privileged. A ship of prosperity. These are they which have left the mundane behind. Who are free to explore every avenue of new perversion, and those things which are not new under the sun.

Underneath the stars of Heaven, there is a couple that stands. But this, a couple in subversion. A couple in hiding. Two women, who have abandoned their husbands in secret so long ago, yet unbeknownst to them. Two women, who are safely hidden in full public view, that two female friends together on a cruise is nothing to raise and eyebrow at. Two women, in the faded early evening light, nearby the nighttime stars of heaven. Where the skies over the waters are crystal clear, and the truth of God's glory can be seen from earth to infinity.

Two women. Whose spirits are intertwined as one in the Sapphic, whose bodies ache even now from memories of the distant morning, where one doth awaken the other with her face down below, at the center of the other's life and living. Those two women, whose husbands are none the wiser, who cannot fathom the adulterous friendship, nor of what pleasures they hath wrought in secret. Their husbands cannot fathom what pleasures they have felt, when their wives have laid together on the living room sofa, fully clothed in fine dress cloth, their bodies pressed together with not a single zipper or button undone, locked in an embrace tight enough to take one another's breath, where the one is laid upon her back with stocking legs open, as the other is pressed in missionary with hardly a grinding motion easily perceived, both of them swollen to agony inside underwear cloth unremoved.

This is the unimaginable truth, these two. These suburban friends, whom the world would call friends with benefits. These two, who have engaged one another's burning fire with malice of forethought, having burned away the chastity of their marital loyalty, having melted away the innocence of fidelity in grinding heat. These two, who stand on the deck of the ship in blissful repose. These two, who are the first to see the approach of the gliding silhouette in the evening day, beneath the stars of heaven.

One of the two mothers opens her mouth with hardly a sound, while the other foretells the end of days in a nighttime declaration, that natural alarm that women possess, which is a scream for the ages.

*T*heir screams ignite a flame of fear among the other passengers, in a rumbling and murmuring response that flows through

the ship, as more and more people begin to hurry from the banquet

hall and casino bar lounge, some even from the leisure of their private cabins where they have retired for the night. As to exactly where they are going, they don't really know, nor do they really understand exactly why. *Somebody on deck is screaming their head off*, someone is heard to say. *A woman's being attacked outside*, someone else chimes in as if they know, so happy to be ready as a looker on—as someone who can spit and judge with venom, to ride in on their white horse of self righteous indignation and aggressive willingness to judge, though having no real knowledge of why the woman is screaming.

Before long, an alert young crewman releases the most appropriate of the four letter sounds into the air around him, *"shit,"* he says, amidst the expression of awe and devastation, when he sees the source of the woman's scream, gliding in early evening silhouette high above the ship. The man turns and runs, breaking rudely through the crowd to get to the cockpit, to alert the captain and the rest of the crew. Those present are held by the iceberg stare, that look of shock and amazement unique to those at sea, when the spirit of impending disaster looms nearby. But there is no port in this storm, and no one to call who can bring any solution for hiding in. There are no warships in the vicinity, to shoot and spray feeble hope into the sky in nighttime firepower. By now, it is known that fleets and squadrons of ships and planes are glorified death missions, that get too close to the monster is like getting too close to a Kansas whirlwind. Attacks on these creatures inevitably do more harm than good, making the surrounding landscape or city skyline look like the aftermath of World War III.

Well, shouldn't we call somebody? says the young cruise ship officer. *There's nobody* to *call,* says the captain, the shock and awe of his expression having faded to the calm of uneasy acceptance. At that moment, the foghorn voice rings though the approaching night, to settle the spirit of fear among them. And as it is written, the types of fear are indeed many, and uniquely distinguished. Among these is the Fear of Death, isolated in the dark, tropical waters of the southern Atlantic, presaged by the Fear of Pain, either by burning, or by the razor teeth of this eschatology, clamped unmercifully around them.

The single scream on board the doomed ship cascades into crescendo, as if the endless shrieking can somehow call forth a miracle from somewhere over the darkened seascape. But all aboard are prisoners of a quiet realization, that no help is coming, neither from God nor man, and there is nothing left to do *but* scream, and wait for Death's slow and painful arrival. *I don't' see it,* one of the men is heard to say, attempting to neutralize some of the scalding, some of the acid of screaming around him. And this false calm spreads across the deck, serving only to silence the voice of Fear alone, though not its prickly and icy touch upon their skin.

Then suddenly, the surface of hope is shattered, scattered like a battering ram through a glass window, when all 300 feet of snow white death splashes up from the waters directly beside the ship, rising high into the tropical night above them. As the screams rise again, this time in a single chorus of Hellish intensity, a handful of passengers are spared the indignity of terror, when the nighttime world around them swoons into a haze, and they fall helplessly to the deck unconscious and are trampled by the crowd stomping over them, so many of them conscious of the people they step on to get away from the dragon Smyrna.

The warm, wet wind that swirls around them is born from the majestic beating of the white monster's wings, as he positions himself for the task at hand, to exercise his calling along the timeline. The sound of his voice deafens the ears of the endtime people as they run, rattling through their bodies in waves of revelation while they scramble anywhere inside the ship, as if there were truly places to hide. The monster settles upon the surface of the water, held up by the skilled parachuting of white wings barely moving, as it watches the two legged things running in futility.

These are they who dare not focus on the tall, white creature made aglow by the light of the ship. These are they that dare not look upon the eyes that glow with azurean flame. These are they which dare not notice the blue glowing of the underside of his wings, the phantom that appears in heated warning of what is to come. These are they who call upon the name of the Lord in blasphemy, when the dragon's head lurches smoothly forward, and the blue flame pours from his mouth through the nighttime air, exploding across the deck of the ship, melting the rails almost instantaneously, incinerating the flesh and blood of so many of them to vapor, while setting the rest of those nearby on blue fire, causing them to run wildly about, some of them dropping to the deck of the burning ship, while others jump overboard in madness, falling like flaming blue stars down to the dark, tropical waters below.

30

*T*wo Asian flowers ride the wind. To where a tale of two sisters must begin. Rachel Lynn Chao. Sophisticated. Beautiful. Ivy League bred. Dr. Rachel Lynn Chao. Dr.Chao. Psychiatrist extraordinaire. Revolving door practice—overrrun with patients on the eve of the Second Coming. A progressive and private place of prosperity. Where depravity of the heart is queen. Where mother daughter therapy is king. Where female perversion from along many timelines comes together in one space. A space guarded by a Goddess of Perversion. The proverbial choir that is preached to about what churns beneath cultured civility. A supporter and purveyer of mother daughter punishment therapy. Where mothers and daughters in conflict submit to a hard paddling from one another in the privacy of her office. Paddling to provoke submission. To teach the bitchy, domineering mother to submit emotionally to the daughter.

To learn the agony of subjugation. The pain of oppression. A paddling mile in her daughter's shoes, so to speak. To endure the paddle for as long as it takes. For as long as it takes for the mother to learn respect. To learn respect for her full grown daughter.

The argumentative pair, the two of them were. The lady judge and her brunette Skinny-Minnie of a daughter The 31 year old spoiled, bitch off the old block that is her mother. Thirty one year old corporate queen, the Skinny-Minnie. Tall, elegant. Long, brown hair, pale skin. Big, doleful eyes. Possessing only the strength to fight the woman who gave her life in battle. A woman of luck and false confidence born. A woman racked with pain and bitterness over the brunette woman of law. A woman of deep curves. Deep Latin ancestry hidden in white and W.A.S.P. sound spoken forth. *She looks Spanish enough to be a judge in Mexico,* Dr. Chao thinks. Beauty hidden n the middle aged thickness of motherhood. Bound in the curves of repression.

The wealthy lady judge. The spoiled lady corporate daughter. The mother daughter dynamic unrestrained. The end of a burning world unveiled.

I want to give her punishment therapy, the uppity, corporate queen says. *I want her to feel what its like to be on the other end of it. How it feels to be hit.*

Two Asian flowers ride the wind. Under the curse of the golden flower, they ride.

Rachel Lynn. Dr. Chao. Her mind ablaze in the heart of memory. Recalling the Latin looking judge. Made to bear her breasts in private. For her daughter's edification. For her epic humiliation.

Dr. Chao remembers the Lady judge in her skin. Stripped topless before her daughter, leaned against the back of the leather sofa, standing up behind it. Dr. Chao remembers the sound of fireworks exploding around them, to bring joy to her sadist's heart.

Dr. Chao remembers the embarrassment on the lady judge's face. The tighter grip on the sofa. The angry look of the tall, thin daughter. The mousy Minnie. The corporate queen in elegant burgundy cloth. Dr. Chao remembers the seventh whack into the woman's big buttock from her daughter, and the long, strained voice of suppressed agony.

Dr. Chao remembers the shaking of the woman's breasts. The tightening of the dark brown areolas—the new protrusion of the nipples in cold humiliation, in the heat of provocation. From whenceforth cometh thine arousal, Mother Dear? Thine daughter's discipline is pure agony. The eighth, ninth and tenth bring the loud, deep and angry yells. Though not yells of surrender. No. The lady judge must be beaten into submission.

Dr. Chao remembers the approach to critical mass. The forward countdown. Seventeen. Eighteen. Nineteen. Dr. Chao remembers the 19th blow. The change of the lady judge's cry. From bellowing anger, to a high pitch scream. Followed by a profound shaking of her head "no." A squirming of the body. A descent into weeping. A squeaking, sobbing contrition.

Dr. Chao remembers the sobbing, topless woman of tears. Hugging her daughter in sorrow. A weeping of apologies. A daughter's darkest dream realized. A mother's nightmare unfurled. Dr. Chao remembers the 700 dollar session. Three hundred fifty from the two of them. Money from the end of the age. From the twilight of human history.

Two sisters ride the wind. Rachel Lynn Chao, psychiatrist. And her younger sister born of the Rose. Leah Rose Chao. Failed violinist. Music store worker. Tried for four years sot find her place in an orchestra. Doomed to failure. Cursed with talent and no opportunity. A fate worse than death.

Rose Chao. Violinist Extraordinaire. She walks a tightrope on the violin string. She sings a song of eschatology. Leah Rose Chao. The least pretty of the two. The flower whose petals are smaller in bloom. A flower not so spectacular as the other. Bound by shyness. A plain faced prisoner. Prettiness concealed by plainness. Beauty unadorned. Cursed with a macromastia hidden away. Hidden by the loose shirts. By the bra that lets them lie flattened underneath. A thin and boyish figure, where two of the longest breasts in creation hang gigantic and hidden. The blessing and the curse of God. Breasts with old scars healed by time. Concealed by attrition. Two of the longest, loppiest bosoms along the timeline. In the history of thin and attractive Asian women. Two marvels of nature in hiding. In grieving to remain hidden. In suffering to be free from pain.

Leah Rose Chao. Witness to the impossible. Victim of eschatology. Friendliness in Asian cuteness, interviewing for the job at the musical instrument store. Rossini's Warehouse, it is called. A paradise for the wayward musician. A quiet superstore of violins, cellos and the like.

Instruments so expensive and so beautiful. Pricy enough to bring a commission. The pianos are the Holy Grail. *In a good year you can earn 65,000 dollars,* the owner says in the interview. *That makes this a position that a lot of people are competing for. They think their MBA's and music performance degrees will make a damn bit of difference,* she says. *And its not who you know either, or even what you know. They think just because their father-in-law conducted some no name orchestra for a season that they can just walk in here and tell me that and I'll praise the Heavenly Father and beg them to work here.*

The sixty-six year old woman stares in eyes of knowing. An expression of wisdom. Short, blonded hair. Thick makeup over the skin in desperation to age. Tell tale lines about the corners of the mouth. Beauty aged to the limits of acceptability. At the far edges of what is still sensual. A voice deepened by time. A voice rich with desire.

With bonuses and overtime, she says, *you can take home much more than sixty five thousand,* she says. *I hire people, not résumés.*

The older woman stares at the rose. In unbelieving eyes. Eyes filled with repressed awe at what she suspects. That what is hidden underneath this thin, demure Asian girl's shirt is too implausible to be believed. That it is incredible. Seen perhaps once in a great lifetime of living.

Ms. Sylvia Greenwood stands up in fine business repose. Charcoal gray business jacket and matching pants, bright red blouse underneath. Walking to the door of the office. Closing it tight. Locking it.

Ms. Greenwood glides the carpet of dreams. Back to the fine desk of mysterious darkwood. Wood glossed in success burnished in upper class privilege. Highlighted and finished in money.

I think you might just be the kind of girl we're looking for. Rossini's Warehouse is one of the only surviving storefronts for what we sell. So much of the business is trying to go online. There's still a place for hands on browsing of a musical instrument. Especially the pianos. They'll never be able to take that to the web, no matter how much they try.

Leah Rose smiles. A smile of sweetness. A smile of demurity. Of submission. The elder Greenwood looks on. Up and down the young woman's body hidden in the midnight blue button down. To match the midnight blue skirt over her thinness. Beautiful legs exposed below the knee. Legs silky smooth in the greenwood memory.

I hope you don't mind me saying this, Ms. Chao, but I think you're a very beautiful young woman.

The Chao smile turns to shyness. To an innocence of epic proportions. Juxtaposed in the Greenwood mind, to what gargantuan delights she suspects that exist, and are so well hidden down below.

Would you do me a favor...may I call you Leah? Would you stand up for me? Walk over this way, so I can get a good look at who just might be our newest salesgirl.

Lea stands up in mystery. Confusion disguised in obedience.

Would you do me a big favor? Would you unbutton your blouse?

Upon what gentle breeze of predestiny, doth words whisper and flow? Lea Rose can only tuck her lips. Raising her eyebrows in fascination. In the disbeliev of hearing. In pleading to know if what was said is truly the same as what she heard.

Unbutton your blouse, comes the Greenwood psychology in refrain. In nervous compliance, this, Leah Rose sets out to do. She undresses every button to her skirt. Driven forward by instinct. Compelled by an engine of fear.

The sixty six year old woman looks on. Standing up in something close to awestruck curiosity. Like the explorer who sees the exotic creature in the nearby distance. Who learns that the Golden Emperor Swan does exist.

You can take it off, she says. And what she sees is the beginning of the end. The end of her world of want. The devastation of her greatest need.

Take off your bra for me.

Oh, sister of secrecy, what words caress the hand of whispered Fate and Predestiny? What hand of obedience is this that trembles in compliance, to reach up behind you, and unlatch the gigantic bra that is too small and ill fitting, that processes them down and against your body in hiding?

When the white bra is removed, so too is the barrier to the Greenwood hypocrisy, which is devastated by the third part of the Truth, which is cataclysm. There, hanging down the girl's waist are the largest and longest breasts she has ever seen upon a woman of fair skin, reminiscent in size and shape of the National Geographic exploitation of the African breast queens, but on the fit and trimmed body of a 25 year old Asian American woman. Breasts of such magnificent size and length as to inspire awe, and the spark of epic desire at the soul of women and men. Breasts flattened by their great length, and areolas at the bottom remarkably pointed forward instead of downward, to where the nipple would then be at the lips of what woman or child below who were blessed to give suck to them.

I think, says the lady Greenwood, that they are the most beautiful thing I've ever seen. And this, she says in wrinkled brow, and choked voice, and the rising of pain that appears in overflow down her face from one eye, such tear as she does not wipe away.

These are the breasts of time. The breasts of fertility. A butcher surgeon's dream, to get his corrupted, evil and money grubbing hands and knives to them. These are the breasts of legend. The breasts of a goddess in demurity.

Sylvia Greenwood takes the steps. The steps over the benchmark of mankind, in his journey toward the end of the age. The steps of endtime woman, and her calling to what is wanton. To what is wayward.

The woman of music takes the final steps along this path chosen. Chosen by predestiny. Taking one of the great, elongated bosoms into both hands, turning it upward to her gaze. To look with authority upon the nipple. To watch the areola in soft earthtone remain so impossible big around, to frame the nipple already so big to see. Brow wrinkled, her beautiful, mature face stained with a single tear, she reaches down to the Great Rose Bosom to give suck, pulling he rose nipple so far and deep into her mouth.

Two sisters ride the wind. Two Asian flowers in the flow of time and history. In the aftermath of when their mother was killed upon the red bridge, by the creature with burning eyes of blue.

3 1

*I*n the rising fires of contempt, the sisters arrive, one of them blazing a fire of hidden rage for the other, as only a sibling can. The older Chao sits quietly in the passenger side of Prius silliness in silver, being driven by the younger sister's pathetic energy of defeat, seeming to hear, to feel the epic notes from the violin that flow from young Leah's spirit. There is only a quiet tolerance that cushions the blow of their reunion. A somber and silent duet of inner voices, as the ghosts of strings and keyboards long since dead and gone. Leah drives her pathetic Prius down the simple suburban streets, the asphalt path to doll house heaven, and behind closed doors luxuries in passing miniature.

The beige and gray mini-castles of her older sister's neighborhood do shimmer in the mist of a new fallen rain, as the raindrops form without compromise on the glass all around them. Wiped away in technological fury in front, swishing, switching back and forth hopelessly, failing to prevent the perpetual formation of a new infinity of tears fallen from the sky. Leah cruises these California suburban streets, streets that were once underneath a sunny canopy of unearthly hope and blue. But these days have brought the descent of a protracted and melancholy gray, that loom in the confidence of promises threatened as prophecy, and fulfilled every hour of night and day. Through the weeping gray mist, the sisters ride, unable to hide behind feeble politeness, nor the spirit of phoniness and fungalooga.

In Prius pride and post modern perfection, the violinist turned music salesgirl glides the left turn to luxury, into the driveway of perverted orderliness obeyed, where the garage door is perpetually closed for what reason the Fates have decided. The psychiatrist and former piano student opens the passenger side door into the light rain, undeterred by the welcome mist upon her pretty Asian features, letting the heat of painful recollection flicker and threaten to die in the summer cold.

But even as she looks upward, to defy the tiny droplets of rain into her eyes, there is no quenching the fires of the spirit that burn, the arrival of a renewed agony of endtime memory. Frozen, but for a moment, under the skies that now weep like those over the Pacific Northwest, the older Chao looks away from the clouds of approaching doom with tears upon her face, but not of her own. These are the tears fallen from the sky in mourning. Raindrops formed and sent in grieving to the blissfully ignorant souls far below. Souls ignorant of what messages are unspoken, secrets of what powers and principalities plan, of what tragedies there must be, of what torments and tribulations must fall like sheets of pouring rain.

She moves suburban bones miraculously unbroken, hidden underneath the stylish, tight legged dark blue jeans, denim slid up and wrapped around hips born from the woman who died. She moves these stylish suburban hips through the all knowing mist of rain, towards the pathetic Leah, who is at the front suburban door, pushing in the silver suburban key, sliding the white door open into the unspacious suburban living room, where the base of the stairs awaits an exhausted suburban safari to the upper room. Leah opens the door and steps inside her older sister's home out of the rain. Her eyes are drawn to Jules Breton, as *The Weeders* are captured by the spirit of divinity in mourning.

Leah lets her black travel bag slide to the floor, as she wanders over to the painting of women without hope, weeding a grassy field after sunset, under the light of a waxing crescent moon. Leah chooses not to feel the spirits that have descended, those that inhabit the halls, and stylish gray walls of luxury. Leah does not engage the haunting of these fervent spirits, that move and moan silently about, those that grieve to warn, those that grieve to give false hope of escape, those that grieve to turn to the darkness of their true selves. Leah chooses not to feel the carpeted footsteps, borne into silence from their brief time on the hardwood foyer, footsteps of her older sister Rachel Lynn, the oldest daughter of Lena Ling Chao.

Rachel glides smoothly over to the upright piano against the wall, sliding her lovely fingers across, remembering her nude sessions as a teenager, and the agony of the cane upon her back as she played. The agony of a dream unrealized by an Asian mother, of a music school audition where there were dissonant chords unhidden, the agony of a naked belt whipping that same night, the agony of an anal raping from the broken hearted mother, the agony of a spirit broken for all time.

This is the quiet and forceful tone. Spoken in the native Cantonese tongue. Spoken by the older Chao, the sophisticated worldly psychiatrist. The one who is the giver of the blue flame. The blue flame tinted the color of night. And upon Leah's last step into the space of what aura that burns, she feels a massive slap across her face that rattles her bran against her skull, and flashes a bolt of lightning somewhere in the back of her vision. And then to accompany this is the monumental hair pull, to color the shock of trauma with pain.

"Skinny little girl with big long tits," comes the Cantonese accent poured so heavy upon the English tone. The accent of her mother's land. A spirit passed from farmlands east, and pain passed through the generations across land and sea.

"I'll watch your tits swing to the floor when you crawl."

This, the beauty and the purity of her mother's tongue, as though lept upward from her mother's premature death and burial to come.

"Please," speaks the younger sister, an answer in this selfsame native tongue.

"Huh?"

"Please," the sound comes again, both women immersed in every Chinese syllable and inflection, as it was when they were raised in the fires of their mother's will and power. From whence hath they learned the language of their mother's homeland! From the heart and soul of depravity that hath ridden from the east, burning blue and black fire.

"Save your tears for when I fuck you," comes the psychiatrist's lovely voice in Cantonese, pitched dark, bitten by the demons Vitriol and Spite.

"Go upstairs, and take off your clothes." Rachel Lynn watches her younger sister turn in disillusionment. Watching her walk away in despair. Feeling her take the steps forward in the shadows of time itself, down the shared portion, the dark and woodsy path along the timeline. Watching her move defeatedly into the cavern of her unknown future, to revisit the echo of a past they both have known. Rachel curses the spirits of pity and compassion, stroking the white keys gently once more, as she moves towards the stairs that lead to the divinely appointed upper room.

In hips so extraordinary to behold, she takes each painful and miraculous step from the past where the dragon took her mother, to the immediate future, where she will burn with the eyes of the dragon, to set the younger daughter on fire of Hell.

Rachel Lynn Chao walks the stairs of grieving. At one with the sound of rumbling wisdom from the clouds.

33

*I*n the upper room, in keeping with the fullness of herself, the psychiatrist gathers the instrument of truth in latter day splendor. The tiny silver sword of truth, in the form of so-called technology, placed on a chair and facing the bed. Rachel fiddles and adjusts, until the view through the little camera is centered, and the record of future events begins to drift into this part of the timeline.

What buttons and switches the little camera needs to come alive are clicked and done. Rachel walks over to her sister, to her immolation held captive, standing in the room nude and compliant, knowing already not to feign modesty, but to have her hands clasped behind her back, to reveal the enlarged and elongated breasts to full view. Rachel, even her jaded older sister, student of every human depravity, is held enraptured by macromastia, by the superior enlargement, by the enormously overgrown and overdeveloped breasts, to where casual viewing is hardly possible, and a cavalier dismissal is as that to a passing comet in the evening day.

Somewhere in the phantom scales that exist above the G chord, thoese mountainous melodies do play, hung down flattened against her body and so far over her waist, so that her slim curviness is concerned underneath them. Rachel walks over slowly and filled with a contempt risen so real, with a bitterness so genuine, which rises both her hands as though involuntary, to take hold of both nipples that are naturally pointed down, pulling them up and twisting them without mercy, staring at the lovely grimace of pain that escapes as a smile turned upside down, Leah's eyes closed, her brow wrinkled as her voice begins to escape on its own, to repeat the words in Cantonese tone *"it hurts, it hurts"* over and over again. This, the younger sister voices without compromise, without dignity, as the pain forces her to move her hands forward.

"Put your hands down!" is the sharp Sword of Woman wielded, the bitter, caustic sound of mercy withdrawn, spat at the helpless young woman in the beauty of their native tongue. Satisfied for the moment, Rachel unbuttons the black, simple blouse, pulling it out of her tight capris jeans and tossing it neglected to the floor. Next, she finds herself barefoot on the plush carpet, never taking her eyes from her sister who stands till and trembling, her expression somber and grieving, her tears slow and plentiful. The pain of betrayal reverberates throughout to add fuel to this suburban flame, to add heat to this end of the world fire kindled and grown.

The sophisticated, worldly psychiatrist removes her bra, her own breasts small and perfect, to contrast the massive hip spread, made more dramatic by the tiny waist and deep, inward curve. In front of her grieving younger sister, in front of the talented violinist turned music sales woman, she unzips her pants and slides them down, down away from her hips, as though slightly dancing slowly out of them. In her black underwear cloth barely there, cut so high in the back to expose so hefty a set of haunches hailed from the motherland hips come and gone, she switches this gift of nature over to the mirror dresser, sliding the drawer casually open. She then slips out of her underwear, letting them fall to the floor, to fully expose the hips of strength, the Amazonian curve so deeply feminine. Reaching into the drawer, she pulls the instrument of destruction colored black as night, sliding the harness up to the center of herself, securing it in place, until this weapon is a part of her mind, body and spirit, stroking its realistic shape in knowledge of the truth, in behind closed doors revelation of her inner self, where the mask of public hypocrisy and politeness is removed, to uncover what churns beneath cultured civility.

The sophisticated woman walks over to the shy, humble younger woman, both in the beauty of their Asian ancestry, staring boldly at her younger sister in the eye, to where there is no pretense of what evil lurks in the hearts of women.

"So, bit long tit girl like to cry?"

And what follows is a slap more massive than the last, to send Leah's brain reeling again, and to reactivate the threat of tears to come.

"Go to the dresser," Rachel orders her, pointing. *"Bring the belt from the top drawer."*

The all seeing eye, the all knowing eye of truth captures this breasty walk, as the slim girl with the long, gigantic breasts walks in defeat over to the drawer and pulls the hard leather belt, feeling the phantom itch already, caused by the tinkling of the golden metallic buckle. She carries this belt over to her older sister, who stands in full Amazonia, in the power of this behind closed doors calling. She roughly snatches the belt from her sister, ordering her to stand facing the all seeing eye. Then, without pity or restraint, she takes the leather end of the belt unfurled, and lashes it hard across her sister's breast close to the bottom, nearby where the nipple is pointed forward and unprotected. Another lash with the belt brings a deep scream from Leah, a healthy and robust woman's scream, answered by another barking order from Rachel Lynn, for her to *"put your hands's down! Behind your back or I will tie you up and beat you worse!"*

And this, Lea believes, knowing that she must accept the lesser of two evils, so that her pain can be endured. She holds her hands locked behind her back, while the sophisticated woman whips her sister's breasts to red welts and bruising, sparing not the nipples at least five times apiece, forcing Leah to hold her own breasts upward in the palms of her hands, with the nipples pointed far out forward, so that the belt can find its place among them.

These are the blows that break. These are the cries that unbind. These are the ties that unwind the dignity of the soul, when the strength of them is loosened and undone. Upon these blows to the nipples, Leah is boken and trembling, bent over slightly, unable to care of what grim future promises are made that can never be broken and undone.

She is ordered to put her hands down again, so that Rachel Lynn can complete this cycle of pain, that is started in the breasts of her sister, to where it strikes the fire of her voice to a scream with every blow, through the air and into the mind of Rachel Lynn, where it vibrates down to her own nipples become erect, and lower to the center of where she lives and breathes, extended to the black member that she wears.

She tosses the belt to the floor, upon the final blow unforeseen, grabbing her younger sister by the neck with both hands, *"your tears and your crying make my dick too hard. Okay?"* Done so beautifully in their Cantonese, shaking the sister's neck on the Chinese word equivalent to "okay." And the all seeing eye captures the slight of the breast flopping young woman thrown violently onto the bed by the neck, followed by the older, hippier sister who sits roughly down beside her, the black phallus showing in contrast to her ivory skin, grabbing the younger woman by the hair and punching her in the face, square upon her cheeks and at the corner of her mouth, until the young woman emits a sickening yelp from the sock, raising her arms to try and block the blows. This, she succeeds in only partially, to prevent the cutting of her skin to blood.

When the plateau of this preplay is climbed and achieved, the older sister climbs upon the bed, on top of the younger sister, holding one hand over her mouth, and guiding the member into the front of her with the other. *The lady cock is so big and thick,* is the voice of a spirit whispered into the younger sister's ear from parts unknown, as the pressure slides itself deep, deep, and deeper up inside of her, to keep her mouth and eyes wide open in the shock of fear and disbelief, as her sister takes her hand from her mouth in two fold purpose, so she can pin her breasty sister's arms to her sides, and so that she can listen to her scream.

For every wayward act from along the timeline, she becomes depravity, to channel it without mercy into the body of her helpless younger sister, held prisoner on her back while her older sister is suddenly lost in involuntary motion, to where her shapely hips are squeezed and released of their own accord, until a lightning bold strikes the center of her world, to cause a sound to erupt from her voice as a siren, while her body begins to tremble and shake like the ground across the battlefields of Armageddon.

A Rhapsody in Blue

Eyes of Dawn

"*Y*ou act like it's the end of the world, Meadow, its seven pounds. It went straight to your breasts and your butt anyway. You actually look better for Christ's sake."

Why the pretense, I wonder. Why do I try to act as though my interest in her appearance is only in passing, as if we were somehow normal? As if we had not been crossing the line since she were twelve? When I was Mrs. Oppenheimer, and it was my job to pay blonde hostess during his corporate climb?

"Irene said I was getting fat."

"No, she didn't."

"You remember. She said she was going to *"burn the fat off my little Egyptian ass."*

Yes. I remember. They say that out of the abundance of the heart, the mouth speaketh. Already, I know that the fear and depression Momma Turner feels, that *Irene* feels, is going to manifest itself upon her granddaughter.

"She's one to talk about fat asses," I say. "Where does she think you got it from?"

At the sink running water over the lettuce leaves, she doesn't bother to answer. The answer as to where she gets her hips from is already burned into both of our minds. The naked Amazon's hips are in clarity in her memory, as she remembers the look of them as they squeezed until they shook, as she pushed the strap on member into me just last night. Channeling her life's grief into me, into her forty year old daughter, as her 21 year old daughter watched. And learned.

Truthfully, I can hardly blame her grandmother. I can hardly blame Irene for what Meadow has churned inside her body. Even while I glance over at her, at the sink with her back turned to me, I am tingled inside by the shape of my own daughter, as it hearkens from the Kardashian Land, so remarkably exposed in her faded black jeans and ocean blue t-shirt tucked in. A girl so beautiful as to cause a rumbling in the spirit of those around her, but cursed with no real talent to speak of, and even less self esteem. So much to my own advantage, this has always been, as she is content to hang around the house in luxury and comfort, watching her movies or reading the occasional book, browsing the internet, nurturing her CD collection top heavy with Mozart and Rossini, though she has never shown any inclination towards playing music herself. Whether or not her reclusiveness is my fault, I'll never acknowledge. No, I'll never take the blame for whatever is right or wrong with her. I only know that come Hellfire or dragon fire, come hell or high water, Meadow is mine.

In a flash of my heart's desire, projected onto the theater of my mind, I walk boldly from the tomato cutting counter, boldly but in the stealth of stalking just the same, pressing up against her from behind, placing the six inch, razor sharp blade against her beautiful neck until she is perfectly still and terrified. I then grab the top of her sky blue tee and run the knife through it at the top, cutting the top of it open so that I can grab the cut shirt with both hands, ripping the t-shirt violently from top to bottom as I press myself hard against her. From this flash of day dreaming, I awaken, my heart beating faster in my chest, mouth slightly open so I can breathe. As I watch her break and wash the lettuce leaves, shaped as an earth goddess on the eve of Armageddon, I am compelled to take one of the juicy cuts of sweet tomato and put it in my mouth, letting my lips linger at the tip of my thumb, while I feel my heartbeat return to normal, and the breaths I take are not ripe with the quiet desperation of just a moment ago.

35

*P*amela White surveys the aftermath of trauma. Reverend Pam, she is called. Pastor White, she has been. The lady reverend stands in awe and disbelief. In quiet shock at what she sees in the looming gray mist, a mist of rain that will not die, that threatens to encircle the earth in darkness and gray. In the theater of my mind, I see the lady pastor as she walks the smoldering rubble in the mist, scorched and scattered brick remains of her modern cathedral, her charismatic and corporate church conundrum. This, a puzzling palace of hidden sins and immoralities, no longer resembling what refuge of hypocrisy it once was. Even in the mist of falling rain, there is still radiated the heat of devastation, where the smoke of destruction still lingers nearby the fallen bricks of a charismatic cause, bricks that died in the overwhelming firestorm of blue flame. And even while she glances around the Virginia landscape of buildings, houses and trees that are untouched by this flame, she is unable to escape the inevitable reaching out, the cold, icy hands of truth that she knows better than anyone, that this ground upon which the charred remains like smoldering was judged, and left abandoned for all the world to see.

Even while the reverend Pamela walks the rubble of devastation, she knows, she feels the rising up of every sin confessed and unconfessed, of those that she heard so often in secret, and those that she could feel by divine instinct alone. In her heart, she often wondered how it is that the Almighty could stomach the goings on under the high church ceiling, camouflaged in the movie theater dark of Sunday morning praise and worship, where the adulterers and the adulteresses, the corporate thieves and sharks mix and mingle with the child abusers, all of them hidden in the lights gone dim, so that the musicians and singer shine brighter on stage, so that the giant screen of their endtime display is better enjoyed, so that all of their sins are comfortably hidden, so that they can rest unjudged by one another, left to be judged by the one who is worthy, who will separate the wheat from the chaff, who will remove the weeds of corruption from the rose garden of righteousness and salvation.

In the theater of her mind, reverend Pamela White surveys the smoldering landscape of corrupted memory, grieving for the time of renewal, where the corporate monies will be gathered again, and the church of hypocrisy will rise again. She remembers gazing out over the congregation from Sunday to Sunday, at the prim and proper faces of suburban civility, knowing of what churns underneath—whose daughter is on drugs, whose white husband is having an affair with a Hispanic woman in the projects, whose wealthy husband tortures her behind closed doors with such skill as to leave no bruises but to elicit screams of agony and pleading just the same, what woman emotionally abuses her husband to tears and laughs about it behind his back, what woman is having sex with the man across the street, while her own husband sits unaware of it at home, unaware that when she is taking out the trash and staying for too long, she is not taking in the night air and the stars on a moonlit night, but that she is dropping her sweats to her ankles and bending over the back porch railing for this man across the street—this man that smiles and is friendly to everyone in the light of day. This man who keeps his lawn mowed and green, who keeps himself in shape, who is visited by other women on a regular basis as well.

Reverend Pamela knows. She knows of the single mother and the nine year old little Carmen Doll, that sits in the pews with her arm in a cast and a sling. She knows that it was not the fall from her bike that cracked the bones of her forearm, but that it was the walls of secret, when the woman's strength is released in rage upon the body of a little girl. She knows what churns beneath cultured civility. What mountain of hidden truths lie beneath the iceberg of hypocrisy and lies? Of this truth, she knows of what endtime secrets threaten to be revealed, as the river of molten rock that flows beneath the mountain, that rumbles the ground in warning as to what lies beneath, and what treasure of forbidden truth threatens to blow. Of this, the final frontier, is the modern Mother Daughter Dynamic, where the curse of fathers upon their daughters in secret is passé, and the last great truth before the end of the world must be revealed. It is the truth that Reverend Pamela knows all too well, having heard the post collegiate confession of a daughter who spoke to her in private—a daughter who was *not* fallen away from her mother—a daughter who the power over her world with her graduation from the University of Virginia, where she was left holding the bag, the bag and baggage of her past that she needed to reconcile.

Pastor White remembers the tall, thin blonde, and her mother of like and kind. *Since I was nine years old,* the blonde collegiate told her, *and nobody knows. Nobody in the whole world would ever suspect what Mom does to me. At least once a week since I was nine, right after my father left. She was cold and indifferent to him, and he got tired of her shutting him out and so he left.*

Pastor White remembers. She remembers the way her own heart felt as though a hand had grabbed it to temper its beating, to where she had to grab her chest, listen to the tall, collegiate blonde tell the rest of her story. And this, a woman who is bound by her mother, and worships her mother, who comes to the charismatic cathedral every Sunday with her mother, the two of them. A woman in her mid 40's, a small business owner, volunteerism incarnate, a helpful pillar of the community. The envy of other mothers, whose own daughters are not as tall, are not as thin, are not as blonde, are not as Gwyneth Paltrow-esque in package and form.

This, Reverend Pamela knows. Remembering eye contact made with the young Gwyneth girl, to see if there was a connection made. There wasn't. She remembers the dead eyes. Eyes dead to the truth. Dead to what is real, to what lives underneath the false faces worn in public. Eyes dead to the comfort of down to earth realness that is attacked, eyes dead to the beauty of what lives underneath the face of fungalooga. This, Pamela remembers vividly, as the thunder begins to roll from the clouds of grieving, as she thanks her Almighty God through her Lord and Savior for the gift of umbrellas, and what shelter and protection they may provide. "I know three girls I met in college, the Gwyneth girl had said, and their mothers all do the same thing to them, she said. Of this, the Paster remembers. In quiet disbelief still, that another young woman in the world knows from what tragic river down which she herself has traveled, and of what fires churn beneath cultured civility. It is an endtime truth that threatens to explode from beneath the groundwork of daily living, where mothers will hide their faces in shame, for what things that are done of them in secret.

Reverend Pamela suddenly shivers from the cold. Not the cold of this summer rainstorm that looms. But from the ghostly chill of recollection that passes through her soul from somewhere along the timeline, from when she herself was a teenager in a broken home, and her single mother visited upon her this amazing tragedy.

Pamela White listens to the thunder. To the voice of a rising wind. Part of her wishes that the storm would exact judgment upon her, and strike her with a spark from the clouds. Is that part of why she wanders through the ashes of this church condemned to Hell, with an umbrella raised in an approaching lightning storm? This, she cannot tell. Cursing herself again for her own stupidity, her own lack of judgment and self control. Giving them an excuse to get rid of her, even before fires of judgment came down. Sunday morning at 11:30am, when the curch was filled to capacity, drawn to the heart of scandal like wolves to a lonely campfire. To witness the aftermath of a killing, to hear the announcement that Pamela White will no longer be preaching at this First Assembly of God Church. The church was more packed than it had been in years. Standing room only, as if the local news shows had been advertising for an even. To see and hear the talk coalesced into action. To see what the seminary school graduate would have to endure, in the wake of what changes had been laid. Will she be there? Will she have the nerve to explain or justify? Will she try and dismiss it as a lie? How will Pastor White, the Reverend Pamela White, how will she escape the jaws of the lion? The lion of public shame and scandal, that had her held tight in the tooth and fang of its hunger grip?

In the winds and gentle rains of yesterday, every member and non-member showed up, quietly disapproving that the victim was no where in sight. The mingled masses of hypocrites and liars, the self-proclaimed righteous hoarde, so happy to sit in judgment of one of their own, especially one who was supposed to be their moral guide, a refuge of goodness and piety in the endtime storm of immorality. They came to see the woman of

God stripped and laid bare, to watch her breasts wobble free and exposed, to see her hips wiggle and jiggle as she is turned and tied into place to be whipped in their minds, in the souls of their darkest

and most delightfully depraved desire. This, the grandest scandal in the history of their church, where two young prostitutes came forth, claiming that they are not doing it for the money, but for the truth, to claim that this lady minister had been visiting them for years, paying them in secret, while she wore upon her naked body that which pertaineth to a man.

Pamela White listens to the storm. Hearing the voice of warning in the breeze, and in the gentle mist of rain. Understanding that yes, there is such a place as Hell on earth, and she is now a prisoner there. Remembering herself in the un-cheap hotel room of the far city, another town some 50 miles away. Remembering herself nude in front of the big bathroom mirror, her mouth tightly gagged with her own black stocking, her hands tied behind her back, legs tied together above the knee, while the realistic male member hangs down from in front of her, gripped in the lovely young prostitute's hand, pulled and jerked upon until her vision hazes, until she can no longer perceive the flow of time nor the death of space around her, and her ears are filled with the muffled sound of her own screaming, as the cock merges itself as part of her being, to cause her entire body to tremble and shake without mercy.

Where have you gone, Pamela White? Why do you think you can hide your sin in the cloak of distance, under the shadow of a gloomy and rainy fall of night? Don't you know that the eyes of the Lord are in every place…beholding he evil and the good? Is what they're saying about her true at all, Pamela White, that you paid prostitutes to have sex with you? The lady preacher is a dyke! My breath trembles, the people say to themselves, I cannot breathe from the pleasure and pain! Is this why she and her husband announced their divorce to a shocked and grieving congregation a year ago? Is this why Raymond White left the church for parts unknown? Is their something that he knew about his wife, something so dark, so scandalous as to be unfathomable? What of his early arrival at their suburban home one rare, Sunday afternoon, when the house was filled with the sound of a woman's voice in painful ecstasy? What of his hurried trip up the stairs of their suburban Paradise over a year ago? What of his quiet steps down the hall, to a view through the open bedroom door, where there was his wife nude on her back at the corner of the bed? What of the neighbor's troubled 16 year old daughter standing naked and strapped on, ramming his wife anally while she calls to God and Christ, her legs up in the air and braced on the troubled girl's shoulder? What of the girl's own close—eyed ecstatic look of burning bliss, where the edge of an orgasm through her lady cock was nearby to be achieved? What of this troubled 16 year old from down the street, who had sent his wife into an orbit of ecstasy that he himself never even knew existed? What of the pissing stream he sees from his wife, coming up from between her legs as she orgasms, as she screams for mercy from the throne of God?

Reverend Pamela White listens to the storm. Wishing that she had been among the congregation, when the fire from the dragon Thyatira blazed down from the sky, and melted the glass and bricks with fervent heat, of the world's most beautiful, and hottest blue flame.

A Rhapsody in Blue

36

The judge's beautiful wife rides the wind. Comfortable in the upper classed, upper middle aged comfort that comes with money, from the benefits of a good marriage to a good breadwinner, $175,000 dollars a year base salary. Income achieved and dispensed from the slot machine of modern corporate capitalism, dispensed in millions to a lucky few. Stocks bought and sold, jackpots hit like a bullseye many times over the years, as corporate success is passed from generation to generation.

Judge Johnson's wife rides the wind. Complacent. Compliant to her life's calling. Committed to carrying out the power and purpose she must provide, in the splendor of 50 years come and gone. Retired early from the corporate grind, from the cushy, cushion comfort of corporate law. How is Margaret Johnson to be refused a position here—her husband is Judge Michael Johnson, Harvard graduate, new Jersey Supreme court justice. How can we refuse anything this woman asks of us? Time off, more money, her name on the door up front. How so we break the spell she has over us, Miss Boston University, Miss Big Wigglehips in the tight corporate skirts, Miss short, jet black hair and fair skin, Miss blue eyed beauty pageant beauty? Who has ever refused a request from her blessed lips? In the history of a so-called llife, what is more of a ride than a struggle, having no understanding of the three part formula of success—which is Talent, Perseverance, and Opportunity? Early retirement from her easy corporate climb—dollars left to her by a father passed to the next world—so middling, so piddlina a paltry five million, to cause her to say with a straight face more than once in her life—*I'm not rich, I worked for everything I've got.* Seven million dollars in pure savings, Mama Johnson carries in the upper class mind. Under pressure to cause it to sustain itself. Under pressure and hope to watch it grow like a flower in the night.

Sensuality and beauty ride the wind. In the plane high above the earthbound madness, high above the ocean of the east coast—high above the madness and fear of eschatology. Cruising in safety and contentment above the storm clouds beneath her stocking feet and high heeled pumps. Breathing in the first class air. Looking out over the endless carpet of grey clouds beneath the plane, and a sky long past the amber sunlight, as the earth turns toward the evening day. Rising high above the gray, grieving storm below, cruising the miles toward the island Jamaica, in the heart of the Caribbean sea. This, to find the young beauty of like brunette lovliness, this Princes Diana Johnson, inspired to marry her latest man in Jamaica. A man sorter than shee, not as inclined to beauty as shee, but quite so lovely in his white naval uniform, and in the flower bed of pedigree. He is somebody, who came from somebody, who is always going to be somebody, Miss Maggie advised, until she convinced Diana that this rich young man whose father headed a multi million dollar acquisitions company (a company that collects and eats smaller companies), she convinced Diana that she loved this little *White And So Pretty* sailor boy with the rich daddy he hardly knew and the skinny pretty mother with the earthy dark blonde hair. A woman whose skinny, curveless body hath caused none a sleepless night for this woman down below, who keeps her sensuality bound and pent up, to channel it though which avenues as she sees fit. A lifetime of behind closed doors discipline to five daughters, punishments done in secret, done in the name of correction. In full pretense that none of the breast canings, none of the nipple twisting, none of the chokings, none of the hairbrush paddlings, none of the belt lashings were given in perversion, but in the name of secret, mother daughter discipline alone—discipline, thy name is pain. In full pretense, that the phantom burnings she feels even to this day upon her bare buttocks is no factor, when her daughters must be disciplined for every poor grade, every missed curfew, every smart remark, every wayward nighttime phonecall, every boy-time rendezvous, as every boy is forbidden until graduation from high school. Three more daughters still at home and waiting, one almost thirty years old, too shy to break the bonds of maternity, too cozy to leave the feathered nest of luxury. Then, two others still in their teens, two great beauties, they are, who have not been spared the rod of Maggie Johnson. This, the rod of Mother Daughter Perversion, as it is dispensed in acceptable form, in corporal punishments ad nauseam to infinity.

Margaret Johnson rides the wind. The summer wind above the clouds of grieving. Comforted by the many flashes of electric blue within the gray clouds far and wide, feeling safe and untouched by whatever storms that torment the poor inhabitants below. Intrigued by the sudden and wayward tingle in her bosom that rises from nowhere, to cast a light upon the theater of her mind, to pull her soul into the heart of memory.

Upon the brightest flash of energy from the clouds, amidst the rumble of thunder reaching out to them so quietly from the distance, the face of her oldest disappointment appears, and of what necessities that must have come and gone. Her oldest daughter Amber, who chose love over money so many years ago, to marry a man with a bad temper and no future—a man both Margaret and Judge Michael despised for 20 years, while he spent those years adrift, in failure from job to job, eventually giving up to stay at home, so support his wife emotionally as she worked—this poor husband, this hated son-in-law—burdened by a calling to write that he did not understand—staying at home out of world weariness and social anxiety. Unaware of what was churning beneath the cultured civility of his own marriage. Unaware of conversations had in secret over the hone, from the Philadelphia suburb to the suburb in New Jersey State, between daughter Amber and mother Margaret, when the mother hit her promised land high above 45, and the Margaret libido became too mountainous to behold, where such things that are done of women alone in secret would boggle the mind of the prudish and the ignorant of heart and soul, of those unaquainted with the spirit of deep perversion, and of what may make a woman have to put the vacuum hose at her nipple, or to tie her own ankles together while she lies upon her stomach on the bed, plugged up so tight in anal ecstasy, her hands underneath her, pressed so completely upon the center of her life and libido. Where the orgasms come with hardly a motion of her fingers while she thinks of how to destroy her oldest daughter's marriage, her howling siren screamed and pitched so high and muffled into the mattress under her face pushed into it. Her body literally convulsing at the middle aged hips spread and seasoned just so, as she screams into her mattress, muffled from the nosy ears of what spirits that lurk nearby a house empty and devoid of life. this, a year ago, when she said goodbye to the corporate grind, and hello to the behind closed doors secret grind, in her libidinous year at age 49.

Margaret Johnson rides the wind. Burning now with the memory of what perversions must rise and fall, for when the hatred of a broke son in law is enhanced by the superior, snobbish attitude that must see him eradicated, and finally cut free from her oldest daughter's life. *How are you and your friend across the street doing,* she would ask Amber. *You're getting closer? Good, its good you have someone else beside that bum to talk too…*

159

Maggie Johnson rides the wind. Cruising the Wealthen Stream above the clouds. In memory of advice so un-surreptitiously given. Dispensed without pretense. *You need to take care of yourself—all those years you worked and supported him while he did nothing, while he was nothing, if you have an opportunity to get love from another man then you need to get it while you can...have the affair,* was the advice unspoken. *Get love where you can, take care of yourself,* was the advice so boldly spoken.

You've got to work on your husband. Stop sleeping with him. Stop being nice to him. Stop giving him money. Stop taking advice from him. Stop letting him tell you what to do. You've got to treat him like the piece of shit that he is until he breaks, until you can get him to put his hands on you. Then you can have his ass thrown out of the house.

Margaret remembers the joy. The celebration in the wealthy New Jersey neighborhood home, when the big fight was reported. When the restraining order went down. When her and her oldest daughter's plan came to fruition. When her stupid, worthless, nothing of a husband was show the door, after having not worked outside the home for 10 years, being an unemployable mess, having to fall from the middle class—from his wife's physical therapist's salary to no salary at all, into the waiting claws of the deepest poverty imaginable. *If you ever get back with him again, you'll be cut off I swear,* the mother tells her, in front of the mirror of her daughter's own bathroom, her 30 year old daughter's blouse and bra off, as she stood topless before the mirror, with Margaret behind her, twisting her oldest daughter's nipples without mercy until she drew tears and pleading, and swears to God and Christ of eternal loyalty. And then, a complete disrobing of the two of them, and a fervent and brutal hand spanking upon her oldest daughter's ample backside, a hard and swift hand spanking to bruises and agony, where the humiliation of her oldest daughter is epic, rising the height of what sorrow is possible, to match the height of what plateau must be inside the mother Margaret.

And then, guided by unseen hands of escort, to guide her naked body into place behind her 30 year old daughter, to stand her there behind her married daughter, to say the words *now you'll divorce that son of a bitch, you'll never speak to his broke ass again for the rest of your life—do you hear me,* she says in roughness, as the roughness comes out of her voice on its own, pressing herself in full heat raised and swollen against the back of her daughter without such as a twitch of motion, grabbing her daughter's breasts from behind as if to anchor herself, unable to contain the gruff, bellowing howl that rumbles from her mouth in her daughter ear like a calf being branded, much to her oldest daughter's shock and tortured disbelief.

Margaret Johnson rides the wind. In fearful witness to a sudden brightness of blue that engulfs the world outside the window, and the sound of the captain's voice in fevered chaos amidst the screams all around her, and the feeling of a rapid descent from on high. Through the fiery blue window, she catches a glimpse of an engine on the wing explode in a burst of bright orange, as the view of the sky above is suddenly replaced by the gray world of storm clouds, made barely visible through the thinning blue fire that seems to engulf the plane around them.

Margaret Johnson rides the wind. In the terror of a rapid descent through the stormy clouds over the ocean, where the feeling in her soul rises to a fear from beyond terror that grips her insides like an icy cold, invisible hand, as she falls from the sky in a wave of human shrieks and screaming, that appears from the clouds like a flaming earth comet, burning blue and white fire across the rainy, stormy sky toward the dark, churning ocean waters far away and down below.

37

The freeway is alive with news from the wire, car radios buzzing with news of the latest attack. As the people drive the busy Carolina freeways of the Triangle cities, they listen in nervous awe, to what happened to an International Airport in the northeast, and a 300 passenger jet bound for Jamaica over the Atlantic. And this plane's fiery demise was seen headed this way, they hear, flying with determined lightning speed from off the Carolina coast at Hatteras, nearby where the blue fire was seen streaking from the sky at dusk. Now, under the rainy clouds of early nightfall, the people ride and wait, believing that they are somehow immune in the Bible Belt from God's endtime judgment, that the fires of this Hell will not, and cannot burn here. No matter that the earthquake rumblings through the Carolinas have not ceased since the creature's arrival. Despite the fact that some were unlucky enough to be on the highway north to Knob Hill, formally known as Pilot Mountain, as the famous and strange plateau was blown into a million fiery red pieces, as Pilot Mountain became the newest volcano in the world, its majestic and monstrous peak crumbled and blasted away, transformed into a chimney of glowing ashes and soot, and the source of a river of bright orange molten rock flowing to the forests down below. This, having blown away so much of the Carolina tranquility unearned, so much of the pastoral peace so graciously given. Pilot Mountain is now one of Hell's chimneys, filling the skies with towers of dust and smoke from far beneath the earth, with showers of glowing melted and molten rocks and lava sprayed to the world down below. The most cataclysmic volcanic eruption ever recorded, they say, making access to the mountain something of the far and distant past, where even the roads that were nearby are no longer safe to travel.

These are the souls of Pilot Mountain's awakening. The souls of Pilot Mountain's demise. Riding their freeways of rainy nighttime safety, far east of the mountain that glows in the night. Comfortable in the arms of concrete civilization, where they believe that they are not subject to the weakness of mountains and forest wood. Of what interest would an endtime monster have for these safe and solid city streets, where the nighttime traffic weaves lighted, thorough out their concrete and urban fall of night. These lighted cars and trucks drive onward, chariots of wealth and poverty held in secret, unknown to one another as they pass, but all who share the same unspoken fear of what tragedies loom in the skies over their southern tranquility down east, nearby the corn and summer greenleaf tobacco country.

The lighted chariots roll on, down the freeway of earthly progression, until a scream goes unheard by none but the one who unleashes it, as her car weaves and swerves over the rain soaked highway, as she stops short at 60 miles an hour down to zero, as if it could make her disappear from the sight—of the line of blue fire being sprayed onto the highway from the towering white dragon's mouth in the dark. The cars behind her take their requisite places among the unfortunate, those cars who are given no time to stop when the tail lights in front of them flash bright red in warning. In terror, in the fear that grips the soul, the nighttime drivers slam on brakes and slide into the cars in front of them, as they watch the cars up ahead disappear in the line of fire, in the flames that ignite the highway as if it were composed of asphalt soaked in gasoline.

Those far enough away are witness to what was once only imagined or heard of, that which had only threatened the cities and suburbs, the forests and fields of elsewhere, as the towering white creature, in full, angelic beauty and power, raises its head to draw a second breath, while the burning liquid drips from its mouth in brightly glowing blue, then lunges forward while evil eyed purposes, blasting an explosion of blue fire from its mouth like a gigantic flame thrower, in the noise of deep rumbling as the road and the cars a mile away are engulfed in blue flame. They are witness to the origins of a flame that reacts with the air itself, expanding to explosive force and power when it leaves the dragon's mouth.

And some take notice that these are the most beautiful animals on the face of the earth, with scales pitched in snowy white, and eyes that burn in royal alabaster blue.

This is one of the out of the way places. A place untouched by the ghost of modernity. A hopeless plot of nothing, a few acres of nothing. Hidden somewhere north of the mountain that burns, near the mountain woods of the Southern Appalachians. One of the few living witnesses to when the top of the Carolina mountain was blown away by the eons of pressure built up. By forces placed upon it from within.

In the fall of this rainy mountain night, the Woman feels the rumbling beneath her feet. In the kitchen of lost hope, as she stands at the window with the southern mountain view. A view that once was benign after the fall of night, where there was nothing but the length of space between here and nowhere, the nearby forest trees going on forever in evening and nighttime silhouette.

The daytime horizon was once hidden by the fall of night, where the loneliness falls like a blanket over the mountain forest landscape. Loneliness replete with the end tome sorrow. Sorrow that is now replaced with fear. This, the fear of impending judgment, when all sacrifice for sin has come and gone. When the devil is listened to, and given a door by which to enter through and through. *The little bitch,* her twelve year old daughter has in her mind. In her soul. In her spirit. The little bitch, in the days before the mountain exploded. This, the heart of a single mother drowned in sorrow. Drowned in regret, in hatred for herself, her life, and the life that was the daughter she knew.

These are the days of little Dawn Norwood, as they burden the heart and mind. As Delilah Norwood looks on from the kitchen window, in the shadow of lost hope. The shadow that falls over the entire earth, beneath the fall of night. Delilah sips her coffee to the television drone—to the monotony of female voiced hopelessness spread through the night. The news chatter over the little box TV signal, no satellite or cable. Just the mercy of an antennae patched in, where the brief signal from the modern world gets through. The briefest glimpse of eschatology.

Tonight, it is in the voice of the newswoman that speaks, that tells of the dragon attacks many miles north, at the northeast International Airport. The Jamaica flight that went down in blue flame. And the freeway traffic attack near the capital city—all done this same evening and night, in the heart of this end of the world storm that grows. A storm that has arisen en masse, to carry the wind and rain from one side of the world to the other, where the promise of God is in the rainbow covenant, that holds the weeping clouds at bay. That dispenses devastation in whirlwinds two miles wide, and hailstones of volleyball sized annihilation. Roofs, hoods and trunks of cars caved in, with the occasional skull or two.

Delilah Norwood listens to the fear. To the disconnected voice of reason that cannot hide the bewilderment. That cannot mask the worldwide terror. On the heels of nightmares come and gone—Delilah must gather her raincloak, and move out into the windblown rain and oppressive dark. Unable to recover from the memory of the energy waves that passed through her this afternoon. When the ground rumbled and shook her cabin beneath her feet.

Delilah goes out into the fearful storm—driven forward by a greater fear. A supernatural terror, pricked into her soul by the eyes of dawn. Eyes aglow with the light of the hidden Moon, under hair as long and black as night. The Eyes of Dawn, having appeared to her seven times in her dreams—always peering at her with righteous malevolence—with the instinct of vengeance tinted black and blue.

Delilah Norwood crossed the massive space of a back lawn, big enough for what cropfield that may or may not ever be planted again. Stepping clumsily over the wet, grassy field with the hand held light all aglow. Illuminating her path to the edge of the woods. Illuminating the hopeless drops of rain forlorn. She walks underneath the clouds aglow with flashes of warning, pushed along towards fear itself. Pushed along by a greater fear. The kind that draws one into the dark cavern of the rest of an empty house to investigate a wayward sound. Sounds of the natural. Or the supernatural.

In the rising wind and rain, long past the bedtime hour, Delilah goes to the edge of the Appalachian Woods, guided inside by the light of memory. Through the darkness of her misdeed. Walking through the woods to the mound of raised earth—unflattened, uncovered by grass and leaves. The set space of earth raised up, to mark where her daughter was buried. But this, the only marker, its no other grave marker would ever be given. A daughter who had never been allowed to go to school. A daughter who was born in backwoods secrecy. A daughter who was raised in isolation. A daughter burdened by the perversions of a woman tortured to madness by grief. A daughter whose body bears the scars of her mother's sickness. Of her mother's depravity. A daughter whose neck bears the bruise of this sickness in full bloom. The full flowering of her mother's psychology.

Delilah Norwood studies the grave in the light. From the flash of light above the forest tree canopy. Trembling inside from the blast of thunder. Burdened now by the images projected. Burned upon the theater of her mind. Feeling the cold of heat revisited in memory, that sends chills down a wayward spine. Memories of the small rope bound to the little wooden stick in garotte. Memories of her leaned over naked, over her twelve year old daughter's back—the rope around her daughter's neck, twisting the stick, tightening the rope—hearing her little daughter's choking grow more impossible to fathom. Reveling in every twitch of twelve year old muscles. Feeling the agony in her breasts, activated by her daughter's struggle. The agony in her breasts mashed against her daughter's back. The agony which spreads to the pit of her stomach, through her womb to her groin. Marveling the impossibility of having received the first part of the Witch's Crown. The explosion of a lifetime of repressed craving into her body without stimulus down below. Feeling her daughter begin to shake from the struggle to breathe. From the struggle to scream. Struggling to hold the rope tight through their ordeal. Through her body's loss of itself, as she begins to feel the falling down through space. Unaware of her own strength as she holds on. As she holds on to the twisted stick. As the siren erupts of its own accord from her mouth. As her own flesh is jiggled and shaken by convulsion. By the twitching of uncorked

Witch's Brew.

Delilah Norwood breathes the mountain air. Content that the dirt of her daughter's grave has not been breached. Has not been broken by a cold, dead hand.

Delilah Norwood stares at her daughter's grave, in the Southern Appalachian Wood. On the winds of fear and regret, she turns to begin the trip across the mountain cropfield, marveling at the sound of thunder from the ground, and the glow of the mountain in the distance. Her soul is aflame with memory, the pain of truth denied, that the very next evening after her daughter was buried, there was the sound of cataclysm as she had never imagined, which made her go outside to see whatever a plane had exploded nearby or not—amazed to see the shower of glowing rock moving up and away from Pilot Mountain so near, yet so far away in the distance. In the silhouette of smoke and ashe that towered high above the southern mountain, there were flashes of orange light throughout, as the glowing rock was spewed upward into the ashe cloude which towered high into the fall of night, where it was illuminated by the steady streams of rock more molten by the hour, and the occasional flash of blue streaks of lightning. Undernearth the ashe cloud dimly lit was the flow of molten rock, glowing orange touched and kissed by white heat, flowing down the mountain in slow, steady streams. This, she has watched nightly in fear, as the orange light continues to flow from the mountain beneath the clouds, while the ashe cloud has already been taken into the clouds by the passing winds.

Delilah Norwood arrives at the house of fear. Taking the lonely steps into the house of terror. In grieving to have the lovely Eyes of Dawn back from the dead, back from those that torment her dreams every night, to where she is afraid to close her eyes tonight, for fear that Dawn will creep to the back door of her isolation in otherworldly strength and determination, to make light work of the back door into the kitchen, to lumber toward her in pale skinned, white eyed witchery, to step toward her in demonic force and power, until her hands are at her throat, to choke the life from her slowly in grieving. As the mountain ground begins to rumble without ceasing, she can no longer hear herself think with clarity, feeling the need to step outside the house in the open air, lest she be buried alive in the rubble of her house fallen down around her. The nighttime trees do the Armageddon Sway, rocking back and forth in darkened silhouette, as Delilah stares in disbelief at the mountain which erupts anew in the distance, and the appearance of a fissure of light in the clearing.

Oh, what can you do, dear Delilah, but run into thine house and pray! From the kitchen window, she sees the earth begin to open up in the darkness, glowing from the light of orange heat risen rapidly to the surface coming at her from the distance in serpentine, with the life of evil incarnate, cracking and splitting the nighttime earth toward the cabin.

Run, Dear Delilah! Run to the field of dreams! There, you will find the absolution you seek, as you run in terror toward the nighttime woods! You stop and turn to your house of isolation. In awe of what feast the ground doth make of it.

Delilah Norwood watches the ground open up in bright orange glow, swallowing the property and what remains of her refuge in the storm. Then to her shock and dismay, the faultline breaks outward from itself, moving slowly toward Delilah in the open field, until she knows again to run, perhaps to the safety of the darkened woods. To hide from the wrath of vengeance until the rainy morning light, then, to make her way down the mountain to the highway of civilization, to show her unadorned country beauty to them. To get the help from then she has always found.

But upon the instant of this thought, there blasts from the air around her the voice of the Trump of God, from the mouth of *Philadelphia* in silhouette, whose neck rises thrice the height of the darkened forest, as the wings begin to glow bright blue in the night, to contrast the glowing eyes of royal blue. The head from which these eyes of vengeance stares leans back upon the gigantic neck in serpentine darkness, leaning forward suddenly to open its mouth, sending a wall of fire taller than the trees at the screaming woman down below.

Delilah Norwood screams a death scream. A noise hidden by the rumbling from beneath the earth, in the harmony of an explosion of deep blue flame, where her body is swept into the swirling of fervent heat, as the Southern Appalachians are suddenly and swiftly set on fire of Hell.

39

he lighting of the forest has lit a fire in us all. Along with the appearance of the Southern Appalachian Fault, we know that our time among the suburban Virginia trees and houses has come to a timely end, as we can see in the great and far away distance the world's newest volcano at night, and the burning of the Great Southern Forest as well, which glows our nighttime horizon the color of the ocean.

"That's not a bad idea," Mother says. "Lets move to the beach. At least we can die with a view of the ocean." And die, we surely would, but not even at the mouth of a dragon. It would certainly be at the mouth of the ocean itself, which has begun to react with fury at the goings on near and about, in gale force winds and hurricane like surf making into piles of wood what was once boardwalks and piers and harbours, with many coastal towns already being half under water.

"I've already bought us a place," I say. "I knew it the second I laid eyes on it. It's a huge farm west of here—a good distance away from any woods or forests. There's only a few small trees nearby, and the rest is open grassland like a prairie as far as the eye can see. It looks like Kansas. The more open and isolated we are, the better chance we'll have of being missed by those damned dragons."

"Well," she says, all hips and sophistication on the kitchen stool, afternoon drink firmly in hand, "avoiding those 'damned dragons' can't really be done, can it?" This, she asks on the cusp of a divine swallowing, to try and drown the demons Loss and Grief, those left when her husband, when my father Dale Turner was taken. And though she was a tower of independence when my father was alive, comfortable in her role as Grand MILF of the 21st century, I know that down inside she was deeply devoted to my father, and carried a torch for him that never went unlit, even to the days beyond his departure, where there is nothing but a photograph in the coffin we pretended to bury him in. And yet, I know that while she represses talk of this love, I can see the after affects of the grief in her daily retreats into the red wine, her red lipstick the color of blood when she lifts to her lovely lips. I don't know for sure whether or not—wait, that is a lie. I know as surely as I know the eyes of the dragon, that she is not aware of how obvious her grieving is, that Meadow and I can see it in the drinking, the flashes of bitterness, the long belts of silence and reclusivity, and even the staring out into the looming gray mist of a world we live in. Plaintiff staring, it is indeed, where there is a distant longing, a profound, indefinable sadness. And I have noticed that as to our perversions that we do, her dispensing of pain has become more uncompromising than ever, her climbs to the top of Orgasm Hill more intensely strange, her treks through the jungles of Eros more wildly

Amazonian, as though she channels the spirit of Estros possessed by Testosteros himself. Her strapped on pushings into the back of me have become more angry and fevered, sometimes to the better part of a half hour, where she is always bound and determined to not leave the river without at least one gold nugget in the pan. I have to admit that the viewing of these taped sessions is a revelation of female eroticism, to watch a beautiful older woman such as she pound into a another woman with such passion and devotion—as much as any all girl passion play that exists in the world, as she does it with the prowess of a horse or a dog, as though she is in possession of a gift, where she could likely teach a man how to fuck a woman to within an inch of her life, which is what it feels like I have had done to my every time. Truly, my own husband never fucked me like my own mother has done, as if he ever could have without training.

Mother says it is because men have the privilege of total sensation through their cocks, so that they don't have to work as hard at getting off. But when a woman straps it on, she is at the mercy of how well she can get it rubbed and banged against her clit, so she has to do the extra work to find the right speed, the right rhythm, and the right hardness by which to bang. And when she finds it, it is as if the fake cock is the real deal to feel, and it is as though she is going to blow a load through the front of it and into the lucky woman on the other end. No orgasm, mother says, is as powerful as the ones she gets from the strap on—they send shivers from between her legs and up into her tits, she says. To listen to her talk is a fascinating glimpse into the lustful heart of woman, whose libido stretches far and wide, as opposed to a man's who carries in his body the power and destructive force of a tornado, in contrast to the unearthly devastation of a hurricane.

"I'm coming in my tits" is her favorite vulgarity to spill, I think, which I've noticed almost always happens when she is strapped on and at the cliff ready to fall. If I have the pleasure to straddle her member while she is on her back, the sucking of her nipple at the moment she erupts is enough to make her howl and beg the Lord himself for mercy. This extreme breast sensitivity, we all have it, each generation of us, seeming to have fully flowered in Meadow's heavy hangers, which dwarf my mother's, and are even bigger than my own which are substantial, her leaving both mother and me in awe of her ability to tremble and shake from just the mere sucking of them. I've never seen mother achieve this, though I have on many occasions, but not as easily and as completely as Meadow. Aside from her impossible sweetness and intelligent humility, she is our devoted slave in depravity, making her more prized than a possession could ever be. Her worth is greater than a mine full of diamonds in the rough, greater than an ocean of crude oil beneath the earth, more valuable than a hundred gold and silver deposits hiding as mother lodes undiscovered, her worth is more precious than diamonds, silver and gold. Hers is the beauty of kindness, the glory of meekness and humility displayed from within the body of great physical beauty, which for those lucky enough to be in possession of her love, it is a gift from the Almighty God.

As I hear the voice of doom rising, as the rumbling from the clouds cascades into the air around us for miles and miles, I hear the voices of depravity up the stairs that I am afraid to climb, knowing that mother has engaged her granddaughter in this end of the world perversion of hers passed down. Protectiveness and jealously wrap themselves in ghostly repose about each lung of mine, both touching my heart with a cold hand, making me have to take the stairs as if I might be brave enough to walk in on them. *Not fifteen minutes ago we were talking about moving*, is the thought that pops into my head as I walk towards the bedroom, hearing the tell tale slapping of flesh together like something out of a porno, though it is in real, 3D space behind these closed doors just out of my sight. I know in my heart that my daughter is the victim on her feet bent over, so that mother can watch her breasts hang and swing in the mirror, and then later on her video copy of this Armageddon revelation.

I hear the pitiful whimpering of my daughter as she gets it without mercy from my mother, who has pledged already to me that she is going to *"beat the blood out of her little Egyptian ass,"* and I can hear the echoes of this dangerous malevolence delivered in her voice, which does not reverberate with the same love and patience it has for me, but instead is touched by the sword of evil intent, as I hear mother spewing such vicious depravity as even I am not accustomed to, ending with *"look at what you did you fucking cunt—you little Indian slut, you're making me cum in my tits, I'm cumming in my tits"*—and then I hear the sound of a depraved nightmare in awakening, to activate my memory of what I was shown in the cloak of night, as the sound that comes out of my mother's mouth is as a war on the Amazonian field of battle.

"When are you going back to New York?"

The question breaks the silence of their melancholy world, followed by a tranquil flash of lightning from the gray clouds, and the gentle rolling of the low, rumbling thunder.

"I took an indefinite leave of absence," Leah says. Still laying on her side, facing away from her sister.

"Why?"

"You ask me that, after what you and Mother went through?"

The mention of Lena Chao corresponds with a new, more powerful voice of thunder.

"I understand," Rachel says, as if prompted by a message in the storm, that what old resentments, what old bitterness there is might best be dismissed. Rachel Lynn rolls over in the nighttime bed, close behind her younger sister, putting her arm tightly around her. Leah Rose takes her hand tightly in the spooning, closing her eyes to a tear unheard, suppressing even the sniff that begs to be.

"I didn't hurt you too bad the other day, did I?"

"No," comes the immediate and kind hearted lie. Wishing so desperately that her sister's new tolerance for her, her new soul of caring is for real.

"There's something I've been needing to tell you for a long time," Rachel says. "I guess now that Mother is gone, I feel like I have to say it."

Leah waits without exhaling her next breath, though unaware, wondering what manner of dream or nightmare her older sister's words will be.

"The way I treated you when you were a little girl. The way I've always treated you. Please forgive me."

The weight of her sister's apology is followed by the weight of a kiss upon her cheek. Whether or not this is merely part of Rachel's game of control over her, she does not know. How long will it be, before the sweetness goes the way of sunlight behind a dark cloud? How long before the tragedy of her libido is rased again, and she must endure the pain of another raping, another beating, another domination, another humiliation? One of her earliest memories is of a whipping, where her then 12 year old sister was made to belt whip her when Leah was only five—whippings that continued until Leah was eleven years old, and Rachel graduated from high school. What secrets and behind closed doors realities was Rachel burdened with throughout her teenage years, that she was a prisoner of her Asian mother's perversions, having hem channeled into her, and through her into her little sister. Among these early memories is the feel and the smell of a pillow over her face, to where she nearly passed out, while a naked sixteen year old Rachel Lynn lays on top her naked nine year old sister in a smothering punishment, while Lena Ling Chao sits in a chair nearby and watches it happen.

Among these punishments she remembers is the agony in her eleven year old nipples, as the eighteen year old Rachel Lynn was forced to bite her younger sisters prodigious young breasts until the tears and the sobs were in steady flow. Leah Rose can remember the years of cruelty, as she bears the weight of her sister's profound apology, and the weight of the profound kiss upon her cheek.

She can remember when she was sixteen, when her older sister graduated from college, when she was back in their home for a time. She can remember the pain between her legs, the pinching, wincing pain, as the mother held her by the neck with her arm, while her older sister pinched her vagina to agony. These were the cruelties promised and delivered, punishments prophesied and fulfilled. She can remember the day when the breast tortures served as the benchmark between pretense and what is real, when the mask of hypocrisy came down, and her punishments were no longer about correction, but were in service to a widow's full blown libido. Leah can remember how the death of her father released her mother's inhibitions, dissipating them away like chains broken and dissolved, so that she no longer had to tell herself that Leah Rose was being chastised for wrongdoing, but was suffering simply because her *mother* was suffering, because she suffered an inner lust that burned as a prophecy in the center of her body.

Leah can remember the day when she was sixteen, when her mother stood behind her and held her bid, long breast up to Rachel Lynn's mouth, and telling her to *"suck the nipple until it hurts,"* but spoken in bitter

Cantonese, causing Rachel Lynn to pun an inhuman sucking upon one nipple improperly, until Leah had to scream from the pain. She can remember the struggle that ensued, as her strong mother held her tight, while her older sister sucked her nipple hard enough to cause a sting.

And this, she remembers from the college graduate, the psychology and biology double major, accepted into Harvard Medical School—here she is back at age 23, sucking the tits of her younger sister to blood and agony. Of this, none would believe could happen. None would believe the truth of the matter, that what is going on behind closed doors would blow their minds. And not just *what* is happening, but *who* it is that it is happening to. These are the curses passed down from Eve, the mother of all living, the spirits of the knowledge of good and evil sent through the timeline, to torment mothers and their children throughout history, to settle upon the Mother Daughter Dynamic, here at the end of the age, as the truth is about to be revealed to the modern world. The hyper intellectuals, the high minded, high financed among us, are the victims and perpetrators of the most unbelievable depravities known to man in secret, including those that haunt the motherline, having flowed down to us from the mountains east of Eden.

Leah remembers the pain of realization that day, that the only two people in the world who loved her are content to treat her like an unwanted dog, to abuse her as the object of their wanton instinct and craving. Leah Rose remembers the Death of Hypocrisy, when the walls of pretense fell, to where she began to dread the periodic visits from her Harvard Medical School sister, wondering what depravity had been cooking in Momma Lena's mind. This fear and ongoing terror, she remembers, remembering the day it was justified upon Rachel Lynn's graduation from medical school, which came as such a deep and abiding shock, because it happened not on a visit from her sister to their California home, but in the hotel room in Massachusetts, the night after Rachel Lynn's graduation had come and gone.

Leah was a music school sophomore herself, having to endure another thorn in her side, another lock on the dungeon door, which was that one of her tormentors is now one of the most respected regular people in the civilized world—the kind of person that literary art aspires to, the person that even famous actors and actresses must defer to, the kind of person that famous politicians and famous athletes must defer to: a graduate of Harvard Medical School, who can call herself a Doctor of Psychiatric Medicine. She rememembers 27 year old Rachel Lynn, the sneaky whispering with then 47 year old Momma Lena.

She is in profound disbelief, when she remembers her older sister and her mother—the beautiful older woman with the deeply curved body, naked on the bed with her daughter the night of Rachel's graduation. Leah stands there in obedience, in the Heart of Memory, compliant with her hands clasped in front—a spirit designated as the watcher, to give the two of them the energy of nerves they require—the pressure of performance to enhance the lighting of this pleasure that must be. This, having become Momma Lena's preferred overture to her days and nights of perversion— the longer the distance between sessions, the more intensely convulsive and vocal she tends to be. Leah watches her mother and her newly graduated sister on the bed, the two of them upright on their knees kissing, holding each other behind the head with one hand, with the other hands probing and rubbing each other down below, done with focus and purpose, as though racing to an unseen finish line. Leah stands there as a muse, as their long breasted fertility doll in residence, inspiring this perverted celebration done in private, the privilege of the initiated, of those who have crossed the line into the forbidden. Leah watches them. Unable to resist her own rhythm of heartbeat inspired, feeling herself in her heart and mind in the place of Rachel, having already learned that this is her mother's favorite first orgasm, and that she has helped Mother Lena climb this mountain hill over the last year or so ad nauseam.

Leah watches the deep, heavy kissing ,where their mouths are wide open and clamped tight upon each other, until she can hear her mother's nose breathing become louder, while her body grows more tense with each passing moment. As her mother reaches this lightning strike platueau, Leah's mind is suddenly aflight in a flash of perception, to sense the modern Mother Daughter Dynamic unrestrained, and the passing of female perversion from one generation to the other. In at least three other rooms in the very hotel she is in, the ghosts of this secret haunt the walls and rooms of the unseen, to deliver the world's last taboo in private, to be uncovered by the pornographic mind in the latter day, as the echo of what realities blossom among the genteel in secret.

The spirit of Mother Daughter Perversion burdens the Leah Rose mind, looming large as a prophecy of the endtime, as she hears her mothers voice appear to announce her body's helplessness while the lightning strikes, beginning to twitch and jerk until she must unkiss and double over from the rubbing underneath, struggling to endure the merciless wave of energy from her daughter's hand to her groin. Leah watchers her mother bent over in jerks and deep grunting, unable to continue her own rubbing of her daughter, as the energy wave takes over her mind and body.

Leah watches her mother and her sister. She watches her sister hug and support her mother's grieving body in spasms that pass—holding her in the strength of knowledge, and the wisdom and beauty of understanding. Oh, what profound luck is this, Mother Lena, to have been given a daughter of such understanding beauty! Who may perpetuate and carry your lust to the heights of endtime promises made and fulfilled!

Leah watches them. Hands crossed at the front of her nakedness below. Obedient, compliant. Unable to look away as her sister turns to glance at her in the eye. A satisfied superior glance of pure conceit, laced in the arrogance of achievement, and the self important entitlement of accomplishments done and done. *Watch us, you dumb bitch,* are the words Leah hears unspoken, breathed into her mind as their mother recovers, lying down on her back and taking a deep breath of surrender, her lovely, mature features hearkening from the far east, from the farmlands of the Chinese countryside.

In Cantonese, the mother speaks to her psychiatrist daughter Rachel Lynn, where she responds by going to the travel bags, unzipping one of them and pulling out two of the strap on members inside. Leah watches them. Compliant, obedient. Knowing not to move or speak unless spoken to. She watches Rachel slide one onto mother's shapely hips, hips made more shapely by her position of repose, made wider by her lying down flat on her back. Before long, the member is where it ought to be, in profound erection from what libido of Mother Lena's there still remains, which is considerable.

Leah watches them. In the hotel of prosperity. In the after math of great achievement. Leah watches her sister slide the member up to her massive hips, born from the Kingdom of Kardashia, tightly binding the member to herself, to where it is now the expression of what libido she too has left, which is considerable. In their native tongue, Leah hears the order to go to her sister. Standing there, long breasted, compliant. Obedient. *You ready to choke on my cock,* are the words uttered in their Chinese vernacular. Leah answers with a *yes,* in like manner, nodding her head with her eyes down, her hands still clasped in front of her.

Get onto the bed—on your knees. Leah obeys. Tits dangling so long as she climbs onto the bed, followed by her hippy older sister. As the mother holds on to herself, they watch as Leah proceeds to slide the Rachel member into her mouth, up and down, gently, knowing to go deeper each time, until it causes her to gag, making her sister hold her there by the back of the head. But Leah does not panic, accepting the loss of breath as temporary, the painful choking as a fleeting sorrow. Rachel Lynn has mercy at long last, allowing Leah to raise her head and catch her breath. In the periphery, she sees Mother Lena gripping her own extended self, stroking it as if it were a natural part of her. Leah knows to return to her task at hand, sliding her sister's agony back down to her throat, this time controlling her gag, taking a breath through her nose, sensing her sister's body betray her, as she twitches at least twice from the power of what Leah has done.

"Bring her to my cock," are the words in their native tongue, spoken from the beautiful mother in repose. Rachel ushers the girl to the mother's unnatural, natural self, knowing what is to transpire, knowing already what direction this arrow is flung. She guides Leah astraddle her mother's member, watching Leah slide every inch times eight up inside her. Holding Leah there. Kissing her deeply.

Mother Lena takes hold of both her younger daughters tits, to pull them longer still, while she watches her two daughters deep kiss in full lip and tongue.

"Get behind her," are the words hearkened from the East, causing Rachel to get behind her sister, positioning her extended self to the back of Leah, letting the spit fall the long journey from her mouth to her sister's backside, in the place where the tip of her member rests at the door of Sodom.

While she straddles the mother deep inside the front of her, Leah now feels her sister push into the back of her, to where she must put her head down and yell out, to cry out to the spirits that give a look see to them. Rachel puts her hand over Leah's mouth, and continues the pushing in agony, as the mother holds on to the elongated tits, watching her daughters merge together in shock and awe.

Leah sits there. In double penetration. Trapped between her mother and her sister. Feeling the pressure of two large members, both inside her at the same time. Hearing her own voice in whining, as her sister removes her hand from her mouth. As to what feeling there is, when Rachel begins to rub her down below, this, she cannot tell. She only knows that it sends the pain in her backside to a new place, a place of ecstatic discovery, where the two pressures inside her begin to merge at the center of her, somewhere at the place where the womb and the bowels meet in the aura of feeling, as the pain begins to morph into a pleasure previously unknown.

Her mother's grip upon her nipples suddenly becomes more in tune, to where the strings are played with depth and feeling, pinching and tweaking them to create the pleasure trinity, the triangle of ecstasy, that sparks from her breasts to her buttocks to her groin, causing Leah to suddenly lose herself and begin to bounce, much to her mother and sister's profound feeling and delight. Driven by the unseen, pushed forward by the unknown, Leah can only bounce the rhythm of perversion, as it is given to her to do, until she hears her sister's breathing tell the tale, and she begins to yell something in Cantonese beauty and pain, grabbing onto Leah to anchor her own shaking, while Leah continues to bounce without mercy.

And this lightning through her daughters zaps the Mother Lena mind, causing her to suddenly grip her daughter about the waist, as her entire body tenses her into oblivion, making her have to hold her head back and grit her teeth to survive.

And this energy rises from her mother and her sister, coming together at the center of Leah's body, the irresistible force of Rachel Lynn's devastation, and the immoveable object of her mother's destruction, clashing to become Leah's cosmic annihilation.

A

A loud blast of thunder pulls Leah from the Heart of Memory. The hotel, and the end of the world crashing of energy waves dissolves into the quiet of her sister's bedroom, the sound of her sister's breathing, and the feel of her sister's arm wrapped so strong and peacefully around her.

Meadow's Body

Headed for the Virginia farmlands, my daughter, my mother and me—somewhere far east of the Southern Appalachians, where we will no longer be haunted by them from our upper class, suburban windows. Far away from the newly lit fires of this strange, endtime world we live in, we safely drive the rainy roads east, away from what threatens to become the greatest forest fire in human history, as the Southern Appalachians are suddenly ablaze with fires of alabaster and blue. A blaze lit just over the Virginia Border from North Carolina, nearby the appearance of the Southern Appalachian Fault, which opened up just north of the new volcano at Pilot Mountain. Such are the privileges of money for us, that we were not desperate to haul every stick of our former life with us, leaving the upscale house pretty much intact, so that the ghosts we left behind might still feel at home.

There is a roomy, two story farmhouse that awaits us now, tucked away in the safety of isolation, where we might be free from the eyes of the dragon. But truthfully, what makes me think that we would truly be safe from the dragon's fire out there? Many isolated homes on the open prairies west of us have suffered, as if the dragons have a personal dislike for the wheat fields of Kansas and Oklahoma, setting many of those farmhouses and open fields to burning. But until the attack on the North Carolina freeway, the lands of the Bible Belt had been largely spared, making the eastern farmlands appear as an unspoken refuge from their fiery sight.

But part of me is slightly apprehensive anyway, when I think of what dark promises have been made and partially fulfilled on Meadow's body, as my mother has pledged already to "beat the blood" from her. And I am reminded that sometimes, Fate decides to send us warning confirmation as a nighttime vision, to warn us in our dreams of what lies just over the horizon. I have been tormented to an icy cold awakening more that once already, with my hand over my breast and heart pumping in the night. Waking up from images of burning trees along the roads of our journey, which is understandable of course, where hardly one of the 6 billion souls left on this planet has not felt this image at least threaten their sleep since the dragons' arrival.

But he fear I have known in my dreams has been transformed from fire to fields of eternal sleep, where will see a single grave stone off the side of the road, with an infinity of grassland behind it off to the distance. And I have been tormented and mocked by this dream four times, with both the third and fourth time having me fearful with anticipation as I rode along the highway, as if I knew the grave marker would somehow be there waiting for me. And the fourth time filled me with the most terror, where I had been lulled into a state of tranquility by a passing grove of autumn trees not on fire, with a rarely seen setting sun in orange amber shining through them. I rode along this road of tranquility in my dreams, so thankful that the horizon was not ablaze in fire and vapor of smoke. Then suddenly, our ride slowed to a cruise, as we rolled off the highway into a space of tall grass nearby a grove of summer trees, in contrast to the dying leaves of autumn I had seen just before. We rolled onto the grass unaware, my driver and me, turning and moving further away from the road, until I suddenly noticed that I could see the ground beneath us, and the shorter grass passing under my feet. And as if to mock me, to prick me with an icy terror, there appeared a flattened marker in the ground as we approached it, partially hidden by the grass, as we rolled directly over this grave marker flush with the ground, infusing me with the spirit of fear, as a terror drifted from the ground itself and up through my body, causing me to try and scream in the open air of my night vision.

I awoke from this trauma just last night, having to reach over and turn the bedside lamp on as if my very life depended on it. Light is our best weapon in the demon fight. Light is the weapon that will put these demons in flight. Even the innocent, naïve child knows this, who are not naïve at all when it comes to the spirits of evil that lurk nearby, knowing the power of a nightlight from early on. I left the light on for the better part of an hour, until the shadows lost their strength to cause fear again, and sleep took back its unblessed hold on me.

And I was awakened this morning by the voices of pure clarity, where I saw Meadow in tears, saying *"but Aunt Irene it hurts, please don't do it,"* with Mother answering her angrily, *"just shut up and take your fucking clothes off!"* Grabbing my daughter's head so violently on the vulgar word as to be a total shock, which woke me up startled again, though this time in the early morning light, and not on the edge of a scream in icy terror. But when I marry this image to the ones in reality, where mother has admitted her darkest fantasies to me about Meadow, I have to acknowledge the feeling that shivers me in this cold summer rain we drift through, which has planted a seed of apprehension, which has grown already into a stem and bud of worry, which threatens to open soon into a full blown blossom of fear.

A Rhapsody in Blue

$\mathcal{T}$he earth turns upon the River of Time, moving the remaining population into the seventh month of their fiery captivity. The three of us languish in our new places under the grieving summer clouds, which have buried the world in epic summer and gray. This is the coldest summer on record, where people have abandoned the hope of short sleeves and swimming pools, as the new and frosty, humid cold is impossible to ignore. Summer has taken a leave of absence from the Land of Mist, leaving every condemned soul under the curse of winter misery. Only by the grasses that still blow green in the icy breeze, and by the rich green forests that swish and swirl in the wind and rain—only by the green of these forests and fields does the earth reveal its place along its place along its blue path among the stars, its place though the months of summertime growth and renewal.

In our country mansion by the sea, the three of us drift in this endtime fog of worldwide apprehension, wondering how we're going to make it from one day to the next, without descending into hopelessness and fear. The world has settled into a deeper contemplation of its fate, the entire earth being on alert as one big disaster area, as at least a third of all the trees in the world are either burning or have already burned, with every inch of flame being colored a shade of blue. As it is when weather changes dramatically, and burdens the world with the heaviness of rising winds and rainfall, so too has the rain of fire and brimstone had its affect, causing the entire population to focus on where the next dragon attack will happen.

All eyes have been nervously trained toward Chicago, Illinois for many weeks, being the home of the last great skyscraper on earth still standing, the tall, black arrow that points toward the sky, that is brushed by the bottom of these gray clouds that loom. The building stands largely empty by now, as the workers have relocated to lower and safer spaces around the city, except for the few thousand that have held to the stubbornness of chance, either through bravery or stupidity, having already been warned of the monsters' fiery potential. It seems that collectively, the world is waiting for this tower to come down, while it contemplates the impossibility of what endtime Fate has come. And along with the blue fire is the earthquakes' arrival, which sees the continued destruction of city and freeway infrastructure around the world, until some cities lie in smoldering ruins under the storm's fury. This, being a worldwide storm that is developing slowly but surely, where the rains come and go with regularity, as God continues to hold fast to his reluctant promise, to never again release every drop of water onto the world, nor raise every drop upwards from the fountains of the deep. The earth is in the shadow of the curse of Eden, as the cold of Divine Judgment descends in the air from mountain to shore, while the elements continue to melt with fervent heat.

And though the worldwide storms have begun to continue without ceasing, the rains have no effect on the blue fires that burn. Children around the world, the children of men and the children of God, have all begun to ask no longer how, but *why*—why has the mercy of God been lifted from the earth, and why is the earth suddenly on fire in a mist of rain? There is hardly a sight more terrifying to the country traveler than when around the next curve along the forest road is the small bridge washed out by a new river across the road, while the trees are lit up in bright flames the color that the sky used to be— these that took the fool's flight along the burning forest roads hoping to escape, but being completely stopped by the echo of what the rainbow promise would look like if it were broken. There hath not a promise been made by him that he has broken, including these that have placed this part of the timeline in fiery death and destruction. Escape from what is happening is beginning to crumble everywhere, like the cracks that appear across the highways and runways all over, to give mankind the impression of open imprisonment, as if trapped within the confines of a moving cage. The bars of this cage are made of fire too hot to approach, as the ground shakes and crumbles away from beneath their feet.

The three of us languish here. At one edge of our field of dreams. Trapped with the rest of the world, in this earth sized moving cage, the bars of which are composed in flame. Tormented by the news of new and greater destructions around the world, by the cities swallowed up in chasms opened up anew. By cropfields either burned or taken in by the ground underneath, leaving the tragic scars along the pristine prairies and countrysides, where tranquility is broken up and hauled down, from the fiery surface, to the fiery world that churns below ground. It seems that there is no longer a peace to be had, no longer a time of calm to be gathered and nurtured, as the dove has taken its flight from the winds of fire that burn.

The church world has taken its expected position on these happenings, claiming the dragons as signs from God prophesied, as confirmation that

God himself is real, and so to is the promise of judgment that was made. We only *thought* we understood Revelation, so many of them are beginning to claim, as the number of dragons and their effect on the world is being recovered for all to see, as the world is plunged into the beginning of another dark age. And the secular world has taken its required and expected place at pure skepticism and religious mocking and ridicule. It is the proverbial coming together of the frigid, arctic air with the warm, heated tropical air, to produce the spinning of dark potential, and the rising winds of devastation, which I saw represented in news images as profoundly disturbing as the fiery tornadoes that have whirled into being, when two female personalities on a respected, national news and information program were allowed to come to blows on camera, as a female atheist called a fire and brimstone lady preacher a "stupid Christian bitch" before the world media, which prompted a rising, as the female evangelist stood up mysteriously, stepping over to the chair the atheist was in and slapping her very hard in the face. As if unable to move, the female interviewer put her hand over her mouth in disbelief as the two middle aged, middle class women quietly came to represent a century of energy building up, exploding in a violence unimagined before among women of such sophisticated and learned manner, as what churns beneath cultured civility rumbled forth from beneath the surface of pretence and hypocrisy. It was as though the spirits had made their decision that this was it, as the two W.A.S.P. women, both fully formed and well packed into their expensive TV skirts, blazers and high heels, were allowed to fight each other down to the floor in a perfect storm of inactivity around them, as a full 27 seconds passed before the Christian woman was pulled off the screaming atheist woman, whom it was discovered was bitten to blood through her open blouse to her breast. Those in the newsroom claimed and feigned ignorance and confusion, as if they didn't understand whether it was real or not, or whether they should touch the two women and possibly be pulled into the impending lawsuits and worldwide humiliation, no one wanting their image on camera being seen involved with pulling the two fighting women apart. A viral video to end all viral videos, viewed over half a billion times after it was posted and reposted online, so that the entire world could see the violent heart of woman presage the Second Coming.

The two women were finally pulled apart by authorized security, who had to work hard to separate hands from pulled hair at the end, as the blonde Christian woman was pulled form off top of the atheist woman, whose white blouse betrayed the source of her scream with the large spot of blood on her white fabric at the top of her breast. Though the lady evangelist was seen by most as the victor, it was a costly one, as she was arrested for assault, appearing in court with a bruised eye and a broken wrist, where she had bear hugged and slammed the atheist woman to the floor so hard that she broke her own wrist in the process, sacrificing her face to many punches, just before she clamped her teeth down at the atheist woman's breast to elicit a scream for the ages, which did nothing to make a single soul nearby touch the two of them. *The Best Catfight Ever Filmed,* those given to vulgarity were inclined to concede, or *Amazon Women On the Moon,* or *Babes in Boyland*, or *Hell's Angels*, or *"Don't' Call A Christian Evangelist a Bitch*, or any number of posted titles ad nauseam, as the two successful, attractive, and law abiding white women were brought low by what lies beneath, and the inability to agree to disagree.

In the wake of this fascination, the world moves toward the Evening Day, mesmerized by every type of dragon which may appear.

My daughter and I are languished in the mist of tragedy. The two of us on the front porch of our new country home, in the light wind and rain, studying the trees waving their endtime message in the breeze, braving the cold, wet wind upon our faces in brief, as we take this short respite in the open air to breathe free.

I stand at the porch railing, just behind my twenty one year old beauty, my arms wrapped tightly around her waist as she stares off into the distance, trying to hear what words are spoken by the rumbling thunder, and what is being written on the clouds by the rivers of blue lightning that spread out underneath them. It is as though I can draw strength from her in the midst of the storm, though I act as if I am providing strength to her. What I feel for her is a longing that goes deeper than love. It is a profound passiveness—the joy of ownership that satisfies every instinct. I feel as though I cannot live without her presence, without her comfort in these end of the world happenings all around us. I am more than content to hold on to this girl for dear life, to breathe in the scent of her silken hair, and enjoy the cushiony feel of her body against mine.

"Meadow," is the sound in the air that breaks the spell I am in, coming at us from the beautiful woman named Irene at the screen door, whose arms are crossed as she stares at us, a stern look so heavily burdened by the edges of a frown. She need not call again, as I let her go, in something that might be called apprehension, were it not so strong. Meadow turns away from our front porch view over the country farmland, leaving me alone leaving me alone with the nearby trees and infinity of house bushes nearby, walking obediently to where Irene waits at the screen door. I do not look away as she opens the door and walks in, as Mother takes her casually, but firmly, by her arm and escorts her from my sight.

Turning back to the message in the storm, I listen hopelessly for the sound of their ascent, as they climb the stairs to the country version of the upper room, while the thunder continues to speak to me in waves, and the lightning flashes its hidden warning in the endtime clouds of grieving.

Meadow Oppenheimer is one of the most beautiful women in the world. In the three years since she has graduated from high school, the 21 year old girl's body has gathered a perfect storm of features, to where it is no wonder that Fate has decreed that she be given no self esteem in life, misinterpreting the strangeness of her interactions with the world as negativity. From the time she was a senior in high school, through the years wandering from one meaningless job to the next, having never failed an interview in her young life, she has been cursed with a beauty unknown and unnatural for the girl next door, even in our expected corner of the white woods. The neighborhood mother have every reason to be proud of their little blonde and lanky skinny pretties to be sure, so many of them spending time at our house through Meadow's teenage years, inextricably drawn to the exotic and beautiful girl with the model's looks, who was always down on herself for being fat, though the only true fatness on her body was about the breasts and hips. And as a fully grown young woman, this curviness has settled into eschatology, into what is a profound and end of the world absoluteness of majesty, as noticeable and disturbing as the height of the Himalayas, or the depth of the path carved in Northern Arizona, that famous Brady Bunch canyon they erroneously believe was carved by the Colorado River.

Her hair is raven black, and grows past her shoulders and half the length of her back, full bodies as shiny, soft and silky smooth to the touch.

Her eyes are as an Egyptian goddess, large and hypnotic to behold, touched by the blessing of the Asian countryside, from high up into her father's family tree. Her fair skin is tinted the deepest shade of ivory, so that too much time in the sun darkens it to a golden hue further along the color spectrum, until it is impossible to perceive her as all Anglo Saxon white, seeming to be hearkened from some far away land or culture, until some have even mistaken her for Indian.

These last three years of her maturity have closed the gap further between us, until it seems we cannot really be mother and daughter in everyone's eyes, but surely aunt and niece, or the requisite sister blonde and brunette. And when she disrobes, Meadow's naked body is an artist's desperation, every dream of Eve realized. Having inherited the macromastic breast growth from me, although they are entirely too large for even her curved, Amazonian frame. As it is with two other women I have known in the theater of my mind, two Asian women besides, her breasts, though gigantic as are mine, hang more impressively long and low, until her grandmother has taken to using them to attack her already feeble self esteem, calling her Lizzie Long Boobs, from Meadow's middle name perverted, the name which is above every other female name, which holds within it the promise of God. My own breasts are huge, to be sure, but very wide at the top, to give them far too much support, making me look as chesty as I do busty, with shoulders and a back wide enough to support them. But her breasts are every square inch disproportionate to her curvy frame, though still Amazonian about the legs and hips, this inherited from my Mother Irene. And when she is nude, her beautiful face takes on a somber, melancholy expression she is often pained to hide, to produce in innocence, a shyness and demurity that is breathtaking to behold. Believing somehow that she is the physical inferior to her hip heavy grandmother and top heavy mother, both of us markedly misshapen in comparison. We are the pear and spinning top to her perfect hourglass, though her waist is partially hidden by the hang of them when she nude. And thought he large, dark areolas are near the bottom of them, they are raised up just enough to be perfectly in front, to give the impression of two great, hanging wineskins, whose sweet elixir awaits uncorking and a sucking drink at the bottom.

If she weren't already rich, perhaps it would not take long, before she found what dark and extremely profitable corner of the topless modeling world she belonged in. Or even the exalted modeling world above ground, where beauty lives in hypocrisy and pretense of virtue. And when she turns around, the spread of her exposed hips is nothing short of extraordinary, to balance the femininity, the fertility goddessness of her eschatological perfection. Truly, when the cat women and wonder women, and the bat girls of their colorful universe are drawn, those who look on in admiration do so believing that their extreme curves are the stuff of fantasy, while I am a living witness to the contrary. I have seen the promised land of her bikini clad body on the private shores of the Caribbean, so yes, you poor, misguided souls in mourning—I know better. There does exist in the world a handful of perfectly beautiful women, but most of them have been ridiculed to ruin, to where they do not wear the hair nor the clothes nor the self esteem to shine their light before the world. And neither does this one that I gave birth to, whose beauty renews itself from without every time I look upon her, and even more remarkably, from somewhere deep within. Perhaps her treatment, the fate she has suffered from me has burned her in blue and black fire, to forge the living example of feminine power and beauty. This, the power of a kind heart, and the beauty of meekness and humility.

The thunder calls the countryside alert in the drowning mist. It nearly shocks me awake from the daydreams of eve, which is the beauty and humbleness of the woman I bore. I am suddenly in a fearfulness, a deep and abiding apprehension for her, having been escorted upstairs by the penis envying pervert who is her beautiful grandmother. But who am I to label with such distinction? Am I not the one who first threw her into this dark well of grieving? Did I not shove her face first into the cold waters of revelation.? Did I not pick from the tree of knowledge, and feed to her the sweet impossibility of what forbidden nourishment they provide? When she was but a girl of 16, did I not lay in her lap and undo her pale blue denim shirt, and work what was then only a G cup from her bra? Did I not lay there and let the huge nipple rest against my lips while I looked playfully up at her shocked face, my own expression lost in the depth of mischief and unhidden delight? Did I not breathe a sigh from my body's own reaction, from the feel of her nipple pulled deeply into my mouth, laying there with my eyes closed and relaxed as if I were a babe at suckling meal? And perhaps, I was. At the infancy of this new relationship, which had already happened in reverse when she was only a child of eleven, when I placed my breast in her mouth while we stood in front of the bathroom mirror, unable to contain the deep, trembling moan that started in my groin, shaking through my jiggly flesh and up into my lungs and out through my voice until I had to double over and grunt like a she bear in the woods.

Oh, what devastation must there have been, when her mother's body shook the ground beneath her feet! This was but the lowly prerumbling, the tremor that warns of the earth shattering devastation yet to come. And as I climb the stairs of our isolated farmhouse in wary, nervous apprehension, I can feel these self same spirits of breast lust and mammarynthia, knowing what promises from my mother are apt to be fulfilled in this strength of our timeline, *"I'm gonna suck 'em 'til we can milk her like a cow."*

$\mathcal{R}$achel Lynn is resigned to the understanding, the profound realization that behind closed doors, she is a case study for the ages. Something that her colleagues probe and mine the brains and histories of their patients for, just to find even the smallest trace of gold in these rocks, in the slabs of dreariness and pain these people call lives. In the secret closet of her own privacy, deep in the drowning rains from San Francisco Bay, she is determined to pull her sister downward, to make sure that she can never climb out of this same abyss she is condemned to live and die in—often wondering that even if Mother Lena had never crossed her into the forbidden, would she still have tapped her sister as an outlet for perversion.

It is a fire that burns so hot and so deep—her time with her younger sister is so completely an answer to a depraved prayer she never knew she had prayed, that her movements and motions, every motivation is born from instinct, and has taken upon itself the character of what is involuntary, inevitable, and inconceivable to behold. This, after a night at the San Francisco Opera, to watch Rossini's Queen Semiramide dominate her dark world in the brightness of melodic ingenuity. The burning, bright blue melodies are tinted white hot in her spirit, as she must wrap the beige packing tape around the tops of her sister's flattened, elongated breasts, grabbing the back of Leah's hair when she is done, holding her head back in agony, to achieve the beginnings of their deep and slippery tongue kisses that slip a slurp every now and then. This, they do by natural instinct and training, brought forth by memories of the woman who gave them life, and took it from them so abundantly.

In the midst of these wet and wild kisses, she pulls away unmercifully, ushering Leah and her taped breasts down to the bed on her back, loudly unrolling another length of tape around them to raise them up just enough, so that their extreme flop and floppability is partially contained.

The older sister Rachel stares down at her captive, mouth partially hung open from lust and desire, stroking her lady member strapped on as she positions herself at the edge of their queen sized bed. Sliding herself deep into the swollen front of her sister, whose legs are spread eagle, her expression bearing the strain of the lady cock's fervent entry. Rachel's eyes bear the heat of determination, staring blatantly at Leah's taped up breasts, unable to contemplate the source of this oddity, nor its birth and growth into their reality. In Cantonese, she speaks their recitative, *"You like fucking your older sister? You want it hard, bitch?"* And this, answered by the hopeless, helpless victim, *"Yes, yes please,"* done in the strain of pressure endured, and the pain of pleasures unfettered and secured.

And this, Rachel begins to do without reservation or remorse, as if the required answer to a prayer, or a wish so briefly considered and so vehemently granted. She stops to readjust herself, hips twitching already in the tremor that warns, taking a better grip on her sister's legs resting on her arm, slamming herself deep, hard and fast into the Leah Rose tragedy, listening to her sister's strained and loud exclamations of pain mixed with pleasure, watching the taped up, gargantuan bosoms wave and wobble back and forth in undulation, as the stormy waters of the wide and sounding sea.

This, Rachel does in mesmerization, her eyes locked into place upon the breast waves, her face in the awe of this brief depravity, and the feeling it sends to the center of her body. Her pounding is assured, set into perpetual motion by her body's obedience to her soul, driving her forward as though crawling through a hot wilderness to a cold fountain drink, unable to have mercy, per her sister's begging screams, until her eyes roll back to find God, to inquire as to how she will survive, as her mother's spirit whispers the olden tongue, *"and now you cum,"* causing her body to strike lightning *after* she bends over, to raise the siren wail from deep within, as she falls on top of her tape breasted sister in weeping, and waves of trembling and sorrow.

*M*y mother's lust knows bounds. As it has been from the days of my youth, these sins are passed through the motherline, to encompass all the days of my life, passing by blood and the spirit down to the beauty that is my own daughter. And perhaps the purity of this lust, the intensity of it has skipped a generation, as I know that when this grandmother and granddaughter connect, it will be as the plugging of a power chord into a wall socket. I know that before long, the milk of this last generation will soon flow freely, to nourish the mind and body of the wicked generation that has come before. Part of me is genuinely worried that I might lose Meadow's loyalty to my mother's perversion, as if what it is that I do cannot certainly be called the same. But although what we do can certainly be called electric by my own twisted perception, surely what they do can be called explosive, given the great chasm of an age difference between them, which I know feeds my mother's lust like warm air into the vortex of a twister.

And this, I have known about this woman so intimately, moreso than what any other soul could even suspect, being that the feel of her lips and tongue doing the vacuum pull at my nipples happened when I was but a child of nine. *Let Mommy show you something,* she had said after a bath, typically I suppose, *let Mommy show you something that feels really good.* And though it happened almost a generation of years ago, I can still feel the vacuum pull at my undeveloped nipples in the heart of memory, which had reached down to the center of my little body, to make me feel as though I might need to wet myself, though there was truly none there that needed forthcoming. To this day, I don't believe I have ever felt anything quite like it, which must surely encompass the years of sessions we shared, because of every perversion that passed between us, nothing trembles my body quite like the nursing of my mother's lips at my bosom.

And this odd breast sensitivity I know is passed to my daughter, but even to a greater degree, having merely the shortest and gentlest sucking be necessary to cause her shapely young body to begin a fervent twitching. This, I learned early with Meadow, even before her breasts developed to their elongated magnificence, that she is a true breast queen, a prodigy of the breast, possessing that rare ability to spasm from breast stimulation alone, as if orgasmic energy is actually self contained in them. It is a beautiful and remarkable thing to behold—to strip her completely nude and stand behind her, rubbing her hand and forearm across both her breasts for a few minutes uninterrupted, until her beautiful face is locked in grimace, and the length and breadth of every wayward pound of her body begins to quiver. To nurse at Meadow's breasts is to light the fuse of a firework, that hisses slowly and invisibly up into the air as if disappeared, only to manifest in a gigantic burst of white that opens up in the air like a fiery dandelion, then sparkles like shimmering silver earth stars as it vanishes away.

This is the method of my daughter's madness, through no fault of her own, to be sure, as I know this tendency toward breast orgasm is surely inherited from her grandmother Irene. Irene Turner. Whom I was privy to like no other, like not even my own father could have ever imagined, teaching me breast games when I was only eleven, that were composed of me pinching what little flesh I could squeeze into my hands so I could push my little breast outward, while she held fast her firm and spongy D minors with her nipple pressed against mine, rubbing the nipple hard and fast against my eleven year old nipple as if she were trying to start a fire, her face in the anger and anguish of effort, until her trademark announcement was made, but introduced by *Momma's gonna cum...* then the announcement, *I'm gonna cum in my tits,* before the feeling gripped her completely, always doubling her over to where she could no longer concentrate on holding her breast against mine, falling forward against me in full to where I would have to struggle to keep us from falling over. And there I would be. An eleven year old little nothing, struggling to help a 30 year old woman carry her cross in private, a weight that is truly too heavy for one so young to bear.

Is this the scene that plays in my spirit so often, when I would have Meadow friction her nipple hard against mine, holding my own nipple against hers with one hand, while my other hand is buried so deeply into myself down below? What scenes play the theaters of our minds unbeknownst, when we become prisoners of our behind closed doors depravity? Is Irene's spirit still in the bathroom with her mother from a generation ago, standing in front of her as she sits nude, spread so hippy on her throne, legs closed, her lips vacuuming little Irene's nipples to relax herself to defecation? Can Irene still feel the swoon of near fainting when her mother did this to her, when the energy buildup and reverse in her young body made her cry out so loud, her mother put her hand over her young mouth but kept going still? Does my mother Irene, still remember her eleven year old self standing in front of her mother that day, when the suckling at her breast gave her body its first explosion from within?

This is the motherline. The motherline energy that flows like a rushing mighty river, crashing from somewhere high above, gathering its momentum as it flows downward, pouring over the precipice like Angel Falls, to rain in glory what things must be done of her in secret. What

As to what feeling that twitched and trembled me as I laid upon Meadow when she was 13, of this, I profoundly know. As to what feeling her mother's hands caress into her down below, of this, little 13 year old Meadow does not know.

As the endtime thunder rumbles from the clouds, as I hear the voice of the pouring sheets of rain, the fuse is lit in the theater of my mind, as I hardly have to imagine my mother naked at the edge of her bed, with Meadow standing upright in front of her, breasts hung so low and gigantic at my mother's mouth in the nursing. As my apprehension grows, so too does the feeling inside the breasts of my daughter, which rises to a Nova, reaching down to the center of her shapely body, quivering it to spasms and grieving.

Jonathan Lovejoy

The Black Tower

*I*n the storm that rages over the city, above the black tower that rises into the sky, there are seven figures that form the great circle in the rain and lightning, having arrived in the arrow formation like so many geese at flight, but being the seven wonders of this post apocalyptic world. The seven monsters have flown in the wake of emergency announcements spread throughout the northern city, throughout the whole Great Lakes area, in futile warning of their arrival at the tower. The monument to capitalism unfettered, colored so tragically as the dark of pitch, the house that Sears and Roebuck built stands as the beacon that calls the seven dragons to a climactic fury, which begins in the dramatic circle they take to at the top, then breaking this circle of death to scatter to the four winds across the city, with the great dragon Ephesus landing heavily among the stubborn passengers and rainsoaked pedestrians down below, who scream their disbelieving chorus of fear and terror, amidst the rumbling quake of the monster's earth shattering arrival. As their screams rise into the storm of drowning rain, they hear the answer given unto them in the booming, spirit rumbling key of C Major, with the soul of animalistic rage toned and colored in, to announce the end of fiery games played, and the beginning of what is tragic and real.

All over the northern city, screams and wailing hath begun in earnest in the buses, on the trains above ground—in the subway stations, in the restaurants fine and dandy, in the churches, in the art museums, from the fools along the clay streets, as the buildings, the blades of park grass, the leaves of suburban trees, the asphalt of every street, road and highway, none could be shown mercy by the falling rain, which cannot put out the dragon's fiery light. And many of these condemned souls were granted a reprieve from the truth that fortold their demise, which began at the lower floors of the Black Tower, in the Illinois northern city. This, in the fires of Ephesus, after having sounded his trump of warning, hath reared back his beautiful, snow white head, his eyes aglow in the royal light of blue, the underside of his wings so faintly blue as the mourning dove—this monster lowers its head from the height of 30 stories, opening its mouth in the gloomy daytime darkness of the storm, to explode a river of the bluest flame in God's Creation tinted with white heat, which blows the blackened skyscraper windows to oblivion, on its way to the melting of the girders no longer hidden by the burnt away walls, floors, and accoutrements of modern office life.

As Pre-destiny would have it, every living soul inside this condemned building was ordered far and away from it, as if it could do anything to keep them from being taken this very day, by the fires that burn elsewhere in the city. But this tower of western greed stands empty, devoid of those destined for either eternal life, or eternal death and damnation. From a distance that can hardly be construed as safe in the impending firestorm of their arrival, the television cameras zoom in on what the end of human history hath wrought, as the bottom of the tower is engulfed in flame, and begins to melt in the fires of blue.

And before too many tickings of the clock, the tell tale wobble and lean begins, to continue in the flashing of a great noise, that of an end of the world creaking sound, as the mysteries of engineering gone awry begin. Those unlucky enough to be a witness with the naked eye, are privy to a glass and steel tower that reaches for the heavens begin to break, spewing the fragments of itself in the joints of its demise from the ground up, while the foundation gives no place to its desire to break into pieces, folding under the melting of itself in the fire, giving place instantaneously to the infinite weight of one thousand feet of concrete and steel. To the disbelief of the nation, to the terror of the world at large, the top of the black tower angles away from ninety degrees, leaning further away from straight up, as the world's last great tower of capitalism verves into the motion of *falling,* to shake the collective heads of the earth's population in "no," as the Great Northern Tower begins to die in rapid, leaning descent from the heights of glory, falling intact as it tries so desperately to break apart as it falls, but being unable, crashing into the city floor as one, devastating city blocks for a quarter of a mile in a single direction, raising a cloud of living dust and debris in the lightning and the rain. The tower dies in a sound like thunder, rumbling and quaking the earth for miles in each direction around it, as the white dragon emerges from the cloud of dust in winged triumph, and snow white power and glory.

*T*he Violin Sonata in F Major plays an unhappy tune, in the midst

of eschatology, on the eve of the Second Coming. This, the

Tempi di Minuetto, the slow and lyrical minuet of K. 377, as one of the

many happy tears that Mozart cried. This, pitched so sharply upward just

so, so that the two sisters may shed a tear for the grieving earth as they

play, and for the woman whom they loved, who gave them life, and then

had her own taken in the fire of the dragon's pain. This, the pain of rage

unfettered, and vengeance poured out upon the earth in the rain.

These two Asian beauties hath taken their place in the Heart of Melody, to try and escape what hath entranced the rest of the world, who sit with their collective mouths open, and their eyes wide with awe, as they watch blue fire devastate the foundation of stability, causing the last of the great skyscrapers to topple over like a sequoia in 1910.

The beautiful amateur sits at the piano in behind closed doors confidence, to set up the question and answer session in the air around them in melody, questions asked on the black and white keys answered by the professional on the violin, who whines the latter day message into the still of the daytime darkness they hide in. These two beauties, in concert and exposed before God, choosing not to dishonor him by false modesty, refusing to wear a single stitch of clothing on their bodies as they perform. And these two are naked, and are not ashamed, as that which is born in darkness is unaware of their arrival in the fall of night.

They play the soft and beautiful sonata in unison, in duet, unaware of the fall of the Illinois tower as being the beginning of the end of the northern city, every square foot of which has been charred or set on fire of Hell. It is the burning on the grandest scale of cityscapes thus far, as it is seen from the northern lake, which itself burns at the surface in many patches of blue. Even in the rising wind and rain, the water itself cannot quench the fiery debris that floats upon it, even when it is swallowed beneath the churning waves and surf.

Every city building and suburban home, every city and suburban tree is touched by flame in this city, every famed ball park and arena, every house of high art and ill repute, as if someone had pushed the proverbial button from elsewhere, and sent the nuclear fire upon the city. But these are the fires of eschatology that burn, that light up the gloomy daylight as none other fire in history hath done. As the storm rages in the skies above the city, the firestorm rages in the ground below, until over two million souls have departed.

These two Asian beauties pay on. These Armageddon flowers, choosing not to join the rest of the world in their desperation, as they watch the northern city and every surrounding suburb burn to the ground. These sisters play on. As though entranced by the memory of one who hath departed, who often commissioned a performance from them both in the nude, while she would sit and watch them in private, so intimately in secret admiration and natural affection, of the kind that rises to the level of love, to cause her to sit in her bra and underwear in aform of sorrow, shedding tears of joy and pain.

Beethoven or Mozart. Schubert or Mendelssohn. The beauties of Handel or Vivaldi transcribed, her daughters could read the music and handle the business of melody as though inspired—playing as a team committed to a single cause, as two who become one, to channel the voice of God, and the mysteries of an endtime message unknown. Truth is so much stranger than the fiction of our dreams. The fantasies and psychological dumping ground of our minds' creations. Yes, there are at least two sisters in the world who hath done this thing, who hath taken a divinely wrought hammer to the barriers of what is normal, to bring them own like the Walls of Jericho.

In secret, while the outside world prepares to be burned off the maps of history, these two are aware of what calling it is that they must answer, of what instincts in their minds and bodies that must be adhered to and obeyed. In the truth of this divine melody, the two sisters partake, until the final question is asked by the amateur's solemn piano chords, and the artist's whining violin cries whatever mysterious answer is apt to be given.

The earth flows the river of time, from the burning of the northern city, to the waves of acceptance that begin to flow around the world and settle. There is nothing for the world to do not but look over their shoulder in fearful waiting, for the appearance of the fiery hand of judgment. In the Theatre of My Mind, I am as a spirit of the northern lake overlooking the city, witnessing the descent of the seven white angels over the skyline, seeing them break their circle around the tower and take their places around the city, to begin lighting every inch of the manmade ground on fire.

And as I am drifted against my will to a place near the bottom of the great tower, I feel the heat of the thunderous flame that explodes from the dragon's mouth. As I watch the white dragon Ephesus burn the bottom of the tower, there rises from the chorus of screams one that is shockingly familiar, which grows louder and louder still, until I am zapped awake as though electrified, hearing Meadow screaming from somewhere upstairs. The protective, possessive part of who I am raises me up from half sleep to fight and flight mode, running me up the stairs with the intent of rescuing my daughter from this latest agony, and to put a stop to my Mother's perversion upon my daughter once and for all.

I take the last step up into the upstairs hall in a hurry, feeling as through my legs are weighted down, suddenly enveloped by the force of my daughter's screams crashing around me like storm surf over a pier in Lake Michigan. I round the next corner from the hall into the cavern of a bathroom, seeing my daughter kneeling at the bathtub and screaming, while I try to make sense of why there is so much blood on the floor and smeared along the side of the tub.

Through this hazy mist of sight and sound, I make my way into the clearing, into the clarity of thought and vision, where I can see now the empty wine glass nearby the bathtub on the floor, in companion to a white prescription bottle that I pick up to see it is just as empty. In the clearing of the mist, I see my daughter come at me as a beautiful phantom ghost with outstretched arms, wrapping herself around me in sobs and weeping, to pull me down into an ever widening pit of revelation, that the blood I see was poured from the wrist of the naked woman who lies lifeless in the tub, half covered in water stained as red as the white pebbles at the foot of the cross at Calvary.

$\mathcal{A}$cross the landscape of the burning city, the winds howl and gather into themselves the future of this world's demise, whirling the fires of recompense up into themselves, until it seems that twisters made of pure fire have been sent down to char the concrete and every splinter of wood, until the manmade portrait bears no resemblance to its former self, having been broken and burned into a raging apocalypse, where survivors are scattered in cracked buildings and broken homes throughout. There are many spots and spaces of mercy that survive in the midst of the roaring fire, so that he people in the crumbling apartment buildings not on fire can look out their windows as first hand witnesses to this tragedy, being on the inside looking out, at the fire that twists and turns and swirls in the world around them. They brave the unbearable feeling of being a prisoner of the dragon's fire, knowing that a trip down the stairwells and out into the rain is a fruitless proposition, except that it be made into a long and dreary walk to another place in time, where the buses and trains, where the planes and automobiles have not been melted or exploded into oblivion. For them, the trickling of the misty rainfall is a mockery, which only serves to flicker the burning fires into greater anger and malcontent.

These are the fires that burn as a sign unto them, of what grim woes and dark promises must be, of which their worm dieth not, and the fire is not quenched. The earth is gripped by the spirit of fear, where some have been spared the tribulation of things to come, their bodies succumbing to swoons and heart failure. And so many who are unlucky enough to be kept alive to see it happening, are swept into the fires of a new epidemic, that which has begun inside the fires of the northern city, and begun to spread into the hearts and minds of the condemned, causing many lives to be sacrificed on the altar of self martyrdom.

Hidden by the waves of flame that rise throughout the city, are the young mothers who have lost the ability to think and reason, who have seen their best judgment be taken as paper inside an inferno, believing that they are doing the work of God as they lay atop their squirming infants until they breathe no more, then giving themselves over to whatever may double as a hangman's rope, or even the cutting knife blade, or pills and a glass of wine. And along one of the few streets not ablaze in the wind and rain, there are the eyes of hopelessness and melancholy that stare from inside a basement window, a window too small to have provided any hope for escape. These are the eyes of little twelve year old Kirsten Benedict, the eyes of the disillusioned and the displaced, of those that have been acquainted with the dark side of life, having been held prisoner in this basement near onto a year in waiting, where her mother and her mother's lady lover have kept her half starved and in constant pain from daily beatings, some which the two women have done until the girl lies bleeding on the basement floor, unable to open her eyes and focus on the two nude women who had just beaten her with their hands and fists.

Kirsten Benedict looks out through the tiny basement window, at the houses she can see across the street on fire in the storm. Wondering where it is that her beloved mother could have gone. From the eyes of little Kirsten Benedict in the heart of the city, across the field of swirling blue flame, to the Church of the Holy Mother spared the wickedness of the fire without, as the nuns cower inside, in the burning of fires ignited from deep within. Those having given themselves over to the perverted punishments in the name of discipline, where the young, wayward nuns are made to endure those things that are unspeakable—these in the name of the Holy Mother, and of the Lord of Hosts—secret punishments dreamed up by the Mother Superiors of the convent, given by "a revelation from our Lord," they believe, to administer special discipline to God's chosen, to place them on the path of righteousness for his name sake.

These are the Ladies of the cloth, who stand protected in the church of stained glass and brick, the mother superior alone in her office, gazing at the storm of fire that rages outside her window, believing that her prayers and supplications have kept her and her flock safe, so that she may continue to do God's work when the flames have come and gone. She hath prayed to God, to spare her little corner of fanaticism from judgment, that she may continue these private punishments wrought, where the punishment for unconsciousness is beyond severe and three fold, beginning with when one of the nuns who disciplines wears that which pertaineth to a man, and the offending nun is anally raped, that through the agony of this pain she might find repentance. After the raping of the wayward nun in private, where only the Mother Superior and one other administer this discipline, the young nun is tied to a cross of wood in this hidden, forbidden room, and she is caned until her back and her buttocks are streaked with blood, so that she may find repentance from the agony of this pain. And then, she is tied to this cross in reverse, so that her breasts hand free and exposed, to where she is acknowledged to *"hold on to the Holy Mother in your heart, take the hand of her blessed son Jesus and pray for strength and forgiveness."* And her breasts are pulled outward, and a large, strong safety pin is pushed through the base of the nipple and latched, one breast at a time, until both breasts hang exposed and bleeding, where the blood runs to a brief dripping in two slow, steady streams.

Of this discipline that grows in the dark, there are *none* who would believe, to give this secret discipline its power and ingenuity, to produce the most loyal and dedicated young sister of the cloth, to make the other nuns marvel at her attitude adjustment, and her transformation before one and all. This revelation to the Mother Superior, put into practice seven times by her over the years, always knowing who to give it to and when, so that the secret remains, and so that secrecy will abound, and so that repentance can be found, from within the agony of pain. Of this truth I am made aware, so deeply hidden from the rest of the world, of a certain Mother Superior, at the Church of the Holy Mother, in the heart of the burning city by the lake, the heart of the burning northern city.

A Rhapsody in Blue

Jonathan Lovejoy

The White Coffin

......

Two sisters ride the wind and the rain. In the Aftermath of fiery devastation. After finally submitting to the pressure. To the pressures of truth and knowing. These two sisters ride the wind and rain. The rain of a rising wind, drifting them from the California suburb, to the grassy outskirts of the West Coast city. Two souls adrift, powered by the grief of memories. The pain of a hopeless future. Having played the sonata to the memory and beauty of she who hath departed. Having accepted the end of the great northern city.

These two sisters brave the winds that threaten, that seek to cause fear and dread. That seek to bring warning from the clouds of gray and melancholy. A message before the end of the epoch. These two sisters follow the chariot in pitch. The Death Chariot of Ling Ling Chao. Two sisters in solo procession, having called no one from the old, country or the new. Having no stomach for the Old World speech, politeness received and given in New World incorrectness. The phony bowing, the tired and false humility they'd have to show to Ling Ling's mother and father, to her many sisters who may have come. Who may have braved the skies of endtime danger.

Two sisters ride the wind and rain. Disembarking their earthly Chariot into the gray. Umbrellas in tow, as white as the purity of their silken white attire in Asian pattern. Both women in the rain as two Armageddon Flowers, whose petals are snowy white. In contrast to the muddy, bloody ground from whence they came. Two sisters dressed in Asian White. The sophisticate. The innocent. Braving the West Coast storm that looms. To stand in the blinding sheets of blowing rainfall undeterred. To see the white coffin be lowered into the ground, below where the photograph of the beautiful Asian woman is affixed stubbornly upon the white marble headstone. Decorated by roses the color of lily white.

The two sisters stand still in the rain. Obedient. Compliant, as the men lower their mother's coffin in the ground.

A strange, strong gust of wind. Pulling at the younger's umbrella. She fights, until the older sister takes hold of her wrist, to tell her in her mother's tongue, *"let it go."* The younger opens her hand. To obey the wind's cruel and selfish desire. The two of them stand under the older's white umbrella. Holding it tight. Joined together as one. Watching the spirit of the Wind take the umbrella across the open lawn, to the wooded grove of trees so near, and so far away from them. Both knowing. In solemn understanding. Quiet as the white umbrella bounces, whirls and flies away from them. Vanishing beyond the edge of the forest grove. The grove so far and so near.

The older sister looks at the younger. Watching her stare after the umbrella taken in the wind. Watching her turn again to look at the face of beauty. The face so firmly affixed upon the tombstone. The face of eschatology.

Two sisters ride the wind and rain. Embarking upon their rolling chariot again. Leaving the body behind to be buried. Braving the resurrection of her, in the grief and pouring rain.

*A*s we join the rest of the world in our vigil, to mourn the passing of a loved one, to gather up memories to honor the dead, I can feel the spirits of universal oppression, pressing down with pressure of depression, to envelop all of us collectively, as we stand in winds and rains in the four corners of the earth. And even while we glide like two phantoms from Irene Turner's grave, the two of us draped from head to toe in black, who I am inside has only been enhanced by the world's dreamy, oppressive mood. And as I walk with my arm firmly around my daughter's waist, part of me is deeply ashamed at what it is I am grieving to do.

How many mothers around the world, in every place along the timeline, have burned in this lust unspeakable, which burdens my heart as I drive us home through the driving rainfall? The new and renewed closeness I feel for her is as much for what she can do for me, as I struggle to support her on this journey through the aftermath of trauma. But truthfully, Meadow has grown into herself despite my presence, and the presence of the one we just laid to rest. There is a power, a quiet strength I feel inside her, even though she is already world weary at 21, possessing a rare ability to adjust and comply, to adapt and overcome the fear that I know has plagued her since she was a little girl. It is a strength that she knew she was going to have to access, an endurance she would have had to raise up as a fortress, to suffer and bear whatever it was that I know mother had in store for her.

And perhaps Meadow was only a day away from the start of one of these blood rituals, to where Mother was going to wield the paddling wood, and cut my daughter's ivory white skin to blood. Of these impending punishments, of these new monuments to my mother's libido, I think she was ready, being somehow more content to live among us in pain and depravity, than to climb the jagged mountains of the outside world. And of what gratitude is there that I owe to Fate itself, that such an extraordinarily beautiful and sensual young woman is the very spirit of quiet and determined humility, as a servant who could have soared to the heights of their own success in the world, but chose instead to obey their calling. And though my concern and love for her are as endless as the sea of clouds above us as we roll the Virginia countryside, my concern is also for my own selfish needs, so that the depraved part of me can have no compassion or pity.

The mere sight of our picturesque country home raised the ire inside of me. A sudden and severe frustration, colored by the pain of loss, and the inability to process that both my mother and my father have been taken. And although I know it to be true, I refuse to accept the fact that one cannot change what is meant to be, and the reason that my mother is gone sits in the passenger side in her long black hair, and her long black raincoat. As surely as I know the apocalyptic implication of our last name, I know why my mother's body now lies beneath the cold, wet ground. It is because Meadow Oppenheimer has encamped about her a shield, an unseen force field to protect her from the curse of death just yet—and though it is impossible to fathom, I know in heart, she had decided to kill her granddaughter.

A swirling gust of wind greets our arrival, blowing the nearby trees in merciless twist and sway. It seems that the storm is no longer content to hold back, grieving to take over where the seven angels have left off, to drive the people that remain behind closed doors, where they will be helpless but to watch the world burn on their television screen. As the world wonders as to the dragons' current whereabouts in the storm, I walk quickly with my daughter across the front lawn to the front porch steps, climbing with her up to the big, country porch that encompasses two whole sides of the big house, hurrying her away from the hands of this great storm that threatens.

The door to our country paradise is our portal to safety, to our refuge from the Earth's grieving anger. The door closes upon a bright flash of lightning from the bottom of the clouds, and a crash of thunder in the world around our new home.

The long, bulbous tits of my daughter. Even among the business of shelter and survival. Even in the aftermath of the trauma of burial. My daughter's tits are literally the first things that come to my grieving mind and spirit, as we close out the wind and rain for now, moving through our gloomy daytime dark, up the staircase to the upstairs hall. The beautiful young woman is content to guide the current of my will and desire, which has already descended on her in shadow form. Hand still around her tiny waist, I escort her away from the safety of her room and her verses, where she has been known to retreat. But she is a condemned and hapless prey, a lonely and oblivious antelope in the tall grass, cursed to be upwind of the lioness, and therefore unaware until it is too late.

In the gloom of repression undone, in the doom of regression unsuppressed, I escort my grieving, traumatized daughter into the bedroom of lost hope, where the spirit of the raven looms, where the white dove has taken flight. We place our purses onto the mirrored dresser, standing to face one another in an epic stare, the blonde mother and her raven haired daughter, still in our long, black coats and high heeled black shoes, with me stepping forward against her, rubbing my pale, white hands through the silken strands of long, black hair.

Under the clouds of endtime bereaving, in the storm that hides the spirits of mankind one from the other, my daughter and me set forth upon the Sea of Tragedy, where the great leviathan swims in waiting, where we are at the mercy of wind and sail. Our lips are drawn together of their own accord, to press their softness against one another, raising up an energy at the center of who I am down below, until I find that a deep breath is not yet possible, my lungs constricted by a phantom's unmerciful embrace.

Our arms are slid noisily around our bodies still dressed in our coats, as I make one last and magic effort to breathe, lest our inner world threaten to sway and swoon. I am suddenly aware of the pressing of great, soft parts of our flesh through the fabric, the collision of worlds where we live and breathe, to bring us both to our knees in devastation, though we stand still and obedient in the storm, resigned to obey unfettered limits of our calling.

Of this, my hands are suddenly in motion on their own, undoing the buttons on her long, black coat. Underneath, the rise under her black dress is extraordinary, where they have been lifted up and stuffed into the black lace bra fabric, to properly contain the hidden chords above and beyond G Major. As she slides out of her coat, I begin to undo the belt and buttons of my own, noticing that even in the black dress, the curves she possesses are magnificent to behold. I watch her turn to the mirror and reach back to the zipper in back of her dress, watching her without mercy, so I can enjoy her struggle to break free. The beautiful young woman unzips her black dress and slides it off her shoulders, down and away from the fabric that holds them in, that lifts them up and away, so that the Nova Curve of her body can be seen, where the inward slope of her waist is awe inspiring to witness, curving outward into wide, rounded hips, where the thighs have already begun to settle into womanhood, giving her buttocks a spread usually reserved for a woman much older, to make her as irresistible from the back as from the front. Meadow Oppenheimer's body is the end of the world. An apocalyptic glimpse at the glory of God in Creation, at the power of the feminine form unbridled, and the devastation of Adam at the hands of Eve.

I watch this full hipped, curve waisted goddess walk over to my queen's throne bed, tossing her dress onto it, not bothering to look at my desperation as I undress in the agony of an aching at my groin, as though I am at a buffet line, held prisoner by a deep and abiding hunger. The sight of her reaching down to remove her black shoes, exposing the gargantuan cleavage, one as deadly as the Great Appalachian Faultline, the sight of it is nearly too much for me to bear, as I notice the new beating of my own heart, and the fluttering of my breath in my lungs.

I have contempt for the athletic thickness of my own waist and lack of hip spread as I glimpse in the mirror, bitter that the beauty of some traits do skip a generation. My extreme top heaviness may be my bodies' saving grace as I bend down to take off my shoes, in grieving to soon be rid of the white bra fabric, so that I may feel the weight of them pulling me toward the bedroom floor. In middle aged strength and natural tightness of form, I walk toward the young woman whose body is partially the opposite, young and soft, supple and fully curved to the eye. The sight of this young woman in her black lace bra and underwear, her black sheer stockings midway up the thighs will allow me no further pretense to demurity, and I slide the straps down from my big bra in cold, clinical fashion, sliding the bra down and away from the mountainous white bosom, turning it around and unlatching it, dropping it unceremoniously to the floor.

I am in my tiny, white underwear cloth, to complete the Amazonian flair, to make me the lady warrior that I am, to cause my heart to be strong and ready in this wilderness of the forbidden. The extreme beauty of her black bra and underwear portrait suddenly give pause to me, and I am compelled to stop her from setting them free from their black lace prison. I stare at her for a moment, stepping forward just enough to brush the nipple against her bra, twitching a shudder which takes my breath, then grunting once from the shock of my other nipple against the fabric. I take her hand and escort her over to the mirror. Standing her there helpless, forcing her to gaze upon her own beauty while I look at her, while I judge and possess her without saying a word.

I slip back into my high heeled shoes, that I may look decisively over her shoulder from behind. I reach around her and grip the two humongous breasts, closing my eyes to listen to the voice inside my head say *"my daughter's tits,"* which I hear again and again, every time I squeeze them like so much bread dough, watching the cleavage spill up over the top of her bra, relaxing her to closing eyes. "Open your eyes," I have to say, as I reach inside her bra and slide the heavy breast out, letting it fall over the bra still latched tight, fascinated by the length and floppiness of its great size and bulbous shape hanging down. The sight of the single breast exposed causes me to have to squeeze myself once so tight against her backside, burying my face into the sweet, silky softness of her hair for a breath of renewal.

It is a sense of pure, unadulterated and outright possession, of a magnitude and depth that perhaps I have never really felt before. Tall and strong in my white underwear cloth and black heels, I reach into her bra from behind her, pulling out her other breast and letting it fall heavy and long in pairing with the other, fascinated by the perfection of the large, dark areolae and the protruding nipples, that seem to draw phantom energy from me through space and time, and I think I already swallow once as a reflex action to what I feel.

Standing strong in my high heels, I gaze at her from the side, until she looks away from our reflection and stares me directly in the eye, as if in wonder of what pain or pleasure, what diversion or perversion she must endure. But this is only the power of possession, the depravity of dominance that I feel, as I look away from her to the mirror again, grabbing the mountains of squish and wibble into my hands, which are truly dwarfed by the sheer size of them. I squeeze and work a massage rhythm, which causes her to have to close her eyes again, struggling to keep them open out of obedience, to watch her mother's hands knead her breasts again like so much bread dough before a feast. Before long, I feel a spark of unfamiliarity at my own breasts pressed against her back, which gives pause for me to consider that yes, my nipples are completely entranced, brought about by the motion of this ocean of movement, and the gathering of a perfect storm of sights, sounds and sensations upon my skin.

I notice that every squeeze raises the Tower of Babel higher over the landscape of my deviation, until I am forced to stop the squeezing motion and hold them still in my hands, perceiving the hardness of her nipples against the palms, which I can feel drawing an arc of invisible energy to prepare a strike to my body. Meadow begins to stare in awe at the blonde woman in the mirror, whose face is anguished over with worry and wait, and whose voice has begun the deep and anticipatory moan of impending doom and devastation, which I am prepared to sacrifice my soul and sanity to. Feeling the two fold pressure building, as the voice inside my head says to me again *"my daughter's tits,"* I allow the flow of this energy to drift out through my moaning voice of inner weeping as my entire body begins to shake and tremble from the inside out, quivering my moaning voice into a shaking, quaking oblivion.

Come to me, Meadow. Come. Crawl thyself unto me. As I lay on my back half devastated, half in demise from thy bosom, descend from on high unto me. Disrobe the rest of thine cloth of pitch, that I may see the fertility of Eve. The loveliness of Diana among us. Thou art Adina, Goddess of the Bosom. Place thine lovely knee upon the bed, and then the other in a kneel to crawl. Bend thyself to thy hands and knees. Crawl thine beauty over unto me. Let me swoon in anticipation of this fervent deviation, as you crawl yourself unto me. Swing thine gigantic and ringing bells downward, let me hear this freedom ring. The freedom of the forbidden. The freedom of what courses through my veins. This is the refuge of mine, Meadow Oppenheimer, as you fly these missiles of annihilation to me. As the promise of your future milk fires devastation in me.

Now, rest thy bosom to my lips, my loving daughter. Encompass me with thy love. Embrace this secret thing that we must partake, behind the walls of secret. Behind the barriers that hide us from them. Wiggle. Wobble thineself to my face, that I may give suck to my heart's desire. Allow me to touch them with my hand, my dearest Meadow, that I may guide them more powerfully unto myself. More agonizingly unto me. Let me hold myself, my dear daughter, through the devastation that must be. Rest above me as the kine that gives suckle to the calf, to ease the suffering of this life dependant.

Now, rest thineself beside me, dearest Meadow, that I may feel your skin against mine, as I nurse this pleasure from deep within. Brave the vulgar bellowing from inside me, the crass and feverish shaking of my head as I writhe.

And now, dearest Meadow, what hast thou done to me! What destruction is this I feel under the clouds of this storm, when I feel thine hand at the center of me! To rub. To caress. To touch and feel my most fervent doom, to pre-tremble the surface of my body in warning as I suckle, as I give suck unto thee. What impossibility is this I feel, as my lips pull your nipple so deeply into my mouth, while your hand rubs the swollen center of me? What height is this mountain that I climb, that rises above all others, over the landscape of my darkest dream. Do you hear the whimpering that has begun, dear Meadow, as you settle into the rubbing rhythm against mine? As I put both your nipples in my mouth at the same time? What does this do to your sensibility, dear Meadow? What does it do to the curves in your body? As I focus again on the single breast at my lips, what does my writhing, my pitiful whimpering do to thee? You have not felt yet, perhaps in the whole of thine young life, the annihilation that looms over my horizon. The explosion of this energy that threatens to do me in.

We are as one now, you and I. This circular connection I feel, the ring which is made from you and me. This ring of devotion, this secret diversion to ignite this new path for us, this new inferno that desires to burn. From the center of me, up into my breasts, grounded by my lips at your suckling nipple pulled in, I must allow this pain to come out through my voice, dear Meadow, the siren which opens my mouth to begin my death, cascading up, then quickly downward from the heights of my terror, to reduce me to a convulsion of spasms, bellowing and deep grunting from the judgment of God.

Come to me, Meadow. Come. Crawl thyself unto me.

The Green of the Eastern Wood

Jonathan Lovejoy

*T*he generations of Rachel and Lea Chao, as they burden the heart and mind. From the rain soaked landscape of the cemetery, up and above the flow of time and history. To where Ling Chao walked the Hong Kong fields of Green, as the child Ling Wu, daughter of Nana Mei Wu, in the pristine fields of plenty. From whenceforth cometh this spirit of blood, this sacrifice and flood of pain?

Under the gray Hong Kong sky, before the arrival of the rain, Na Na Mei calls in her native tongue to her daughter, that they must take a walk to the far side of the grassy field, nearby the Hong Kong woods. To leave her two younger sisters to their meal, so that Na Na Mei and Ling can take a walk. In their native tongue, where pretense is covered only so slightly, where the anger of promises is softened by the tranquility of promises kept, Na Na Mei, Mei Wu takes her 12 year old daughter by the boyish waist, to usher her in false hope away from her two younger sisters, who look on in the apprehension of sorrow, in the nervousness of knowing, as Na Na Mei escorts Ling from their hut as the condemned, to where it is that they themselves have already been. This, with the cane so firmly, so unashamedly in her hand, as the clouds have gathered to threaten the daytime of the impending mist of rain.

To the far edge of the grassy field, their world hidden behind the slopes of the Hong Kong country side, Mei Wu takes her tight pullover top off, to reveal the great, dangling source of long breasted majesty passed down, sharply ordering her daughter to strip her dress and her underwear off, while Ling Wu watches in fear her mother bend over to retrieve the cane, her great, long breast hanging impossibly, as great bells of dark and forbidden wisdom unknown.

Na Na Mei stands un-idly by, to judge her twelve year old Ling strip to her bare skin, enjoying the defeated and pitiful look in her eyes unspoiled by bravery, as she slides her underwear down and away, to reveal the whole of her young self, to stand exposed and humiliated already under the skies of grieving. Without further hesitation, she grabs her daughter's arm with her free hand, to swing her round and about in the violence of the cane's evil voice, which is heard in the quick *whip* and quick *whop* through their brief space, joined by the growing appearance of bloody welts on her daughter's white skin, and the sound of her screaming little voice in their country isolation. Ling watches in her periphery the great breasts swing, the macromastian bosoms do their ring-a-ding-ding, while her mother's arm gathers its strength over and over, to bring the cane down to cut her skin to blood and sting. Through the haze of her own screaming, in the chattering maze of her mother's voice in preaching, she recalls the mother's promise from eight hours ago, because Ling made a bitter face when she told her to feed their young sisters at the breakfast table. A mean little wrinkle of the nose and lips it was, done with hardly a malice of forethought, an instinctual little twitch of irritation because she was busy at her morning lute, trying to gather the energy of a melody visited to her mind from beyond, to give her false hope, that she would play and write melodies for kings someday. But in her farm girl's poverty, she was reminded of her reality, when Mei Wu spoke to her in bitter morning tones, that she was going to *"get the blood stripped from [her] ugly little stick body,"* because she made a *"sassy face."* Ling remembers the slap in front of her younger sisters, who had to stifle a laugh that came from they knew not where, while Mei Wu began to preach and promise the whipping that would come before the sun went down.

Ling Wu remembers the fear in the pit of her stomach that lingered, that evoked a silent prayer that stretched across the hours, that the clouds would voice their displeasure to her mother, and bring about the salvation of thunder and rain. But the skies mocked her throughout the day, until she gave up hope when the late afternoon dinner was served, and Mei Wu told her, *"go and bring me your cane. "*This, she did obediently, to the fear and dismay of her and her sisters, who would have to endure the fear themselves, when their mother escorted ling to where her skin would be cut to blood. Ling Wu screams the melody of this diversion, as the final blows come down across her back and buttocks, to criss cross her in stripes of crimson red.

And Mei Wu stands quiet and short of breath, to watch her naked daughter stand trembling and sobbing so deeply, ordering her to "turn around and look at the woods," so she can better gauge the quality of her work, of what messages she hath wrought upon her daughter's skin. And for the first time, she is compelled to step against her daughter's back, to press the great, long breasts against the bloody welts, to listen to her daughter cry again, and to marvel at the blood stained bosom, and the shock that sparks from her breasts to her groin. In the beauty of this native tongue, she orders her daughter to lie on the ground, to lie on the grass, even though her back is itching already from the caning. The mother looks around with eyes of shame, content that the house is far away from what lies in the grassy field, and the small woods and hills are the barriers of secret that uphold.

She slides her long, peasant skirt down and away, and then the slight, silken underwear cloth besides, getting down to her knees, ordering her daughter to open her legs. Ling Wu is twelve, when the spirit comes to her. Ling Wu is twelve, when the spirit of Mei Wu is come. Na Na Mei crawls upon all fours, to where Ling can feel the brushing of the hardened nipples against her stomach, which stops her mother in the tracks of her motion, to make her rub the hanging breasts of their own accord against her 12 year old's fair skin. Ling lays still. Gazing up at the lying gray clouds, which had promised her a storm of deliverance, but left her sprawled on the ground and bleeding.

Mei Wu moves from the lightning of her nipples brushed against her daughter, to obey her body's calling, to obey the spirit that passes through the motherline, to tell her what it is that she must do. In obedience to the flesh and spirit, Na Na Mei lies down flat upon her daughter, sliding her lower self against her daughter's, until the warmth of what she feels produces a magic reckoning, awakening a part of her bodies' response that had only been imagined in her darkest dreams. She swirls her narrow hips around and about, mashing and rolling the great bosoms pressed down against her daughter's chest, speaking in her mouth's opening upon its own accord, for her daughter to put her arms around her, and she begins that new and tell-tale rhythm, the humping that betrays the inner mechanism born and bred, that causes her hips to rise and fall, to slip and slide the bump and grind of agony, as she feels in the totality of her enormous bosom the rise of fervent heat, that threatens to spark to somewhere in the center of her body.

Ling Ling holds on to her mother. To support herself from the burden of such itching pain in her back as she has never known, and the terror of what feeling that promises to make her scream again. Ling grabs onto her mother, to endure the hazing of the gray sky from her vision, and the ringing in her ears, as her mother's heavy pounding and sliding works her little body into a frenzy of pleasures impossible to endure. As the itching pain in her back merges with the throbbing pleasure in the rest of her, she is unable to open her own eyes, to witness her mother's face of anguish and agony, as her babbling speech is suddenly transformed into a high pitched wailing in her ear. Ling Ling Wu holds on, as the high pitch sound breaks into the low, animal grunting, as her mother smother's her mouth with a fervent kiss, to have an outlet for this pain, to channel the remainder of it so deeply into her daughter's body.

You are twelve, Ling Ling Wu, when the spirit doth come unto thee. You are twelve, Wu Ling, when thy mother's spirit hath come.

The rains of our fear and discontent have haunted us day and night, saturating the world around us like the end of the first epoch. This is a hard and unforgiving rain, as if the earth itself is in grieving to put out the blue fires that can never be quenched. Cities, towns, fields and forests around the world share this grieving and mourning thing in common, as the fires of eschatology continue to burn, as the dreary and ineffectual rains continue to fall.

But for what effect the rains do not have upon the burning land and cityscapes near and abroad, they have delivered to the remaining six billion people a tragic and oppressive mood. And this has settle in upon us here, in our white house by the Virginia countryside, nearby the green of the eastern wood. I have often stood on the majesty of the sheltered front porch and looked out into the storm, either in grief, prayer or worry, but always in the wake of my mother's passing. So many times I have wondered, unable to accept even the existence of the new cold spots that come and go, and the echoes of brief shadows that roam. I have heard of things like this happening to others, who often feel the welcomed or unwelcomed presence of a love one when they have died. Whether these are angels or demons, or even the souls of the dearly departed, who's to say? Perhaps it doesn't matter, when the lights must be turned on to banish away the daytime dark, because another second in the room without light seems impossible. And what of the curious sensation of being in the presence of another person, but turning to find nothing, and no one there time and time again? I'm sure it is just post traumatic nerves we feel, the deep oppressiveness of grief in store.

Meadow is no longer capable of sleeping in her own bed, as the dreams we have expected have begun in earnest, her being a prolific dreamer already. And this, I knew would be enhanced by the accumulation of events, by the culmination of this one, which is the exclamation point at the end of her grandmother's sentence on the timeline. This, the timeline of her mind and body's maturity, as I was able to protect Meadow from my mother's lustful eye until after her eighteenth year had come and gone, the devastation which began the moment I saw Mother kiss Meadow at her high school graduation, even though we were all in public and in broad daylight. The audacity, the possessive ownership in that brave public smack on the lips, the fearlessness in that kiss that announced to the world, *"Yes, I'm soon to be fucking my granddaughter. What of it?"* As I watched them hug that day like lovers reunited after an absence, I wondered if I was the only one who could see this predatory woman over fifty, who had crossed boundaries and barriers so long ago, beginning when I was just a little girl. I remember wondering that day—am I the only one who understands what churns beneath cultured civility, that understands the end of the world nature of behind closed doors reality, and of what would deliver to those who knew an apocalyptic shock. Day and night, we are burdened by the terror of this remembrance, by the heavy weight of her fervent memory, until we have convinced ourselves that the only thing to fear is fear itself, and the bygone memory of one who has come and gone.

And the energy of this spirit recollection grips me in full, as I am suddenly awakened by the sound of my daughter's voice in a deep and powerful scream, of the kind laced with the fear of death, waking me up with the start proverbial and quick, clutching my heart and lungs with terror as I see my mother, naked and strong, draped flat on top of my daughter who lies underneath her, her arms pinned to her sides, screaming for the mercy of God unspoken.

At the edge of heart attack horror in my blood, I am suddenly aware of the gloomy nighttime storm of my reality, looking over at Meadow, who is not really screaming at all, but is resting and breathing so peaceful and sound asleep.

$\mathcal{T}$he days of Wu Ling Chao, as they burden the heart and mind. Knowing already what it is that must be done to her daughter, underneath the Harvest Moon. This, the first October of her oldest daughter's departure, where her youngest daughter and she are left alone. When Rachel Lynn Chao first reaped the benefits of the Tiger Mother Dynamic, and was bestowed the harvest for seeds sown. For a childhood gathered up into the whirlwind of a Mother's Discipline, and scattered to the four corners of her reality. A straight A student, having failed upon the piano, but knowing that an undergraduate acceptance to Harvard University is a calling from God.

Wu Ling and her eleven year old progyny named for the flower, Leah Rose Chao. Wu Ling and Leah Rose are on their way home from the airport, after the sun has said its final farewell, at the far edge of the evening day. Wu Ling drives with her eleven year old beauty which doth remain, already knowing the ghost of what future that must live and breathe, knowing the phantom of what sorrow of the ages there must be.

At the traffic light, somewhere near the California suburb, Wu Ling suffers the whisper from ages gone by, to send energy to her lovely right hand that moves on its own, to the dress worn by the eleven year old daughter. Wu Ling slides her hand up the smoothness of the little girl's thigh without mercy, having not done this to Leah Rose before, not in such tranquil and loving manner as this. Without so much as a single glance to her, without so much as a pleasant twinkle in the eye, she rests her hand at the precipice of tomorrow, where all hope is come and gone, and in the secrecy of their chariot unseen, she pinches hard with her thumb and her forefinger, to cause the young girl to draw a breath of pure shock, a breath of total indecision, as her brain will not disclose the truth of either pleasure or pain. For another moment in time, she holds it there, gauging the conglomeration of spirits out and about, those that whisper and caress, and those that stare at her in judgment through the red traffic light, killed suddenly by the disappearance of crimson, and the appearance of the light in the act of earthen green.

Still holding death in its place betwixt the two of them, as a knife to the throat of a suckling lamb, the mother cruises her daughter through the Wealthen Stream, grieving for the Land of Plenty. She unlocks this uncertain grip, this certain trip through the doors of what must be, sliding her hand down her daughter's thigh again. Slip, sliding the dress fabric back over her young daughter's knee, returning her hand to the wheel, to finish their silver gray luxury journey among the stars that remain hidden, in the fading light of day.

Wu Ling and Leah Rose climb down from the exhausted heights of Lexus SUV luxury, a gift bestowed by Fate, when Dr. Chao was buried. Wu Ling Chao stands in the warm, late afternoon glow of suburbia, waving to the nosy mother across the way, who boils in the lust of gossip, the craving for knowledge as to where the pretty, shapely Asian woman and her think, busty little daughter have been. How is it possible, they ask, that an eleven year old girl has the breasts of a woman? Why does Lena Chao lie about her daughter's age? Why does she drive her to school instead of letting her ride the bus like every other child? Why is a girl that looks like a freshman in high school just going to the sixth grade? How many times has she been left back over the years? Why does Lena Chao never invite us over to her house, why does she never accept an invitation to ours? Her husband was a doctor, I think. How did he die? Did she kill him? Did she trick him into drinking wine laced with some exotic poison from her homeland? Does she think she is sexy, because her big hips and bloopy boobies bounce to an Asian rhythm?

The heavy hipped, big bosomed Asian woman holds out her right hand. Curves bequeathed in power. Shapeliness forged in fires that burn. The small waisted, busty 40 year old Asian woman holds out her hand, to receive the arrival of the eleven year old Asian girl. Leah Rose takes her mother's and in waiting, and the two of them walk together across the patch of grass that masquerades as a lawn, ignoring the mailbox and the patch of grass grown too far up therein. They walk together into the house on Forest Hill Drive, to leave the nosy neighbors behind to their grief, as the earth turns toward the evening day.

All pretenses of the American tongue cease to be, encoded upon the words, *"take off all your clothes,"* answered in the girl's desperation to breathe, in the last gasp of English her mother can tolerate. "But Momma, what did I do?" Believing so completely that a belt whipping is imminent. But such is the renewed patience, and epic satisfaction of the mother, who repeats in a quieter tone, *"take off your clothes."* Lena watches her daughter disrobe, as if in the fires of a fervent command, standing still and quiet as the girl removes her dress, letting it fall to the floor. The Mother looks on in awe, as the uniquely guargantuan bosoms hang down from the girl's tiny body as she bends over, sliding her underwear down and away.

Upon this chord races the mother's beating heart, when the eleven year old daughter stands naked before her. Lena can only swallow the waters of this thirst that beckons, calling for Leah Rose to walk over to her. *"I want you to spank me,"* Lena says to her daughter. *"I want you to spank me as hard as you can."*

Fully clothed, gray skirt pulled so tight across the widened hips, she turns her back to the breasty young girl, already possessing the full development that few woman could dream of, hung bulbous in the key of F major, in equal prowess as her mother, to someday climb the hills of impossibility, to play the J chord in space, that will be hung so flat, long and low against her body. The breasty echoes of this future wobble and beckon, as the young, naked girl raises her hand in obedience, and gives her 40 year old mother a hard, clumsy whack on the backside. The shock that widens her mother's eyes is in full bodied repose, touching every nerve ending from her breasts to her groin, to make her nearly afraid to receive another. *"Again,"* she says breathlessly, *"harder."* And she has her worst fears confirmed, as her mind shows her the naked girl swing hard into her buttocks again, which shoots a lightning bold of warning to the center of herself, to admonish her not to receive another hit from this child, lest she be doubled over in unwanted, premature grunting and trembling.

Her body on fire, her mind ablaze with what to do, she stands up in full curviness, in the middle of their living room, turning to gaze again at the breasty naked girl.

"Come with me upstairs," she says. Walking past her daughter in frustration, not needing to look back, as the daughter follows in stripped down obedience, in bare breasted, bare skinned compliance behind her mother. On the living room floor lay the remains of her daughter's past, in crumpled dress and underwear cloth. Leah Rose follows Lena up thse quiet suburban stairs, turning down the carpeted hall, strolling one by one into the upper room.

"Now, you take my clothes off for me," she says, barely able to restrain her inner beast, which begs to put her hands around the young girl's throat, and choke the last breath from her body. She stands so patiently, in such easy power of her command, in agony to restrain herself, as the fumbling of her daughter's inexperienced hands at her bra causes her to tremble. Soon, the Mother and the Daughter stand naked together, in the glow of the daytime dark, hidden in the suburban upper room.

"Put your mouth to my nipple," she says. *"Suck it like you mean it."* The woman stands a head taller than the beautiful young girl, looking down on her desperation, her pathetic attempt to please. With no knowledge of what it is they must do, with no understanding of inner agonies that beckon, the young girl clamps her lips to her mother's breasts in full, suckling pull— nursing for every drop of approval, for every ounce of affection there my be,

staring once up into her mother's pained, deeply anguished expression. The breast slips out of the girl's mouth in a loud, sucking kiss, reducing her mother to a shudder, twitch and tremble.

"Put the other one in your mouth," she says, *"squeeze my behind with both hands."* And this, her daughter does. To inspire the mother's hand to grip her other nipple, to complete what triangle of ecstasy this is. She relishes her daughter's small hands pressed into the fleshy, sensitive backside, telling her to *"squish and squeeze my bottom. Squeeze it good,"* her voice nearly breaking in the last syllable. *"Hold your hands still,"* she says in Cantonese, *"I don't want to cum yet."* And in the nick of her perverted time, the daughter's hands stop moving, and wiggling the squishling flesh, to keep her mother's body from quaking the Armageddon swing.

"Now, pull my titty with your mouth," she says, *"pull it until it comes out."* This, the daughter does. Obliging the fall, the flopping of the mother's tit down against her body. *"Do it again,"* she says, control of her breathing nearly gone. As her daughter pulls the great breast forward so far and long, her mind phases to the feeling she endured, when her own mother, Na Na Mei Wu, did this self same pulling to her, to watch her young breasts rise and fall.

As if ordered by the unseen, Lena takes hold of her daughter's head when her sucking breaks free, and she kisses her eleven year old daughter deeply, coaxing the girl's tongue to the surface, until both tongues are seen at war with one another in a slow and slippery slide asunder. From this fervent, licking kiss, Lena Chao escorts her daughter to the bed, where she climbs up onto cushioned comfort, in full, naked repose on her back, knowing what it is that she must do.

Both her hands are guided down, down far away below, pressing eh softness of herself apart, so that what is within may rise to its present life and

56

Their fantasy chamber is the bathroom today. The suburban chamber of porcelain secrets and marble depravities hidden. It is the place where two Asian beauties, two sisters stand in front of the mirror, to gather the visual souvenir of their time. It is where the lady psychiatrist, so sophisticated, midnight hair so silken and laid perfect just below the naked shoulders—it is where she stands in the awe of what grief there may be, fascinated by what is driven forth by the spirits that lie within.

Rachel Lynn observes in awe her own naked reflection, the rounded, firm breast perfection raised up in C Major, the pearly white skin, the dark brown areola and protruding nipples that ache to be touched, tickled or tortured, the waist curve cinched in, the Nova Curve, that flares desire in both women and men, and the sojourn outward into a hip spread too remarkable, passed down from the woman whose burdens and pains she bears, from those secrets and depravities she bore. This sophisticated, wide hipped Asian beauty is at the mirror of a waking dream, gazing upon the reflection of herself, and of her divinely inspired immolation, her victim, the charge of her light brigade.

She watches Leah finish the strapping of the member to herself, per her own order and command, marveling at the gigantic, hanging baskets of breast flesh that she sees, attached to a body so fit and so thin. It is truly one of nature's great anomalies, that begs to be studied and marveled upon, ogled and worshipped, reminisced and ridiculed through time. She observes the epic feeling that has begun in her groin already, that has begun to spread outward, threatening to cause a hidden twitch somewhere about the thigh or the nearly massive buttocks, which give the perpetual pear, the bottom heavy hourglass of legend and form. Rachel watches Leah secure the straps to finality, until she can bear it no further, closing her eyes briefly, allowing the sigh in her body to be heard so loud and clear.

And now, the younger Leah joins in the watching, observing the great source of her private shame hanging down from above, to contrast the strapped on shame that now hangs down below. Allowing a certain memory to fuel this fire, of when she was eleven, and when her mother stood fully clothed in front of her. Fueled by the energy from days gone by, her obedience is sparked to bravery, and she wails the tar out of her older sister by a single blow, with the palm of her hand across her sister's bare backside, causing it to wiggle mightily, the slap of it echoing the space of their death and tomb. And she does this a second time with skill, as if obeying a calling bestowed, obeying her older sister's charge on her skin, until the pain turns black and blue.

"I want you to spank a bruise on my ass," are the words in vulgarity, that are laid heavy upon her heart's memory, knowing that to be less than violent is to risk her sister's wrath. In the spirit of frustration nurtured by fear, she

spanks both sides of the massive buttocks bare handed, until the bright red begins to deepen, and the beautiful skin turns into a mottled, deeply bruised monument to pain and suffering. And when the red skin has turned the corner to blue, the giant breasted girl pulls her older sister's hair from a place beyond fear, where frustration morphs into bravery. In their native tongue, she mocks her sister, saying *"I know what the Dr. Whore want now. Hmm?"* This, to precede a hard, repeated slapping to her older sister's face while her hair is pulled, until the skin is red from the trauma, and Rachel's face can no longer hide in a mask of dignity.

"Now, spit in my hand, so I can give the whore what she wants." This, Rachel does. Lowering her beautiful face in humility and shame, spitting generously onto Leah's reddened hand at the fingers, then she stares into her own grieving expression, remembering the familiarity of the fumbling at her backside, as Leah spreads her cheeks open with one hand, and rubs her sister's own spit onto her rectum with the other, pushing her middle finger inside, making Rachel have to close her eyes, where the memory of days past glows loud and clear.

Leah lets her own spittle fall in a slow, steady stream to her sisters' cheeks spread open, to give what final mercy there is to be had, for their journey through the gate to this secret. Leah takes hold of the bottom of her member, to leave the rest of every inch times seven exposed, pushing the head of it into her sister's backside, not looking up to see Rachel's head lowered, undeterred by the gruff, deep yell that escapes into the world around them. Leah presses on, pushing the second of these seven inches exposed inside, and the third, and the fourth, which bring a higher pitch to the gruffness of her yelling—with her hands firmly gripped to the counter, her head now thrown back, then lowered to a fevered and violent shaking of her head back and forth so briefly. But Leah presses on, whacking her sister's big, sore bottom once with authority, pushing past the fifth, then the sixth inch in, as Rachel lowers her beautiful, sophisticated head to persevere the last mile, releasing a yell that has matured into something akin to a scream of pure frustration and anger. But Lea presses on, pushing the seventh exposed inch through her sister's angry, warrior's yell, until every inch times seven plus one is pushed in. Rachel's rebel yell digresses, into a series of long grunts and groans, feeling every inch of pressure inside her rectum.

"Shut up," her sister says, pulling her hair without mercy, her body full against her now from behind. *"I said shut up. You make me cum too quick. Squealing like a sow pig."*

Leah absorbs the energy of suffering from her older sister, which thrills her heartbeat to a flutter, and her soul to fluttering of melancholy delight. *"Dr. Rachel,"* she says into her ear. *"Listen to people's problem."*

Leah begins to slowly, but deliberately push her hips in and out, sliding the member accordingly in an out of her sister's rectum. She watches Rachel's anguish transform from the agony of pain to something else, listening to her bellowing grow more controlled, as her struggle to endure encompasses another feeling, where the line between pain and unedurable pleasure is crossed. Leah reaches around with both hands, taking hold of the big nipples, twisting them both without mercy, until they are burdened again by another fervent scream, in their porcelain and marble chamber.

Leah takes hold of her sister's suffering with her teeth, by way of a bite held down to her ear.

"Your scream make my dick too hard," she says. *"Make me want to cum in my tits. Now, Dr. Rachel have problem."*

With her mouth still at Rachel's ear, Leah slides her hand down below, to the front of her sister's fervent suffering. She slides her hand onto the swollen front of her, closing her eyes to the warm sensation on her hand, feeling the inner thrust of it grown to beyond a second inch of maximum sensitivity.

"Your girl cock too big," she says. *"That why you cum too hard."*

Rachel loses the grip upon herself, taken away by her sister's slow and powerful rubbing at her proper place, her improper place, until the pressure in her bowels transmogrifies, to radiate energy into her buttocks, joined by the rising energy from her sister's rubbing, until the two meet at the center of her body, to send spasms into every muscle, causing her to push back against Leah in violent, electric shaking, that trembles and quakes her voice into a desperate, breathless attempt to plead and beg for mercy.

Jonathan Lovejoy

Cougars, Panthers, and Cheerleaders

I want you to kill that little Egyptian cunt. Or I swear to God...I'll kill you.

As new fires are lit around the world, in me a new fire is lit as well. One that truly, I may not have felt since I was eighteen, that same fire that torments so many of the skinny pretties and busty beauties in high school, whether they hide in loose shirts, sweaters and glasses, or whether they flaunt it in cheerleader thighs spread wide, it is a fear that permeates the pretty girl culture, especially those that are descended from the pretty girls grown up. The ones with the good luck jobs and good luck husbands, who have recognized their daughter's pretty quotient early, and staked claim in the fertile ground of their potential

It is a feeling that truly, I have not felt since I was a twelfth grade cheerleader, when I was reacquainted with the truth. It is the inevitable tide that rises, the typical bravery and rebellion that hits every teen girl on the edge of womanhood. I see this girl in the heart of memory, the laziest and bustiest cheerleader, who can barely jump an inch off the ground but whose tits are so big it doesn't even matter. *"You are such a great cheerleader, you are such a great cheerleader,"* they sing, in protruding ignorance, equating talent with tit size as a cheerleader—when the skinny, plain faced nerd without glasses who can flip like Dominique Dawes is practically ignored by everyone.

So why shouldn't I feel that I am in charge of my own self, then? I'm Carol Ann Turner. I'm everybody's favorite cheerleader. Not you, Mom. You can't tell me what to do, I'm not a little girl anymore. Take your hands off me.

In the Heart of Memory. I see the balloon breasted young thing that Friday morning. Being driven to school in the silver Mercedes SUV. Cozy in my cheerleader costume, the royal blue advertisement to the forbidden. Riding casually with the strong, beautiful rich woman in the driver's seat, the wife of the oil company executive, purveyors of old wealth charmed, channeled forth and displayed. One of the privileged daughters of Miller Creek Crossing. Neighborhood of southern brick mansion homes, somewhere in the loving arms of Richmond.

I cruise upon this Wealthen Stream, on this Friday morning of the frigid Autumn breeze, so uncompromising in its morning unpredictability, under the November Forest Moon. Having felt the line crossed this morning before we left, when I snatched my arm away from her grip as we walked out the front door, refusing to be held in check, angry because Mother has refused to buy me my own chariot to drive. Because who does she think she is, that she will not bow to my teenage wants and needs? Who does she think she is, to not become a slave to my sense of entitlement? Who does she think she is, to not give in to my New World rebellion, and my latter day disrespect and disobedience?

"I don't want to fucking hear it Mom, okay?"

This, I say outright, interrupting her explanation as to why she doesn't think I need car just yet, whether the reason be financial or social. Regardless, I know I don't want to hear it, whispering the *"bitch"* to myself, with my head slightly turned away, hoping in my heart that she heard me. But Mother obediently closes her mouth, continuing our little commute in the fog of tension, where the silence is so thick that the air is actually harder to breathe. As a woman of 40 years, I gaze backward along the timeline, amazed at the audacity of the little big-tittied bitch that I am, at the unabashed temerity, the unmitigated gall with which I conduct myself, as if I truly have a pot to piss in or an inch of ground to pour it out on.

We roll in smooth, silver Mercedes luxury up to the school, but not past the font of the school house like we should. It pisses me off, this little side trip to the parking lot, where she parks us nearby one of the half barren, November trees, whose leaves have already had their death in gold and amber, waiting to be taken up into the cold Autumn breeze, and cast down to their final resting place, to their browning journey beneath the soil.

"Oh, so I have to walk now. Fine." This, I snap at her in witched bitchiness, nearby the fervent sound of automation, as it applies to four locks being clicked shut all around me. In the next instant, I feel the back of my head in the agony of blonde hair pulled tight, married to the hardest pinch to the fat of my inner thigh that can be imagined. The scene nearly degenerates into violence, until I realize that the battle strength I feel from her is twice my own, and the pain coursing through my body from my inner thigh is unendurable. Hand up my cheerleading skirt to my inner thigh, just below where the blue cloth boundary begins, her other hand twisted and buried in my blonde hair pulled, she leans toward me with a calm expression, as though aware of what peril she may be in, as if walking topless in front of an open window at night.

To my inner thigh, she applies another powerful, pinching twist, to hear our inner space resound with my voice, one heavy burdened by the rage of unwanted agony endured. The strong, middle aged blonde woman holds me there, watching the tear stream down my face. Watching the shock of revelation overtake my expression. And then, I feel the mercy of Fate on my skin, as she releases the pinching, twisting hold, resting her hand firmly on my inner thigh, still holding my blonde hair firmly, now gently as I cry.

"I'm picking you up after school," she says.

"What about the game?"

"There'll be no game for you tonight. I'll call the coach and tell her we have to go out of town on family business."

I lower my eyes, with the requisite sniffling, which is the victim's best cry for mercy.

"Did you hear me?" she says, her voice showing signs of a monumental struggle for restraint. I nod my head pitifully, in hopes that the sympathy card has been properly played. She slides her hand down my thigh and away, unraveling her fingers from the yellow blonded hair. I see the effort it takes for her to remain calm, to remain composed as she cranks the car and backs out of the space, rolling us again toward our proper destination. The school suddenly feels oppressively crowded to me, as if I am suddenly wearing invisible clothes, as if every wall of secrecy around me is suddenly made of glass.

"This afternoon," she says. *"Be here."*

"Yes Maam," I say. Like the fool who raises the umbrella after her hair is already soaking wet. I continue this fools errand. Leaning over to kiss her on her beautiful cheek, taking brief satisfaction from her fake smile and pretend kiss. Getting out of the SUV like an actress at a Hollywood premier, feeling the flashbulbs of contempt and judgment going off all around me. In my mind, the looks and stares have nothing to do with the fact that I am all slutted up in blue. In my mind, they all know what happened in the parking lot around the side of the school, and they are all grieving for a look at the bruise on my inner thigh. I turn pitifully to the beautiful woman in the silver

Mercedes ride, waving in full fungalooga regailia, as if it has made any iota of a difference in how she feels toward me. I watch her drive off as if I'm at the airport, or in the parking lot of a bus station, wishing that the separation were not meant to be.

As this 40 year old woman that I am, I gaze fervently into the Heart of Memory, seeing the busty young cheerleader walk the concrete path over the Campus of Dreams, knowing that what she feels in the pit of her stomach is the same energy that I feel, activated by this self same woman, at these two points along the recesses of our time.

The school day moves along like Winter's Molasses, mocking me every second, in every minute of the day, refusing to allow me to forget
the unspoken promise made, and the nagging soreness of the promises kept. The itching and tingling where my hair was pulled converses with the throbbing tenderness where my thigh was pinched, to keep me reminded that my mother's discipline is no joke, and I had recently been spared of it, perhaps too long, literally forgetting my place in the grand scheme of things,

forgetting my place under the sun. I sit at the front of my classes nervously all day, crossing and uncrossing the long, white legs decorated at the top by the brief blue cloth, unable to do little more than study the clock every five minutes, which makes the day drag like the minutes inside the locked door of a prison cell. I am a prisoner of what will descend in the last days, which will cause men and woman's hearts to fail, from the things that are coming upon the earth. I am a prisoner of this, down through every waking hour of the day, until at last, one of my girlfriends has to ask what's on my mind. I want to relax and at least say, *I just had a fight with my mom,* or *my mom's not getting me that car*, or even, *my mother is such a bitch,* which is the refrain we pass around to one another anyway, drowned in the yin yang of the modern mother-daughter dynamic, which is Love and Hatred.

I watch the minutes and the seconds of the hours tick by, amazed at how from eight o'clock this morning until the clock strikes three, I have been unable to relax my nerves. I do not ask for whom the bell tolls. I only jump out of my skin when the chimes ring 3:55, to release all of us prisoners to another few hours of freedom. But I wonder. How many of us are being turned loose from the safety of our confinement, into the danger of this afternoon freedom?

I walk slowly with two of my blue cloth buddies in bouncy hair and bosoms, knowing already that my lie about going out of town with my mother didn't take, and that they are wondering why I'm really not coming to the so-called biggest game of the year, when our school the Richmond Cougars, are going to fight the Panthers of South Richmond. It is the high school nonsense of the year, bigger than the so-called homecoming game, where the adults actually care for once what's going on in their children's lives, and the sporting children are burdened with desperation for approval

275

and victory. Richmond vs South Richmond draws the curious from miles away, even from the exalted heights of university recruitment, as if somehow, this game matters more than any other game in the history of our hopeless lives. But somewhere inside, as I walk the concrete path again, across the campus of dreams, I do care about this event in my young life, and when I see the silver SUV parked in front of the school, my heart is iced cold in fear.

Thunder rolls over the fear of mankind, to gather it up and enhance its dimensions, to spread it out, until the earth is saturated with fear and dread. I too, am a prisoner of this, my own fear made worse by every flash of lightning over our house, and every crash of thunder that rolls over the Virginia countryside. My perverted desire remains for my daughter in repose, as I am burdened still by apprehension, and ghostly beings from the Heart of Memory. Among these spirits are my mother and me, having crossed the miles already to the brick house of secrets in Miller Creek Crossing. Oh, how thankful she is, I know, that Dale Turner is such a traveling busybody and workaholic, lost somewhere in the winds of time and space, separated from who we are by the miles and by Creation itself, so that he could not fathom the heights and depths of his faithful wife's libido. A woman who has never laid claim to lesbianism in her mind, having been with no other female but me, having never allowed herself to admit as to the nature of what fires that burn, of what tranquilities that have whispered her to sleep every night for the 20 years of this marriage, and of what end of the world secrets haunt the halls that lead to his daughter's upper room.

"Who the Hell do you think you are?" she asks, though not rhetorically, grabbing and shaking my head hard enough on the "Hell" syllable to rattle my brain. I stand in my own bedroom with the door closed and locked, though who it is that is being kept out, God only knows, considering that spirits do not make frequent use of doorknobs when entering a room. In full

cheerleader blue, I stand in front of the angry woman, who hast stewed this anger like a roast in a crock pot, until it is beyond ready to serve to myself and she, until we have both had our fill.

"Every penny," she says, her voice deepened with a full days worth of frustration held in. *"There's not a <u>penny</u> of your father's money that doesn't come through me. You think you're entitled to a fucking car? You're entitled to what I say you're entitled to. Do you understand me, disrespectful little cunt?*

I already know not to speak, but to merely nod my head. Neither of us are aware of the full implications of what the spirits bear witness to—of a beautiful, wealthy suburban woman with her fully grown daughter cornered behind a locked bedroom door, with both sides of her daughter's head gripped in her angry hands, as the cycle of fear and rage run its course between the two of them. The daughter looks physically mature enough to have a family of her own. But she is a prisoner to her mother's will, oppressed by the flow of every whim from her mother's rise and fall.

"And you have the nerve to speak filth to me? To call me a bitch? To say that you don't 'fucking' want to hear what <u>I've</u> got to say? The woman who got split open to push your screaming ass into this world? Who fed you with the milk from my own tits? The woman who kept you nice and cool and the summer, warm and cozy in the winter? The woman who made sure your father kept cash money in your pocket since you were in kindergarten? The woman whose food you eat, whose house you have lived in for eighteen goddamned years, this is the woman who you 'fucking' don't want to hear anything from? This is the woman who is a fucking <u>bitch</u>?"

I can only stand there. In full cheerleader regalia. Face wet with the new flow of tears brought forth from the epic fear and sorrow, feeling as though

I am about to be stuffed in a bag, tied to a tree and left in the middle of the woods to die. Across the brief space between us, I think that the rapid pulse I feel is the beating of her angry heart in her chest. As if hearing an order from somewhere deep within, she lets go of my head and stands up straight, the beauty of her face colored by a soul piercing frown.

"Turn to that mirror," she says. This, I do. With my hands clasped in front of me, seeing in the mirror a pretty faced young girl with blue eyes, tears and bright blonde hair, with a pair of the biggest breasts she has ever seen on a woman her size and color

"Roll up your sweater," she says. And though I would like to, I know better than to pretend I don't know what she's talking about. I fold the sweater up one, two, three times for the lady in rage, until the great bosoms are exposed in the big, blue sports bra, which has earned its keep mightily, pushing them up and together like two giant flesh pillows covered and hidden.

Mother stands behind me in the name of discipline. With no pretense toward motherly whispers this time, which I have heard and felt so many times before, preceding her epic grinding and slamming against my backside until she is done. But this time, she is fully clothed in her jeans and long sleeved button down navy blouse. The flash of her diamond and emerald ring set in gold reminds me of who she is, as her beautiful, white hands begin to squeeze both my breasts very hard, her white skin in stark contrast to the navy cloth of my sports bra.

When she is satisfied that the heft and weight of the task has been fully measured, she grabs the bottom of my sports bra with purpose. Pulling it up, up, upward toward revelation. Toward the truth of an endtime generation revealed. I watch the white hands in the mirror, pulling the soft, stretchy blue fabric up, up and away, to where the impossible waits for the melancholy blue curtain to be raised, so that what graces this hidden stage might be performed. It is a symphony somewhere beyond G major that waits to be played, as though the conductor's ivory hands are raised in this quiet command, to see the first notes struck in beauty and power.

The woman's hand pulls the blue fabric up to the limits of its motion, pulling its burden up along with it, until the force of what lies beneath breaks free, and I see two great globes of ivory white flop back down to their natural state—the great, brown areolas framing the nipples unflattened, prortruding their message of future pain and eschatology to me. I am mesmerized by the sight and feel of hat is shown to me, as the woman's hands bury themselves in the great globes, kneading, squeezing them in mashing, until my body is filled with apprehension, and the fear of which road of knowledge I must take.

But the answer grieves to be born of its own accord, when the hands I see take hold of the protruding nipples, and twists them without even the smallest pretense to compassion and mercy. Two separate bolts of lightning join in my body as one, to zap a deep, woman's scream from my eighteen year old mouth, as I am now acquainted with what pain is—born from Mother's hands and through the nipples of my bosom.

"*Uh, huh,*" Mother says, holding on just enough to hear my scream taper down to a squeak and a beg. *"That's what us bitch mother's want to hear, isn't it? Isn't it?"*

"I don't...KNOW!"

My deep, woman's scream returns on the syllable, to sound as if I am screaming the world "no," as if my soul pleads with rage and agony. I can no longer see the breasty girl in the mirror, as my eyes are closed, my head is turned, and my face is pressed so hard against the side of my mother's.

Another twist caused me to bury a scream into her face, with I know raises a current from her cheek to her groin. What trembling there is in my body bears no gratitude to pleasure, but owes its existence to the unendurable, lightning pain that stings, that sings pure heat into every corner of my skin. She releases this pressure just enough, holding on to them tight, listening to me tell her against her face how sorry I am, and how deeply I swear to never say that to her again.

"But I don't think you're really sorry," she says. *"I think you're just sorry that you're in pain."*

"I am sorry," I say, trying to stare her in the eye. *"I swear to God I'm sorry. I won't ever call you another name again I promise…"*

And I feel the twisting pressure return slowly, to cause my voice to raise up to a quiet siren, as I stand with my hands clutching hers, trying so desperately not to move.

"Get your hands down," she says sharply. *"And don't you move or I'll tie you up and do it.."*

"No, Momma…no."

I lower my hands. Gripping Irene on the sides of her jeans, noticing even now how remarkable the hip spread is.

"I'll bet you're sorry now, aren't you?"

"Yes. Yes Momma I'm sorry."

"Then show me. Stand still and take one more like a big girl."

Though I try not to let it happen, only the word *"no"* comes out, along with the shaking of my head.

"I thought you said you were sorry."

"I am. I am."

"Then show me."

It is an uphill climb for me, long after the strength in my legs is gone. But I push forward, to the mark of this higher calling, to where I am submitted to my mother's will, and where I have the greater part of her love and approval.

"Are you ready?"

"Yes...yes, I will..."

And to my shock, the burning pain returns as before, until it feels as if my breasts are on fire, spreading heat through to the rest of my body, causing me to shake all over in pure agony, as I press my lips hard against her face again; to anchor myself in the midst of this fervent scream. And then, the pain ends as quickly as it began, as she slides her hands down and away from my breasts, to let the cool air touch its merciful caress upon them.

"Will you ever disrespect me again?"

"No. I swear I won't."

Then I feel both her hands at the back of me, engaging their fumbling, mysterious motion, until I can hear the quiet, metallic tale being told, of when a zipper is made to undo the magic of its hold. I then see her slip her pants down, staring at my breasts in the mirror the entire time.

Soon, her button down is lifted up and away, and she lifts her bra up to expose the spongy perfection between high C and D minor, pressing them firm against my back exposed under my rolled up blue sweater. Then, against the back of my underwear, underneath the cheerleader skirt, I feel the hard, swollen part of herself bulged against me through her own underwear still up, where she rests herself in quiet determination and deep concentration, resting against me in solemn meditation, until at last she begins to move and rub her front against the back of me, raising up, taking hold of my waist with both her hands, slamming into me as though her phantom member is a part of reality, and she can somehow feel it up inside me. As to my bowels, I can only say that they are rattled and shaken by her pounding, which she does with my cheerleader skirt raised up, staring down at her handiwork as if there were a message to be read.

I watch her with her breasts hanging out from under her bra raised up, staring back and forth from my blue cloth bottom in front of her, to the swinging bells that wiggle in the mirror. I watch her desperation, her fiery concentration take hold, until there is an angry determination on her face, which I can feel in the strength pounding against the back of my body. The motion, I think, is of inhuman power and precision, as if done by a programmed machine, or a creature of this fevered instinct, whose only purpose is to achieve what mighty release that awaits therin.

With her bra turned up, her jeans half way down her thighs, the massive hips partially hidden in their own pink cloth, she slams into me with the depth and precision of a woman possessed, as I watch the look on her face grow more agonized and anguished, with her involuntary *"I'm gonna cum in my tits,"* as her look slips over into shock and awe, as her breathing begins to get away from her, and what motion there is in her body degenerates into an unsteady, full bodied trembling, as a loud, single yelp leaps from her mouth, lurching her forward into the back of me. She takes firm hold of my neck as I lean back, the energy reforming, sending waves through her that cause her characteristic grunting in my ear like some beast of the field.

I can only stand still in awe and wonder, at the pain I felt in my breasts, the quivering I feel in her body, and what it is I might be doing at this moment, had Fate allowed me a normal life, and sent me to the place where cougars, panthers, and cheerleaders go to laugh and play.

Jonathan Lovejoy

Dragon's Breath

I lost my mother to the Dragon's Breath

As the world burns away in blue and black fire

Now she seeks to have my daughter and me in the flames of an angry death

To torture my daughter's life away through the burning of my desire

Jonathan Lovejoy

The spirit of Irene Turner presses down on me, to deliver a deeper and more fervent craving for my daughter. As the world at large prepares for war, I am prepared to do battle in this gloomy isolation, to keep her spirit from reaching out to me in completion, to cause me to do her will and her bidding. I know that there were two lines left to cross on my mother's journey to insanity. A loss of reality , I know, activated by the perfect storm of fear and grief, mixed in with the rising wind of her blood's desire. This, a natural craving that burned her up even since before I was born, through my childhood, and into my adult years until the day she died.

These two lines I know she needed to cross, the first in pleasure, and then the one in pain, that was going to be one of the hidden tragedies in the world, of the kind that no one could ever suspect or believe. The whispers of my mother's inheritance haunt me from head to toe, to have me approach the first line that must be crossed now by me, to partially ease the pressure that she delivers to my soul every day, until I know that it is the only way that my torment will cease. The way that an addict, an alcoholic, an overeater, a smoker or the like—the way that they are haunted until their bodies must give in to the tragedy of their existence, I know this line my mother has set for me must be crossed, and the phantom taste of it already tickles the inside of my mouth and my being.

In the turning of a grieving earth in time, in the burning of my body's cry for this relief sublime, I go to my daughter's refuge of TV and computer isolation, in the confines of her upper room. What's that you're reading, I say, as if I care in the least, as it is only the lasso I use to reel her in, from her internet articale about spirits of the dead.

"I don't know whether you know this or not, but she's here," Meadow says to me.

"You mean *Mother*?"

"That's exactly what I mean," she says. "Sometimes its almost like she never left, and it gives me the creeps. Last night I swear I heard something moving around in the kitchen. If its okay with you, Mom, I think I'm gonna sleep with you tonight."

Like a stranded traveler at an open portal through time, I leepthrough this opportunity with the heat of desperation unbridled. It is as though a tiny twitch has sparked the switch between my thighs.

"I wanted you in my room from the day we got here," I say.

"I know. But I couldn't."

"Because of Mother, right?"

"I felt like you belonged more to her than you did me. I didn't want to get in her way."

"Well, she's not here now. And there's something we have to do. Something that we have to make happen."

Meadow only looks at me. Quiet, Egyptian eyes of vague understanding. Refusing to smile or frown. Refusing to flinch the least little bit, at what perverted story it is that her busty blonde mother's body should have to tell.

"I want you to get undressed," I say. Watching her take the clip from her hair without pretense, so that it falls in full, silken glory.

From across the Great Divide, which is only the length of this massive bedroom, we eye each other, both mother and daughter, as we begin to strip these clothes one by one, until the blonde with the snow white skin gazes upon the brunette with the sun kissed skin of deep ivory.

Our meeting at the bedside is as the collision of worlds, the cataclysm of the force and object irresistible and immoveable, which actually devastates me to a single spasm and quiet exclaim when our nipples touch. But though I know her body is even more sensitive than my own, she is always the pillar of restraint, so that she can watch me succumb to the curse of this perversion passed down. My mouth waters with anticipation of what line this is that must soon be crossed, as I can hear Irene's solemn declaration in my mind, *"Milk her like a cow."* And in the wake of this, I can only lower my head to the great, dark brown nipples of this beauty, and let my mouth attach itself in the violent, vacuum sucking, which brings a quick, gruff sound to my muffled voice, as the memory of Irene and me at the mirror when I was eighteen is burned onto theater of my mind.

I am in grieving to taste my daughter's milk, as I set upon this journey in desperate sucking, in pain to know how many hours of how many days we must engage this passion, until I see the white milk gather itself at her dark'ned nipple, to drip, drip, drip itself to the carpet, then run down the bottom of her breast and thighs in two slow, steady streams.

The slow, steady streams of their tears have come and gone. There is nothing left in the world for the psychiatrist and the girl violinist to do, save lean upon the other for strength, and relief from the melancholy in the drowning rain. These are the last days, the last wishes made, the last battles fought, the last errands run, the last slivers of joy and hope to be found under the sun. These are the days of eternal gray skies, where the earth is made a prisoner in gloom and clouds of melancholy gray. These are the days where the hopes and dreams of mankind have gathered themselves in surrender, to concede that this is the end of the age, where the fires burn on the eve of the Second Coming.

On the winds of eschatology, the two sisters ride. Caring nought for the impending war with the dragons that looms nearby. Understanding that all roads on the earthly plane are of finite duration, and there is always an end somewhere along this endless journey we travel. The two sisters disembark their rolling chariot, strolling toward the airport in their Asian cloth of black and blue, the younger sister Leah Rose in the silken royal, full length Asian dress, with the older sister Rachel Lynn in the silken cloth as black as midnight. These two draw stares from all at the airport within sight of them, among all the busy passers by, all the condemned souls of every age and ethnicity, every class and color thereabouts, wandering in and out, and through the airport along their tired and pathetic paths chosen. All having already given place to the spirit of hopelessness, the companion of the spirit of fear. The world is on the edge of oblivion, they say. It is a greater disaster that must be addressed, the tragic possibility of a bigger problem that must be solved... this, they sing with melancholy glee, to provide themselves with an excuse to throw every piece of ammunition in existence at the those seven monsters, to try and kill them, in hopes of saving what is left of the surface of this planet, before the death toll climbs too high above the summit of a billion souls departed.

I the wake of this stormy, fiery tragedy, the sisters take their steps through the drowning rain, so beautiful in their umbrellas both black and blue, gliding past the interested souls through the big glass doors, and into the busy lobby. Who are all of those desperate souls, bound by the spirit of to and fro? Trapped by the want and need to travel, both born from the necessity to flee, to run from whatever truth it is that haunts them where they live. Sit still, stay put, tend the garden of your own back yard. Of these things, the airport people care nothing for, and cannot be told to go home, and hide from what is coming upon the earth.

Past these souls in flight, the two sisters glide, placing their long umbrellas together in black and blue repose, drawing sleepy, smiling stares from the women and children who take the time to give notice, who cannot pretend that two Asian beauties in long, shiny Asian dresses is irresistible to behold. These two sisters lay their umbrellas together across the arms of one of the chairs, sliding the *pistol* so casually, so inconspicuously out of the small leather purse Rachel Lynn carried in.

In the mist of a latent scream, the older sister in black stands in the gathering circle of onlookers, who fearfully stare as if held prisoner of a show, not knowing whether or not the gun is real, or if this is a scene staged for the benefit of some hidden camera nearby. But in keeping with the nightmare world at large, as if phased in from the grieving, ghost world of wind and rain near and far, the nightmare scene takes on the substance of reality, when the lovely Asian girl in blue places her mouth onto the barrel of the pistol, and the woman in black pulls the trigger, filling their world with the sound of gunpowder blasting a splatter of red from the head of the Asian beauty in blue. She falls without a bending of the legs, her body leaning back, back, backward as if in slow motion, until the Asian blue tower of beauty falls dead to the floor.

Screams are layered one upon the other, with so-called security running in confusion, as chaos spreads like a forest on blue and black fire, as the Asian woman in silken black cloth smiles just a bit and lowers her eyes, placing this self same gun into her mouth, again pulling the trigger, to send the second blast of gunpowder through every soul nearby, as her body takes a stumbling step backward, falling in place at her sister's ivory white legs and feet.

*D*esperation rides the wind and the waves, rolling across the barren desert and wilderness plains, looking for signs of the seven dragons in flight. Being fortunate, or unfortunate enough to discover their whereabouts over and over again, through the passing of the days, which has seen the fleet of seven, fly directly toward the approaching hoarde of airborne planes and gunships, the world coming together as one in the name of international defense. These tragic and lengthy fireworks displays have already gone down in history as mankind's greatest war, his greatest battle fought along the timeline. These monsters no longer give place to hasty retreat, spreading outward in a line from horizon to horizon, spreading their explosive blue lines of fire through the evening day and far into the night, in their endless stream of fiery conquest, causing the planes to melt and explode in groups ad nauseam, some simply streaking a line of blue fire through the sky as they fall. The white, birdlike creatures in flight become fire breathing silhouettes in the evening twilight, becoming invisible sources of explosive fire in the fall of night. They have developed to a place of invulnerability. They act and proceed without weaknesses, having no need to retreat from the endless blasts of glowing red ammunition from the planes and helicopters aflight, sometimes baring their heads down and forward in battering ram repose, shooting through the sky like great white arrows shot from we know not where, exploding the unlucky planes in their paths on contact. They swoop and swerve with effortless grace in motion, being impossible for the pilots to zero in upon, turning, climbing and diving so quickly—as though they are playing the most deadly and determined air game in the history of mankind.

These flights of fancy have continued through the turning of the rainy days, decorating the gray skies in the glow of fiery blue and white, until more than fifty thousand pilots have given their lives under God and Christ, to finally settle in the minds of all involved that here will be no more suicide dragon strikes from the air, when the countries around the world begin to cry out for their flying men in fear. And as if to advertise and confirm their place and calling, there is at least one incident at close range alongside a battleship at sea, where the giant gun is made to call upon the gigantic white creature; the noisy, fiery shot exploding into the monster in mid air, blowing it apparently backward, where the fire and smoke dissipates from around its gigantic white form, then again, then again, then again—until the battleship sailors inside know that there need not be another great shot fired, but merely a preparation for evacuation.

Someone has the intelligent authority, the good judgment gathered up and acted upon, and the battleship soldiers begin to fly over the edge of the ship one by one, but so few having made it in time, to escape the burst of cooking blue heat that pours, and begins to melt the great metallic battleship in two. And soon, there is the grandest seafaring explosion known to man, as the blue fire burning the ship is plumed from within by a ball of orange and black vapor of smoke. And the parts of the great ship that remains are upended high and wide, sliding down beneath the surface of the late daytime waters it lived and died in. Over 100 of these great and small ships from every port at sea have met with their most fervent demise, until there is the quiet understanding that there will be no further suicide sailing for the dragon's fire at sea.

And the quickest and most tragically benign strategies of wilderness attack have had the fastest concession and departure, as the world can withstand no more scenes of tanks being turned into blue fireballs in the rain, where husbands and fathers are being cooked alive by the tens of thousands, until the world at war comes to its quiet understanding that no, there will be

295

no more suicide missions over land to find the dragon's fire, to join those that have made their rise and fall, across the wind and sounding sea.

A Rhapsody in Blue

She is feeding me fantasies about killing my own daughter.

In the rising tide of fear and misery, it is a perverted reality that I must face—as my evil dreams will not cease, where my daughter is being done in by my own hand, or is being in some way tortured and tormented by my mother. This, as the world is made aware of an endtime truth, as the private sins are slowly being uncovered, when news of the airport suicide grips the nation and the world at large, and the sisters' posthumous memoir called *A Rhapsody in Blue*. The disturbing details about he deeply incestuous and abusive triangle between an Asian mother and her two daughters, from their early sessions when the girls were less than 12 years old, to the depravity that continued until the older sister was in her mid 30's. Whether or not the world is prepared to believe Dr. Rachel Lynn Chao may be irrelevant, but it cannot change the truth about who is telling the story. We may not believe the message, but we'll believe the messenger because, face facts, the woman is a California psychiatrist with an MD and PhD from Harvard Medical School. And she chronicles not only her mother's abusive, incestuous upbringing, and what was passed down to her two daughters, but Dr. Chao opens up the doors of her controversial practice for the world to see, with revelations of a video archive of private mother-daughter sessions behind the closed doors of her office, where several mother-daughter couples agreed to spank, paddle or cane one another in the name of progressive therapy, with one mother agreeing to be punished by her daughter anally.

Dr. Chao wrote that the purpose of these sessions was to: "*...remove all barriers between the mother and the daughter, to foster a closeness beyond anything that they could have ever thought possible before. To stop the pretending, to quit the coy game playing and useless back and forth, to literally "cut the shit," and go to places emotionally, spiritually and physically that would bring them together as one, and make future conflict as enemies difficult if not impossible.*" Only one of her C.T.S. Therapy sessions (Catharsis Trauma Salvation or CatharsisTrauma Session, i.e., "*Cut The Shit* Therapy"), only one of them had progressed to the final stage, which was *anal sex* between the two, where this daughter had stood behind her mother in the clinical, comfortable office setting strapped on, sliding it without mercy deep into her mother's rectum. The confiscated videos have been held back from the public, deemed as "too pornographic to show and may constitute a crime." Even with this documentation and confirmation of the psychiatrist's credibility, the world is still unable to process the sisters' private lives, and the truth of Lena Chao's depraved dominance over her two daughters.

But even while the world remains fascinated by daughters and dragons, I remain fascinated by my own, often amazed and bewildered by its very existence, and how it is that the world has finally been made aware. But it is a secret that threatens to remain as such, as those who know still dare not come forward in true confession just yet, and those who care are unable to admit it to anyone but themselves in private. It is the last great secret before the end of the age, as the eve of the Second Coming of Christ unfurls, for those who have allowed themselves to believe that the scriptures are true, and that the fires in which we burn are eschatological to be sure.

As to the Second Coming, I know not when or where. I only know of my own private Second Coming, that concerning the woman who just recently left us behind, and the return of her presence in fear and dread. I often walk the rooms of this house in dreadful anticipation of every corner and trip from one room into another, waiting for a shadow to darken and move, or to hear the call of a deep, ghostly moan. I live in daily terror of this possibility, my daughter and I being partners in this fearful waiting, waiting to take our places among the unfortunate, of those who have learned where it is that their beloved and recently departed mothers could have gone.

Meadow and I spend our days cooking and eating our diet portions, such as they are, with every one of her new seven pounds being at her hips and bosom. And when we are not reading or watching TV, listening to music or driving and shopping for clothes we will never wear, I am engaged in my mysterious and secret hobby, whereas she is the object of my endtime obsession, which is the fervent, protracted nursing of her bosom. From one breast to the other I give suck day and night, to learn the truth about the nursemaid, and whether or not her spirit may be visited upon one who has not yet conceived.

This obsession has grown exponentially since my mother committed suicide, seeming to dominate my every waking hour, until the two of us have grown accustomed to the rising, to the inner call of when these nursing sessions must be. Our time together is more breast centered than ever before, until the touching of them is a place beyond foreplay, and the nursing is our place of completion. One of our favorite positions, beyond my laying in her lap like a feeding child, is for her to strip completely naked and to straddle me while I lay on my back, often fully clothed or in my underwear, nursing the great, long things as they hang down in my face, where their sensitivity is something that I am still not used to, as the nursing alone can often bring her to full orgasm. Even without her moving a muscle, this sensitivity is her gift, a conduit to the pleasure centers of her mind and body, making her perhaps as rare and special as a diamond in the dirt. This ability of hers grew as she did, seeming to blossom in proportion with her breast size—the bigger they got, the more sensitive they got, until we have learned that a massage done long enough is the Milkmaid's Intercourse, and is the same as putting a burning match to a fuse in a stick of dynamite.

This fuse has been lit already for us, as we stand in our favorite place by the bedroom mirror, protecting one another from the ghosts that stare. I stand behind her, pressed tight against her as I squeeze her breasts from behind, mashing and kneading them deeply, pulling gently at the nipples, wobbling them, bouncing them together until she takes that tell tale sigh, closing her eyes and relaxing backward against me, while I continue to massage and rub her bosom with quiet and fevered determination, my own heart racing in anticipation of what I know. And just when I am convinced that this is but a glorified breast massage to nowhere, I hear her swallow quietly, then she readjusts her stance against me, and I hear her begin to moan pitifully, as if the relief she desires is visible, but is a great distance away.

I continue to rub and squeeze this curiosity, this false hope of our want and need, pulling the nipples and shaking the big breasts by them, even clapping the wobbly things together loudly, which makes her begin to moan in frustration, in the torment of hopeless longing, and the pain of unrequited desire. From this clapping, as I hear her voice sing a song of sixpence, I am inspired to work her breasts into an ongoing and squeezing rhythm, working them by this circular pattern, watching her grow tense with the readiness of the impossible, as her voice grows more burdened with pain, this, the agony of a promise unfulfilled, as a pot of gold at the end of a rainbow.

But I am committed to this fantasy, to this end of the world reality I see, to the softness of what I feel, and to the beauty of what I hear. I know that I need but continue this circular squeezing, this kneading of the heavy breast flesh, like the fires of that lit fuse that approacheth, until it vanishes forever from sight, to send the truth exploding into the air like a thousand canons, to roll the countryside like the voice of thunder and tragedy. I watch her glimpse at the pleasure trauma upon her breasts, as I marvel at the *white miracle* that begins to drip from the pinched nipples, her expression suddenly giving in to shock and disbelief as her eyes roll back, and her body begins to shake and tremble as she pushes back against me, with the moan she tries to suppress exploding from her mouth as two great sirens, sounding one right after the other.

65

I want to drown in my daughter's breast milk. I have achieved as earthly paradise for myself, even as the skies continue to rumble with such force and power, and the angry rains continue to fall. I am in heaven when I lie on my back underneath my daughter, both of us stark naked, with one of the great, hanging jugs pulled so far into my mouth, causing the milk to flow in to the point where I might choke on it, so unafraid to let it run down the sides of my mouth and down the side of my face while I lay down, caring nothing for where it goes, what it does to my hair, what it does to the sheet under my head. I am content to suck and drink to my fill from any number of positions, whether in her lap, or on my knees in worship position, or with her on her back, or even the breast sucking 69, where we are at each other's bosom at the same time, which has been enough to shake me to the core more than once. The feel of her wet nipple in my mouth while mine is inside hers…to think of it makes me have to shake my head awake from this daydream more often than not.

I sometimes am burdened with wonder as to these possibilities that run through my blood, how far back past Irene this sickness hearkens from, that keeps me in perpetual lust for my daughter. How many mothers around the world are as I, who have given in to this drug induced coma from the normal, from the mundane, from the ordinary ways of thinking and living which do not involving trading orgasms with my daughter. But somewhere inside, bestowed to me by the spirits that haunt and mourn this grieving earth, I know that mine is a condition that is pervasive, and spread in secret epidemic throughout the world.

But at this moment, my own lust is the only burden I can carry. I languish on all fours on the comfort cushioned carpet floor of the upper room, listening to the rainfall oblige, while feeling her rain breast milk down from above me, onto my back. Somewhere in the depths of my perverted soul is the chiming of the ages, where every erogenous nerve in my body is tingled from the feel, from the image in my mind of my giant breasted daughter standing over me in determined, purposeful submission, squeezing the new milk down from the great wineskins onto her mother's back. But this, we do not engage in with play and fungalooga, it is of the utmost and urgent commitment from the two of us, with the deepest understanding besides, as I know how deeply arousing it is to Meadow to be standing over me, squirting the milk from her tits down onto my lustful and twisted psychology.

I know that part of her enjoys this dark magic she has over me, this addiction she knows that I am a prisoner of behind these walls, perhaps making her as completely depraved as I. I am in such raptured amazement as I relax on all fours, feeling the growth of my lady cock down below, which sends already a shiver through both of my legs unseen.

I raise my head up like the sleepy barnyard cow that I am, raising up to my knees to where I can put my face at the bottom of those great long breasts of hers, so I can access the nipple of this fervent fountain to drink. I gently move her hands away and take hold of one of them, staring directly into the nipple in awe of both the steady dripping, and the steady climb my body makes toward its goal and desire. Only the slightest squeeze brings the steady flow of milk from her, which squirts in the prowess of a showerhead when I squeeze harder, to make me wonder what manner of milkmaid queen is this I have given birth to. The milk *sprays* from her breasts rather than squirts, truthfully, as I tell her to take hold of it again, and to *spray it all over Momma's face, baby*. This, I say with conviction, meaning every word of it, every nuance of vowel and consonant sound, with every deep and breathy syllable of intent. I close my eyes to this shower of white, this milk bath, this white shower, slowly working my face back and forth like an Amazon under a waterfall. I am pushed to the edge of instinct, until I can take no more, moving my face over to where I at one with the member that hangs from her strapped on, looking up at her as if she is my goddess, my queen, as I wait for her to have mercy on my soul.

By this instinct alone, I open my mouth and slide it onto my daughter's cock, feeling my ears ring a chime that goes down to the tip of my nipples, causing me to rub an involuntary squeeze across the two of them. And I am unable to slide my mouth back and away from this sucking, pushing my head forward until my mouth is filled to the back of my throat and beyond, causing me to gag this reflex action, but still having no mercy upon myself, repeating this until the gags descend to muffle coughing, and the spit falls in a stream to my waiting breasts down below. My daughter takes hold of the back of my head, to make me regret this passion, causing me to choke and spit ad nauseam, until I have to pull it out to save my life, stroking the member covered in spit, looking up at her while the tears roll down my face in grieving. But I must go under once more, to taste my daughter's cock again, to feel the pleasures of this suffocating choke, and the rising tide of wishing in pulls from both my nipples and my groin. And I catch one last glimpse of her face, as it slides to the breaking point in the back of my mouth, her eyes closed, her head back in the anguish of revelation, that this member is somehow an extension of her full self, and my choking upon it rings every bell in her from head to toe.

At long last, when my choking exhibition is done, I move up to the corner of the bed on all fours, noticing that I have to resist a visible tremble when she touches me. But when I feel the elongated breasts fall against my back as she leans down against me from behind, squeezing my breasts roughly with both hands, I can no longer hide the truth of who and what I am, and I have to lower my head against the shame of it, as my body convulses a single, mighty spasm that hazes my vision. Oh, Meadow, my tragic Armageddon child, what further devastation doth this pre-lightning bring to thee, when but a mere hugging to your mother's body causes her to shake one quake so powerfully! My daughter takes this signal from my body, raising up to her business in back of me, and I feel her slide it into my swollen self from behind, make me lower my head again as the barnyard cow I am in grazing, with a long, bellowing grunt in surrender.

I think that maybe, I have never felt anything so good in my life, and I know that as surely as my name is Carol Ann Oppenheimer, I am going to cum on my daughter's cock.

66

*I*n the rising wind and rain, in this raging storm of eschatology, I languish on all fours at the corner of the bed, with my daughter standing up behind me. Every inch of her strapped on self is pushed deep inside me, filling me up to my womb, perched on the edge of a lightning strike to every part of my body. But as if inspired, by some unknown instinct, my daughter knows to lie down against my back, where the feel of her breasts nearly pushes my body over the edge again. She presses down firm against me, sucking my earlobe noisily, moving the member inside me nary an inch, rubbing both my breasts across the nipple with one hand. How does one know, pray tell, for whom the bells toll? Yes, my dearest heart, they do indeed toll for me. The stroking of her hand across my nipples warns me of what destruction is about to occur in me, as the tip of the funnel cloud that must climb down from the whirling gray cloude, to begin its irreversible descent to the cowering prairie plain.

This towering promise of destruction begins in me, to make me have to begin the weeping moan, even shaking my head 'no,' understanding that what I am about to endure is going to rise the heights of pleasure that is a cross to bear. Meadow understands from whenceforth this whirlwind cometh that threatens, channeling her prodigious breast understanding into me, both of us knowing that there need not be a single touch anywhere else to my body but here. Of this slow and steady rubbing across my nipples hanging down, she does not cease, nor does she cease the warm touches of her breath to my ear, as the slow and steady climb of the funnel cloud nears its destination downward.

And when I feel my daughter's body lurch itself against me on its own, my spirit flashes to the lurching of my mother's body against me when I was twelve, as I can feel the memory of her massive hips squeezed tight as she lays stretched out naked full on my back, her hands firmly tucked between my legs underneath, causing the whirlwind I feel to make contact, where my body's stability is taken up and scattered, making my moaning voice have to rise to a full, long sob and weeping, as every part of my soul, mind and body is imprisoned by a devastating quake and tremble that has no end, causing my weeping voice to quiver throughout. I hold on as a victim of the whirlwind, shaking uncontrollably underneath my daughter, in weeping prayer for its merciful passing. I hold on, as the quaking makes its way through my bodyguard into the bed underneath me, sending energy somewhere deep into the grieving earth below.

In the aftermath of this weeping, my daughter pulls the member out from me, turning me over onto my back, us still at the corner of the bed, placing a pillow underneath my buttocks to raise me up. Oh, what is the power of déjà vu! The power of predestiny sent from somewhere along the timeline! This selfsame thing I did to Irene when I was but a girl of 13, with the little plastic member strapped on, in the hotel room of our travels! Meadow places the tip of the big member at my place, but pulls it out and downward, to push at the door of my rectum in repose. I can only hold on in waiting, as we do at the tip of the nurse's needle, suffering the pushing of this goddess dick into my bottom. I reach up to grab one of the great hanging breasts for support, staring into those Egyptian eyes of hers, that stare down at what she does without mercy, letting the pain come out through my voice as she slides it in, working it slowly in and out, deeper in and out, deeper in and out, until I feel my bowels filled to their completion.

And I watch this breast goddess settle into her rhythm, closing her eyes to hear the music of this symphony that begins in her body, as she hears the spirit of *"fuck your mother up the ass"* whispered to her spirit in grieving. And this, she does without mercy, while I gather myself to this new sensation, amazed at the completeness of feeling it sends to my groin. She lowers her hand once to my breast, pulling the nipple up in one great, popping suck, watching the big, white breast fall and wobble back into place. I watch this breast goddess anchor herself for the journey, her nipples still damp from the milk, slamming into me with fever and intensity, until I find that the strange feeling in my backside expands a pleasure whose boundaries are unknown, flashing the picture of my mother on her back in the hotel when I was 13. In the theater of my mind, I see my mother tense up in the throes of a siren from her voice, shocked by the fountain that *squirts* up from the front of her, that gushes up onto my stomach at 13, which causes the 40 year old me to tense up from the energy unrestrained, having to scream this self same siren into the air around us in the present day. The quick, violent spasm takes my daughter aback, causing her to stop suddenly, readjusting herself for the pounding that must continue now, if it's the last thing she ever does, neither of us having dreamt that an *anal orgasm* was in our destiny. The heat of it lights her motion up to another fever, until I am again screaming and shaking from the second fall from this mountain, seeing through the haze what appears as a fervent *pissing* from the front of myself, which shocks Meadow's body into its own violent shaking overdue. As to this feeling, we know not where, as she continues to pound down into the back of me, as I cry out continuously from pleasure arisen up beyond itself, to where the endurance of it is agony unfurled.

As I watch the milk drip faster from the goddess' breasts dangling, I am quickly sent back to the precipice of this tragedy, feeling my lower body tense up again on its own to the pissing stream, to turn the switch of quaking on again in my daughter's body, this time without mercy, to where I can see the pain on her face, and the craving for a return to sanity. This, the twisted sanity of our calling. The tranquility of our private devastation, as my daughter lays down on top of me, that we may find our way back to the land of the living, while our bodies exchange the energy of aftershock trembling and quaking passing through.

"*I told you to kill her,*" *Mother says.* "*You disobeyed me. So now, I'm going to have to kill you.*"

This chimes a sequence in my brain, a dark melody of dreariness and foreboding. My daughter and I have ridden the winds of this endtime rain to the shopping palace, this great mall of leisure still undeterred by the dragon's flame. There are pockets of hope and resistance left in this stubborn, Laodicean culture, that refuse to abide by the warning signs, that refuse to be driven in hiding. Among these stubborn, money obsessed souls, we walk in the same inner pride as so many of them, but strengthened and made special by what secret it is that we share. We walk together from store to store in this unnatural closeness, the tallish, brunette beauty with the Egyptian eyes and sun kissed fair skin, with the pretty older blonde twice her age that must surely be her aunt or friend. Surely, it cannot be her mother. Surely, these heavy breasted women are not mother and daughter.

As we follow each other around the Belk shelves and racks, my mind continues this dark melody of anticipation, of expectation, where the image of my mother from last night's dream continues to haunt me. We had both been sitting quietly on my bed, while the intensity of the storm outside was above and beyond possibility, with trees bending as if they might break, and lightning strikes with thunder unrestrained. I can remember most of all the color of my mother's eyes, which seemed to glow with the most beautiful and unnatural shade of blue. When she told me she was going to kill me, I remember how the fear started somewhere in my brain, radiating downward into every extremity, down to the lower parts of my stomach, bowels and womb. I woke up this morning with the smell of her Jergen's lotion in my nostrils, and the sound of her deep, sultry voice in my ears. Even moreso than these past weeks, I now walk in genuine fear, which I work hard to conceal in the complacency of wealth, and the end of the world complacency I share with my daughter.

When this three hundred fifty dollar trip to bountiful is done, we stroll through the half empty paradise of perpetual spending, the exotic brunette beauty and her busty blonde companion, both of us content to cruise this Wealthen Stream without remorse, or consideration for those who are less fortunate, who cannot swipe three hundred fifty dollars away as if it were three dollars and fifty cents, with no consideration of where it came from, and no concern for what frivolity it is going to.

Confident in our privileged place among women and men, we leave the mall and raise our umbrellas to the goddess of thunder, who rages down her angry warning to an endtime generation both day and night. We hurry through the hard, pouring rain to our silver gray luxury, finally climbing aboard to the safety and tranquility of shelter bought and paid for, and dreams of our long and private isolation of realities unseen.

"I had another nightmare last night," Meadow says. "Grandmother scared the Hell out of me again."

"In what way?"

"It was something she said."

Every now and then, precognition strikes a fire, to light one's mind up with revelations of the unknown. "She said she wanted to kill you, didn't she?"

In Meadow's beautiful eyes that stare, in the beautiful lips slacked open without a word, is the terrifying answer screamed so loud and clear. "How did you know that?" she says.

The only answer I can give is a shrug and a sigh, accompanied by a brief shaking of my head, as we cruise out of the parking lot of false hope, onto the rainsoaked highways of shattered dreams come and gone.

$\mathcal{O}$ur complacency is washed away in the deluge, as we splash through the small, grassy puddles of water on our country lawn. We are glad to finally be back and away from our forced trip into town, settling into the isolation of who we are, and our attempt to banish fear and pain away forever. We are alone, my daughter and me, content to spend our days drifting through these dreary but hallowed rooms of peace and comfort, where we endeavor to give no place to the shadows that grieve to see our bodies dead and gone. *Fuck you Irene*, is the vulgarity that pushes at the tip of my tongue, though I am compelled by the solemn memory of her, to speak my farewell respects to the dead.

"Good night, Irene," I say, taking my daughter's hand, gazing up to the high ceiling and beyond. In the turning instant, upon one fervent ticking of the clock, the rainy silence of our world is blasted away in a great noise from outside the house, in the form of a long, booming foghorn of otherworldly truth and revelation made real, as the cavernous, overwhelming voice of doom rattles every window, and trembles every particle of our body and soul. There is no mistaking the voice of the endtime, of the great call from the power of Laodicea, a noise that rises the two of us to what is written: the types of fear are many, and uniquely distinguished. Among these is the Fear of Death, as the booming bass of this voice calls into the air again with greater force and purpose, adding to this terror the fear of the supernatural, and the certainty that under no circumstances, as God sits on his throne in judgment, am I going to look outside that window.

Frozen where I stand, my gaze affixed to nowhere in front of me, the oceanic fear gives birth to a calling, that wells up through my body of its own accord, to compel words from my mouth that have a life of their own. "Lord *Jesus,* help us," is the cry of this desperation, in the brief silence of this temporary reprieve, as Meadow says "the basement," as if repeating the words of unearthly guidance unseen. In the wake of a third, deeply booming B flat that rattles every particle of Creation again, we run hand in hand across the living room and through the kitchen, turning the corner in desperation to the safety of the basement.

And our future is activated upon the touching of the knob, as the sound of the world exploding around us makes us scream the chorus of two, closing the door pointlessly behind us as we hurry down the stairs, feeling the blast of heat at our backs that knocks us both to the bottom of the staircase, just below what is the unmistakable truth in the burning periphery, as the door is blasted away in an explosion of fire and blue. What injuries and pain there may be are unbeknownst to the two of us as we stumble to our feet, Meadow grabbing me by the arm and pulling us to the wall tucked underneath the wooden steps, the sound of the rain lost in the rumble of a house being blasted away in a cauldron of blue and black fire.

*A*fter the turning of another day. When the heat of burning has come and gone. The two of us are able to rise up from the shadows of fear and epic dread. Walking up the stairs that lead to the sound of a storm unsheltered, in the glowing light of gray. We emerge from the soot charred top of the stairs, to the feel of the pouring rain on our faces, and the touch of Autumn's early arrival in the wind. We step onto the charred, blackened remains of the house that once was, which is only burned bits and pieces of manmade hopelessness unrecognizable and gone.

With hardly a steady glance into the hot ashes of where we must step to flee, we can only stare in rapt amazement through the rain into the distance, at the infinity of burned, blackened landscape from east to west, and the scattering of forest trees burning unquenched in the cold, Autumn rain and win

ABOUT THE AUTHOR

Jonathan Lovejoy is a graduate of the University of North Carolina at Greensboro with a B.A. in Religious Studies, Liberty University with an M.A. in Theological Studies, and Grand Canyon University with a Master of Divinity. He currently lives in Mesa, Arizona.

For more info on the author's life and career, visit jonathanlovejoy.com.

www.ingramcontent.com/pod-product-compliance
Lightning Source LLC
Chambersburg PA
CBHW060520180626
46817CB00002B/429